THE
WOMAN
FROM
PRAGUE

Center Point
Large Print

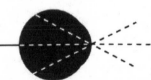

**This Large Print Book carries the
Seal of Approval of N.A.V.H.**

THE WOMAN FROM PRAGUE

ROB HART

CENTER POINT LARGE PRINT
THORNDIKE, MAINE

This Center Point Large Print edition
is published in the year 2017 by arrangement with
Polis Books.

The text of this Large Print edition is unabridged.
In other aspects, this book may vary
from the original edition.
Printed in the United States of America
on permanent paper.
Set in 16-point Times New Roman type.

ISBN: 978-1-68324-575-9

Library of Congress Cataloging-in-Publication Data

Names: Hart, Rob (Fiction writer), author.
Title: The woman from Prague / Rob Hart.
Description: Large print edition. | Thorndike, Maine :
  Center Point Large Print, 2017.
Identifiers: LCCN 2017035899 | ISBN 9781683245759
  (large print : hardcover : acid-free paper)
Subjects: LCSH: Private investigators—Fiction. | Large type books. |
  GSAFD: Suspense fiction. | Mystery fiction.
Classification: LCC PS3608.A7868 W66 2017 | DDC 813/.6—dc23
LC record available at https://lccn.loc.gov/2017035899

THE
WOMAN
FROM
PRAGUE

"You are free, and that is why you are lost."
—*Franz Kafka*

To Bree

ONE

The dishwasher is broken.

At least I think it's broken. The wash cycle has been going for nearly an hour now, even though it usually takes about fifteen minutes. I check the dial to see which setting it's on but that doesn't help anything because the dial settings are in Czech. I've picked up a little of the language in the past two months, but nothing that covers home appliances.

I consider calling someone—one of the local maintenance guys who will undoubtedly look at this, hit a button, and fix it. Then give me a withering look of disappointment that the American needed to be bailed out of something yet again.

Fuck that.

I open my laptop, type the model number of the dishwasher into Google, and find a website offering a PDF of the instruction manual. Bingo. Click on that, but it's also in Czech. Figures.

A little clicking around in the browser reveals a translate option. I click that and the text flashes and re-appears in English. Some of it is nonsensical—I don't know what it means to "re-appropriate soap material"—but there's enough that I can figure out the dishwasher is on the self-cleaning cycle. I turn the knob to the regular cycle and within a few seconds it stops and drains.

Score one for the moderately clever.

With the dishwasher draining, the apartment is a good bit quieter and I can hear the faint sound of bells ringing in the distance. Probably the astronomical clock in Old Town Square, chiming on the hour.

There's a faint odor of pot in here. I open the windows even though it's cold and a light snow is falling. The bells get a little louder. The Scandinavian backpackers who had been staying here the past week weren't supposed to smoke inside, but the trip downstairs and outside is a long one, so I don't entirely blame them. A few minutes and it'll be fine. Probably not worth going after them for the security deposit.

This apartment is clear for the next three days. This is where I've set up base for now, which means I could use some groceries. I step into the hallway, make sure the door locks behind me, head down the dark, winding staircase that looks transposed from a gothic cathedral. Down to the courtyard at the center of the apartment complex. The air is cold and sharp but also a little pleasant.

A calico cat with bright yellow eyes pads through the snow and meows at me, then disappears behind the line of trash bins. I push through the courtyard door, into a long, empty hallway that leads to the front of the building, my footsteps echoing in the dim space.

Outside it's crowded, mid-day and close enough to Old Town Square there's spillover of the hordes of tourists. Snowflakes spiral around me, leaving a light dusting on the ground, the area crisscrossed with footprints. To my left, the sea-green spires of the Church of St. Havel stick into the stone gray sky. It's the kind of church that's stunning against any other background, and here is just another beautiful building lost in a sea of beautiful buildings.

Without even making a conscious decision to do it, I walk toward the church and enter. It's quiet inside, and warm, the space permeated with the intoxicating smell of incense. At the front of the pews is a sign forbidding photography, which means less incentive for gawkers, so as per usual, it's nearly empty. Only one other person, seated up toward the front. Someone kneeling and hunched over, lost in silent prayer.

I take a seat in the back pew and look around. Contemplate the ornate altar that culminates in a sun-inspired sculpture perched at the top. Soak in the silence and the seclusion. Look at all the beautiful decorations and architectural flourishes I don't know the names for. I do know the Church of St. Havel is also known as the Church of St. Gall. Established in the 1200s by King Wenceslas I, named after an Irish monk who helped introduce Christianity to Europe. It was rebuilt in the Baroque style sometime in the seventeenth century.

At least, that's what the internet tells me.

The woman sitting up front slowly lifts herself to a standing position, makes the sign of the cross, and shuffles out of the pew. She walks slowly down the aisle, giving me a small smile as she passes, which I return. After the door falls shut behind her, the sound of it echoing through the space, I look around to verify that I'm alone.

When I'm alone, I'm able to breathe deeper. My muscles unfurl and relax. It's when I'm alone and it's quiet I feel most like myself. For a very long time, I felt afraid of the silence. That it would force me to face the things all the noise was covering up. But I'm not afraid anymore. Instead, I've found it can be quite nice to be alone in a quiet place.

My stomach rumbles. Hunger wins out over contemplation. I slide out of the pew and back into the cold. Pull up my collar and cut through the market at the end of the block, traversing narrow, cobbled streets. Sidestepping people who are walking backwards to take photos on their phones, not paying attention to where they're going. Dodging the occasional kamikaze biker. The chaos of it makes me wistful for home.

I stop at a kiosk to grab a trdelník, which is essentially a donut shaped like a beer can. My second one today. I'm glad this is a good walking town. If it weren't, with the way I've been eating, I'd need to buy new clothes.

Another few blocks and three near-collisions, I find my destination: a blank building with a small, open doorway that leads into a pool of shadow. I step into the gloom, to an indoor shopping plaza. You'd never know it was here if you weren't looking for it. There's a luggage store, a travel agency, and most important to my needs right now, a grocery store.

I grab a basket and wander the aisles. Grocery stores are my favorite thing about being here. In America, you get used to a certain layout—fruit and vegetables on one end, dairy on the other, meat along the back wall, everything else in the middle. The layout is different here. The meat counter is off in one corner, and the freezer case is in the other. The aisles are different lengths, so you get the feeling you're playing Pac-Man. Plus, nearly everything is in Czech. It's a bizarro version of a grocery store, and sometimes, even when I don't need anything, I'll go to one and stroll around, mostly looking for what's familiar, but occasionally grabbing something I don't know to see if I can figure out what it is. Like my own personal game show, where sometimes you end up with really delicious potato dumplings, and sometimes you end up with meat of unknown provenance.

I fill my basket with bread and eggs and bacon and apples and frozen vegetables and chips and other assorted items that'll get me through the next few days. The girl at the checkout counter is a thin brunette with a pixie cut, her small boy body swimming in a yellow polo shirt. She smiles and scans the items and I smile back. I'm sure she speaks English because she's young—most young people in Prague do—but I say "*Ahoj*" anyway because it makes me feel like I'm assimilating.

"*Jak se máš?*" she asks. How are you?

"*Dobry,*" I tell her. Good.

She smiles again, recognizing from my stuttered inflection that I'm not a native, but at least I'm trying.

I pay the bill and head back toward the apartment. As I exit the building, I nearly bump into a tall man with a sharp nose and cheesy ponytail and reflective aviator glasses. He puts up his hands, showing off fine leather gloves, and says, "*Prominte.*" Sorry.

He lingers for a second, looking into my face like maybe he recognizes me, which happens every now and then. I must look like a lot of people. After a moment he smiles again, this time giving me a flash of dazzling, nearly-glowing teeth, and turns away from me.

As he turns, he says it again. "*Prominte.*"

Weirdo.

I've always had an ear for languages. Growing up in New York will do that. Not that I can speak anything fluently, but I can usually get the gist if the person is speaking slow enough. This town has been my first true test of how good I am, and the answer is: not very. The way people speak when they're home is fast, loose, comfortable. They slow it down when they go somewhere else. That's why I was able to pick things up. Here, I feel like I'm watching a foreign film at double speed with no subtitles.

Not that it matters. I've found when you're in a foreign country, there are six things you need to be able to say.

Just six. The first is "sorry."

The rest are:

Please. *Prosím.*

Thank you. *Dekuji.*

Bathroom. *Toaleta.*

Beer. *Pivo.*

Cheers. *Na zdraví.*

Everything else comes in time, but if you're able to do those, you're pretty much set. Prague isn't too bad with the language barrier. I keep a translation guide in my back pocket and I can count on one hand the number of times I've had to take it out.

Back at the apartment building, I fish the key fob out of my pocket. It's the size of a quarter, connected to a small leather strap. I hold it up to the black box next to the door and a green light flashes. The door clicks. I push through and head upstairs. Inside the apartment, I unload the groceries and close the window, sit at the counter with an apple and open up Google Maps, zoom out until I'm looking at the whole of Europe and Asia.

I've been here a little more than two months and my visa is only good for three. My boss, Stanislav, has offered to hire me full time so I can stay here—he likes me a lot—but I'm not sure. I really do like Prague. It's gorgeous and everything is cheap because even though they're in the European Union, they're on the crown instead of the euro. The exchange rate is bonkers. I can go out and have a beer and get a nice meal for a couple of bucks.

But there's something off about this place.

I can't say that I'm stuck. That's melodramatic. I feel like I'm in a car, driving down an empty stretch of highway, and the place I'm headed to may be over the next rise or a hundred miles way, and there's no way for me to tell. So I keep driving, wondering when I'm going to stumble across my destination.

Wait. That was *way* more melodramatic.

Let's go back to stuck.

Stanislav is the cousin of an old friend from back home. He owns dozens of apartments across the city he rents out through an online service called Crash Hop. The site was intended for people to rent out their homes to make a little extra cash. But an entire industry has popped up around services like these. It's a nice setup, and for a lot of travelers, preferable to a hotel. You get a kitchen and a few bedrooms and if you go in with a couple of people, it ends up being pretty cheap. There's something nice about being forced to fend for yourself rather than having a front desk do everything for you. A little more of an authentic experience than staying at the Best Western in Kinsky Garden.

For example, you get to go to the grocery store.

My role here is jack-of-all-trades. Cleaning vacated apartments, fixing stuff, delivering packages. It's a far cry from my previous jobs: amateur private detective, amateur bouncer, amateur chef, in that order. Though, truthfully, the detective thing never goes away, even though I've tried.

And I've accepted that. I'm the guy who can't sit by while something bad happens.

Acceptance is the first step.

Not that I've figured out what to do with that.

So where do I roam to next? There are other places in the world I want to see. Ireland, because that's where my family is from. I'd love to visit Paris, because who doesn't want to visit Paris? Tokyo is high on my list, because it's a country built from neon and strict honor codes and Hello Kitty and sexual repression. Sounds fun.

I could also go home.

Back to New York City.

It's been more than a year since I left. And there are things I miss about it. But I'm not sure if I'm ready. Considering the number of bridges I nuked in my wake, I'm not exactly keen to buy my return ticket yet.

And anyway, there's something I like about the solitude of travel. There are entire days where I don't have to talk to anyone. It's oddly comforting. For a very long time I haven't done a good job of being myself. This allows me the space to do that.

All I know is, if I'm going to leave, I need to visit the Sedlec Ossuary at Kutná Hora. I promised someone. Someone I met once for only a few minutes, but hey, a promise is a promise.

I take a deep breath. Feels like a beehive buzzing in my brain. I'm done thinking for a little while. I close the laptop, chuck the apple core into the trash, kick off my boots, and head into the living room. Drop onto the couch and turn on the television.

The Simpsons is on. *The Simpsons* is always on. This episode is from after season twelve, when the show stopped being good, which means normally I would skip over it, but there's something about the Czech dubbing, making you focus on the visual gags, that it ends up being pretty entertaining. I settle in, figure on watching this episode and working up the energy to make myself an actual meal to eat, or call Kaz to meet for a drink.

There's a knocking sound from the front of the apartment.

I figure it's for the apartment across the way, because no one knows I'm here or would have any cause to visit me, but then I hear it again, a little more insistent this time. I head toward the front and open the door.

The man who bumped into me outside the grocery store is standing there in the dark hallway, still wearing his sunglasses. I can see myself in them and I don't like the way he's smiling. Like he wants to sell me something that's broken.

"Ashley McKenna?" he asks.

"How the fuck do you know my name?"

"I have a job offer to discuss with you," he says, like this is a perfectly normal thing to say to a stranger in a strange city.

"I already have a job," I tell him. "Fuck off."

Before I can close the door, two thick men in jeans and heavy coats step out from either side of the door, flanking the first man. They are very big, heavy-browed men who both exude an "angry caveman" vibe. I can rumble and I get a little ahead of myself sometimes, but these are two guys I would not fuck with.

"This isn't the kind of job you get to turn

21

down," the man says. He smiles, and even though I imagine it's the confusion and adrenaline warping my vision, his bright white teeth look slightly sharper than human teeth should.

"I know that's supposed to scare me, but I stick with my original answer," I tell him. "Fuck off."

He nods. "Thought so."

The man on the left reaches inside his jacket and comes out with a small pistol. He points it at my gut as the man on the right pulls out a gun, too. He holds his in front of him, like he's uncomfortable with it.

Not that it matters. Their two guns trump my zero.

"I guess we should have this conversation inside," I tell them.

TWO

The apartment has a living-dining room combo on the other side of the kitchen. Which means a sofa unit on one side and a cheap Ikea-style table on the other, with a couple of straight-backed, uncomfortable chairs around it.

This meeting feels too formal for the couch. I sit on the far end of the table and wait for the others to take their seats. The whole time wondering what the hell is going on.

There's not much information I can glean from these guys. The sidekicks look local. Weary, stone expressions that indicate they wouldn't understand or appreciate sarcasm. They're not going to like me.

One guy, his face is chubby and bunched, like a pug dog, his bottom lip protruding as if he's actively sticking it out. The other is solid muscle, and given the odd proportions, I imagine he gets those muscles as much from drugs as he does from working out.

Pug and Hulk for short, until they introduce themselves.

They stash their guns and sit on either end of the table. I sit on the long end, my back against the wall.

I hate how appropriate that feels.

The man in the aviator glasses picks up the remote off the couch. He turns off the television as Homer is gesticulating wildly at Bart.

"Aww, c'mon," I tell him. "Can't we at least finish this episode?"

He doesn't answer. Doesn't even acknowledge I said anything. He takes the free seat, across from me, and places the remote down in front of him on the table. He removes his sunglasses and places them down next to the remote. His eyes are small and dark. There's deliberateness to his movements that seem almost alien. Once he's got the glasses perfectly lined up with the remote, he looks up at me and smiles.

"So, Ashley McKenna," he says. "That's an interesting name."

"It's a girl's name. What do you want?"

"You're awful cavalier for someone being held at gunpoint by three strangers."

"Not my first rodeo, fuckface."

He winces at my casual use of profanity. Hard to get a read off him, otherwise. Accent is completely flat. Features tell me maybe he's Italian or Greek, but I wouldn't be shocked to find out he was Middle Eastern. His clothes are expensive. Under the jacket, which he hasn't removed, is a dark sweater with a thread count so high it shimmers in the light.

I still can't tell if he's dangerous.

The guys he's with, yes, absolutely. But there's

something about this guy that strikes me as both sinister and . . . soft? Either I'm not smart enough to be afraid of him, or I have no reason to be.

"You know my name," I tell him. "What do I call you?"

"You can call me Mr. X," he says.

"No."

He purses his lips and inhales sharply, like he's about to laugh. "What do you mean, no?"

"I mean that's a dumb nickname. I'm not calling you that with a straight face. Think of something else."

"Fine. Call me Roman."

"Okay, Roman. That's much better. So, Roman, what do you want?"

"First things first," he says. "Are you expecting anyone?"

"Nope. Not until you and your asshole friends came and fucked that up."

Pug and Hulk don't bristle at this. I wonder if it's because they don't understand English or don't care what I have to say.

"First, it's important to me that you're truthful," Roman says. "Because if someone else walks through that door, I'm going to shoot them dead. Second, can you please stop with the profanity? It's . . . uncouth."

"We're alone," I tell him. *Asshole.*

He shakes his head, pushes the edge of his sunglasses with a fingertip until they're parallel to the long end of the table, forming an L with the remote. "You don't seem all that flustered by this."

"Like I said, it's not my first time," I tell him. "I call it the John McClane Paradox of Bullshit."

"I don't know who that is."

"You've never seen *Die Hard*?"

He shakes his head.

"You're lame, on top of everything else," I tell him.

He clears his throat. "So, about why I'm here. First, let me ask you, do you know what a golem is?"

"Little weirdo with a jewelry obsession. Hangs around Mount Doom."

He shakes his head. "Golem. G-O-L-E-M. The golem is a very famous Prague legend. It is a beast of Jewish folklore, a creature created from clay by a rabbi. It is given life by magic to serve at the behest of its creator. A golem is a big, brutish thing. Strong, but not clever. Completely obedient."

"C'mon. Rip the bandage off. Tell me what you want."

He glances toward the ceiling—I think rolling his eyes—and looks back at me. "Foul language aside, I like you. You're bold. You're going to be a good fit for this. I represent the United States government. The agency I work for, you've probably never heard of it. Most people haven't.

When we do our job right, no one hears about us."

"You're . . . what? A spy or something?"

"I am a creator of golems," he says. "It is really very hard to maintain the identities of covert agents. As soon as something goes on a computer, some fourteen-year-old kid in China has it. Every now and then we find ourselves with a job that's important, but not important enough to risk one of our primary assets. Think of real spies as the high-value pieces arranged alongside the back of a chessboard. Do you play chess?"

"Occasionally."

He nods. "The knights and rooks and bishops. You don't risk them unless utterly necessary. The pawns, meanwhile, are expendable."

"And . . . you want me to be a pawn, or a golem, or whatever?"

"Yes."

"You want me to be a spy?"

"No, I want you to do a job for me."

This is where I start laughing. Pug and Hulk don't flinch, but Roman looks disappointed.

"Fuck off, dude," I tell him. "This is nonsense."

"I thought you might say that."

Roman removes his leather gloves and places them on the table, next to the remote. Then he takes a piece of paper, folded in thirds, out from inside his jacket pocket. He unfolds it and pushes everything—the remote, the gloves, the glasses—

off to the side. He runs his fingers along the creases of the page to smooth it out. There's a lot of compact handwriting I can't read.

"Ashley Florian McKenna," he says. "Father died on 9/11. I'm sorry to hear that."

"Fuck yourself."

"A little over a year ago you were still living in New York," he says, looking at the text, not at me. "You have some loose associations with Ginny Tonic, a known drug distributor. Before you left, the police were looking at you for the murder and rape of one Michelle Long. Though they eventually caught the real perpetrator. You come up a lot in police records. No actual police reports, but your name is in the system." He looks up at me and raises an eyebrow. "I've heard you fancy yourself a private detective."

That's all about right, with a few minor parts missing—I freelanced for Ginny, mostly making deliveries of packages I was smart enough to not look inside.

And I loved Chell. She loved me, too, just not the same way. So when I found the guy who killed her, rather than kill him, which had been my preference, I dimed him out to the cops. Figured it might be nice to break the cycle of violence.

"It wasn't professional, the detective thing," I tell him. "I helped people and sometimes they gave me money and sometimes they gave me booze or drugs. I was comfortable operating on a barter system. I was more of a blunt instrument."

Roman smiles. "Blunt instrument. I like that." He looks down at the paper. "So you left New York and six months later you're living in Portland, where a couple of interesting things happen. Mike Fletcher, who was running for Congress, ends up the focus of a federal investigation. Among the complaints was harassing the employees at a strip club where you worked. And one of his employees, Chris Wilson, was found buried in a hole under a tree off a hiking trail. Neck broken. He got buried around the time you left Portland, best as I can tell."

This is the first I'm hearing Wilson had been found. Something happens to my face because Roman narrows his eyes, realizing he's hit a nerve.

And yes, I did kill Wilson, but it was mostly an accident, and anyway, it was to protect two people—Crystal, a dancer at the club, and her daughter, Rose. I really do not like the direction this is headed. My stomach twists and the bits of apple I ate are threatening to make a re-appearance.

"A few months after that, you're living in a hippie commune down in the Georgia woods," he says. "Two people died. And a fracking derrick got blown up. There are rumors that a militant environmental group is involved . . . the Soldiers of Gaia." He stops reading from the paper and looks up at me. "So, there are two interesting conclusions to draw from this. One is bad things happen and you run. Which makes me draw the second conclusion: you are very good at getting into and then out of trouble."

This is getting worse and worse. The involvement of the Soldiers was supposed to be covered up. That was the entire point—blow the derrick, save the community, stop the militant assholes from making a name off it. Where the hell is he getting all this?

"Yeah, I don't know about any of that," I tell him, trying to play it cool, though I can't help but look away.

"Here's the thing," he says, folding up the piece of paper, pressing down hard on the creased edges until it lays flat. "I don't know what you have or haven't done. Maybe you weren't involved in any of this. But you have to understand that this all looks very bad for you." He taps the folded paper. "Someplace in here is something I can take advantage of. And I will. I can make your life very, very difficult. At the same time, there are records I can strategically eliminate, so even if someone sat with all of this information, your name wouldn't be so prevalent."

Well. It was only a matter of time, I guess.

Karma finally came to collect.

This, though, is not my jam. I have never been

good at following orders, and I don't aim to get into the habit.

"Sorry," I tell him. "I'm not going to be blackmailed into doing some asshole's bidding. Especially some government stooge. I reiterate my original request: fuck off. You want to throw this shit at me, go ahead. We'll see how it plays out. I've got nothing to lose."

Pug huffs and shakes his head. Maybe he does speak English. Though my response might transcend language.

Roman licks his lips and raises an eyebrow, not even a little surprised. "I thought it might come to this. I really did. So, there's one piece of information I would like you to consider before confirming for me that this is your final decision."

He removes a very fancy fountain pen from inside his jacket and scribbles something on the folded piece of paper. He turns it around so what he wrote is facing me, and slides it across the table.

It's my mother's address.

My whole world goes red.

"That's a funny way to commit suicide," I tell him, and throw myself across table, grabbing him by his collar, and I don't care if those two assholes have guns, I am going to do my best to put his face through the floor.

Before I've even got a good grip on Roman,

Pug and Hulk grab my arms. Once I'm off-balance, Pug lets go of me and Hulk pulls me to his side, wraps his arms around me, lifts me into the air, and slams me down on the table. It creaks but surprisingly doesn't break. Good on Ikea.

I throw my elbow hard into Hulk's gut and catch him square. He staggers back, gasping for breath, and I try to roll off the table. Pug grabs me by the shirt and drags me toward him. I slide off and hit the floor hard, knocking the little bit of wind out of my lungs. I twist to get up, but Roman's leather loafer presses into my throat. I grab it by the toe and heel, try to move it, but it doesn't budge.

He's stronger that I would have guessed.

He is also very angry.

The smile is gone. The cool, bemused demeanor has dissipated. He's leaving me enough room to breathe, but barely. Within seconds, dark patches float on the edge of my vision.

"The flight time from here to New York is eight hours and forty-two minutes," he says. "I can be on a chartered jet in under an hour. Depending on the time of day, it could take anywhere from thirty minutes to an hour to get from the airport to your mother's doorstep. I could be in her kitchen in approximately ten hours if the timing works out. Would that be preferable?"

"Fuck . . . you," I tell him.

"I'm sorry?"

"Fine," I tell him.

"Convince me that you are sincere," he says, letting off the pressure a little. "Because given your attitude, I'm not so sure you won't take another dive at me."

"I promise," I tell him.

And I mean it, too.

The pressure increases again. Like he has to think about it.

After a moment, he lets go. I sit up and look at Hulk, who's cradling his midsection and looks like all he wants in this world is to stomp my head until it ruptures like an overripe pumpkin.

"Sorry," I tell him. "Honestly, can you blame me though?"

He shrugs, like he gets it.

The chairs got knocked over in the scuffle. We right them and seat ourselves. Roman sits down, smiling again, like none of what happened actually happened.

There's not even room for negotiation at this point. He's got me and he knows it.

"Tell me what you want me to do," I say.

He smiles again. "See? That was easy."

"No, it wasn't. It was so very not easy."

Pug reaches into his coat and hands Roman an envelope. Roman opens it and places a photograph on the table. A black-and-white shot of a petite blonde. She's a little plain, in a high school sweetheart way. Like you'd expect her to make a scrunchy face and cough after having a sip of beer.

"Samantha Sobolik," Roman says. "Czech, late twenties. She works for Hemera Global, a bank based in the United States with offices here in Prague. Sometime tonight, she's going to receive some information that we would very much like to have. Probably on a thumb drive or a small laptop. You're going to retrieve it for us."

"I don't even know how to start with that," I tell him.

"You're going to figure it out," he says. "You have to understand, the information she has is very valuable and very dangerous. You'll be doing your country a service."

"Fuck my country," I tell him. "Priority number one is my mom."

"We'll leave this photograph with you. On the back is her address, as well as locations in her neighborhood she is known to frequent. Memorize it and destroy it. Then get to work."

"Say I get whatever it is you're looking for. What then?"

"Don't worry," he says. "I'll find you."

"If I do this, what? Free and clear? You don't bother me or my mom?"

"Never again," he says. "This is a one-off."

"This Samantha," I say, nodding toward the photo. "Is she dangerous?"

"If this were difficult, I'd put one of my men

on it," he says. "But I'm afraid she might be under surveillance and my men are known in this country and could be compromised. Hence you. Nobody knows you here. I don't need finesse. I need a tool. A blunt instrument, if you will."

Roman stands and brushes off his coat, like the act of being in this apartment has sullied him. Pug and Hulk stand behind him. "I know this is a little odd, but I'm a serious person and I suggest you take this seriously. It'll be done before you know it."

They turn to leave and I tell him, "One thing."

The three of them turn.

"You rang a bell you can't unring," I tell Roman. "If I get even the hint that my mother is in any kind of danger, I will come after you. I get that you're a cool guy with thugs and guns and shit. But I'm a born and bred New Yorker with anger management issues. So even if I don't kill you, you best believe I'm going to take a chunk out of you before you put me down."

Roman smiles again. "As I said before, I like you."

As he's walking to the front, he stops at the kitchen counter, by the neat little pile I made when I came in and emptied my pockets. Phone, wallet, and passport. He picks up the first two, places them to the side, and holds up my passport.

"I'm keeping this for now," he says before disappearing from view.

The door at the front of the apartment slams to signal their departure.

What the actual fuck?

I sit back, rest my head against the wall, and stare at the ceiling.

This whole thing is so ridiculous, part of me believes it didn't even happen. And I might fully believe that if not for the soreness of my throat and the overwhelming feeling of dread hanging in the air like a toxic cloud.

I get up and go to the kitchen, pour myself a glass of water, and down it, pour another and place it on the counter, not sure if I want it. I pick up my phone and text Kaz: *Need help.*

THREE

Pats is my favorite kind of bar: perpetually empty, so I have to wonder how it is they stay open.

Gray light is streaming through the windows and "Lost in the Supermarket" by The Clash is playing a little too loud for mid-day. The bartender, who looks like he should be living under a bridge and asking people riddles, puts a golden pint of Pilsner Urquell in front of me before I'm even settled on the stool. It's a beer I wouldn't drink back home, but here it's like Guinness in Dublin. It's made locally, and you drink it here because it's best when fresh.

I toss some coins onto the bar and the bartender takes them without acknowledging me.

"*Na zdraví*," I say as he moves to the other end of the bar.

People think the Czechs are rude. I don't see it like that. They share a lot in common with New Yorkers. You live in a big, old city, in a relentless crush of people, you're bound to develop a callus. This city is way older than New York, plus it's been through a lot, with the revolutions and regime changes. The thing we have in common is we just want a little peace and quiet.

Pats is a good place for that. Always the same

bartender, infrequent crowds, and the décor is very much my aesthetic: old-school punk rock posters in Czech, covering every available inch of space on the walls.

The door opens and I hear Kaz before I see him. The clinking of the thick chain hanging from the belt loop on his jeans, disappearing into his pocket and connected to his wallet.

Then I smell him. The cloud of cologne that precedes him is so thick I'm surprised I can't see it. He hops onto the stool next to me, wearing a sheepskin Russian-style military hat, a black sweater, and red and black plaid pants with boots made for stomping heads in mosh pits. The outfit looks wrong on him somehow, with his soft, boyish face, and jittery energy. He's past thirty, but I wouldn't fault anyone for guessing he was twenty.

"You smell like a French hooker," I tell him.

"It is very manly smell," he says, his Russian accent leaning heavy onto his words. "You are jealous. I will lend you some."

The bartender puts a beer in front of him. We hoist our glasses and clink them. He downs half of it and says, "*Vashe zrodovy*, my friend."

I met Kaz on one of my first nights here. I was wandering the city by myself, completely lost, when I heard the sound of a punk klezmer band playing "Hava Nagila."

I had nothing to do and nowhere to go so I followed the music. That's music you follow. I found myself inside a small bar, the band alternating between Eastern European folk songs with a punk-rock tilt. I bought a beer for fifty cents American and mixed into the crowd and the surge of it pushed me forward until I was right in front of the stage.

The floor was plywood and it shook when everyone jumped but I jumped with them. Sweaty bodies were pressed into me and there was a mess of languages buzzing in the air.

And then the band cut into a cover of "Folsom Prison Blues" and every single person in that place began to sing it.

Every single person.

It was a moment I'll carry with me the rest of my life. Half a world away and alone and a little afraid and lonely and here was something so familiar. People finding connection through music. Johnny Cash, no less.

Halfway through the song, I felt an arm around me. It was Kaz. He was singing and I was singing, and we finished strong, so close to the stage now we were practically singing into the mic.

We sang Johnny Cash and we hugged and he bought me a beer. I don't have brothers but I imagine that's what it must feel like to have them. After that, he invited me out for more beers, and even though I didn't take him up on the drinks, I still went out and we had a good time.

He's been my one and only friend in the time I've been here.

I like having one friend. Keeps things concise.

Even better, that friendship blossomed into a pretty solid business relationship.

"Before we get to it, may we conduct our business?" Kaz asks. "This way it is done."

I take an envelope out of my coat and put it on the bar. He picks it up and peeks inside, finds a list of apartments that'll be free and empty for the next couple of days. He nods and takes out a tightly-packed roll of Czech bills and holds it toward me. I stuff them into my pocket.

This is my side-gig. One that Stanislav would probably not be thrilled about. Kaz is in a line of business that requires empty apartments. I have no idea why and I've never asked. It's just a thing we came around to in conversation one night.

I make about five thousand crown per "rental," which works out to a little over two hundred dollars. It's a nice partnership, because I don't have to do anything and the apartments are always immaculate when he's done with them.

"I do not know what I'm going to do when you leave," he says.

"You'll manage."

"Maybe you stay? I will take care of you," he

says. "You come stay in my apartment. I have a beautiful apartment. Many rooms." He spins a little in the seat to look at me. "And the women, my friend. I will introduce you to women who are so beautiful you will have no idea why they are even talking to you."

That conjures an image of Crystal. Her hair buzzed to stubble on one side of her head, black hair draping like a curtain on the other. Blue-green tempered glass eyes.

"I already know how that feels," I tell him.

He chugs the last of his beer, waves the empty pint glass at the bartender, who comes over to fill it. He doesn't do anything to mine even though it's nearly empty, because he knows I won't have another.

"So what is the problem?" Kaz asks.

The bartender is out of earshot, down at the other end cleaning some glasses. I've also never heard him speak a word of English so I'm not too worried. The bar is empty save us. I walk him through what happened. It sounds ridiculous, saying it: some government clown is blackmailing me into a one-and-done spy mission.

After I finish, he nods and says, "You sound very fucked." But not at all surprised. Like this is the most normal thing in the world for me to be telling him.

"Thanks. You ever hear of anything like this?"

"I have heard stories," he says. "Expats and

41

tourists get jammed up on this thing or that thing. Sex and drug stuff. Girl notices wedding ring so they go to wife. They know your name, they know your Facebook, your shit is done. But no, never anything like this." He takes a swig of beer. "You are going to do it, then?"

"I don't think I have a choice."

Kaz looks around and lowers his voice, even though we're still alone. "I know people. Good people." He taps his temple. "Smart people. I can have you out of here in a few hours." He flattens his hand and arcs it through the air. "Leaving on the jet plane."

"I'm worried they might actually go after my mom," I tell him.

"I suspect it is bluff. If the job is so easy, it does not seem worth flying all the way to America to murder old lady to motivate you."

I drain the beer, put the empty glass on the coaster. Drop my head forward and rest it against the bar. It's not a terrible point. If I leave, are they really going after her? Or will they find someone else to complete the task?

It's too big an if.

"Can't risk it," I tell him, picking my head back up.

"Maybe tell her to leave town for a little while?"

"I wouldn't even know where to start with that," I tell him. "How do I explain all this? I don't want to scare her."

"Look on the bright side," he says. "You are like James Bond now. Without all the toys and the good looks and ability to seduce women."

"Thanks. The 1970s called. They want you to know the communist punk look was lame even back then."

"We only got this look last year, Mister Fancypants American. Still in style." Kaz drains his beer. "You want weapon? Someone to back you up? I get it for you. Easy."

"I don't think I need to take it that far."

"Good to be safe. I know a guy. Get you whatever you need. For a price, of course. But you will be, what do the Americans say? Strapped."

"I don't think I need to take it that far. I'm more worried about missing the exchange."

"You need me, you call me. Understand?"

"I will, thanks."

"You want another?" Kaz asks. "I will have another."

"You know I try to keep it to one," I tell him, getting up.

Kaz sticks one finger in the air and the bartender nods, takes the empty glasses, and goes to pour a fresh one. "You should build a better tolerance, my friend."

The thing I don't want to tell him is that a few months ago I was self-medicating with whiskey and when the supply ran out, I got hit with a case

43

of the DTs. I probably shouldn't be drinking at all, but beer is practically water and, anyway, it's nice to have a little something to take the edge off.

Also, it's not like I've ever been good at doing the smart thing.

"I'm getting old," I tell him, placing some coins on the bar, enough to cover one of Kaz's beers. I pat him on the shoulder and he puts his hand over mine.

"It will all work out in the end. You will see."

"Yeah. We'll see."

Once I've got the information on the photo memorized, I crumble it up and drop it in a trashcan on a corner. I already know the street with Samantha's apartment—Crash Hop has an place over there. It's across town, which means walking, and that much is nice because Prague is a good walking town. I stick in my earbuds and click over to Bach's cello suites as performed by Yo-Yo Ma, and let that rip.

Good walking town, good walking music.

Leaves me with some space to think. It's a good space for that. Big, sprawling, lots of nooks and crannies to explore. Confusing as shit because I can't pronounce any of the street names, and they zig and zag and stop and reform and circle back on themselves.

This has been my first time out of the country.

What continues to strike me as incredible, even though I've been here for more than two months, is the age of the city. So much of it has been standing for longer than anything in America. It does well at challenging your perspective, and makes you realize how much bigger the world is. How much of it you don't know.

The architecture, in particular, is fascinating to me. I've been learning a little about it. There are buildings here that remind me of buildings in New York. There's a synagogue that looks like the inside of the Village East Cinema. Apparently it's called Moorish revival style. Of course I recognize the Gothic style from St. Patrick's Cathedral, but there's also Romanesque, like the Mercer Hotel, and Renaissance, similar to Casa Belvedere, an Italian cultural center on Staten Island, not too far from where I grew up.

To be clear, I barely understand what any of these terms mean. I can't explain the difference between art nouveau and baroque. But I like the way I can wander around and come across something that reminds me of home, even this far away.

I spend a lot of time wandering and reading, and some of it is beginning to stick. I wish I was this motivated to learn stuff while I was still in school. I would have been a much better student.

I bunch up my coat against a gust of wind. The snow has stopped but it's still pretty damn cold. I move in the general direction of where I think Samantha's apartment is. I should probably consult a map.

I think I've strayed too far but come out on Wenceslas Square, which is actually a half-mile long and shaped like a rectangle, with a wide street and businesses lined up on either side. It's got a boutique feel, more so than the rest of the city. That aside, it's a big, pretty spot, and a popular place for demonstrations.

It takes a little while and a bit of backtracking, but at the other end of the square I find the street I'm looking for: Římská. A few blocks later and I'm outside a bland apartment building. Far less people here. This neighborhood is more residential. No businesses in sight save the coffee shop across the street, and coffee strikes me as a good idea, so I head in and order an Americano to go and sit at a table in the corner.

It's mostly empty, just a few people reading books or poking away at laptops. I take my laptop out of my backpack, find the Wi-Fi network, which is unprotected, and research the list of businesses Samantha is known to frequent, to get a sense of what kind of area I'm working with. There's a dry cleaner and a grocery and two restaurants on the list, besides this coffee shop.

Should have kept the photo. I could take it to the guy working the counter. Ask him if he recognizes her.

I poke around a little on Facebook and Twitter, hoping to find a Samantha Sobolik. I can only find a LinkedIn profile with some of her job information, which sucks, because LinkedIn is about as useful as a handle on a bowling ball.

I get bored with that and figure on clicking around Google to see if there are any good examples of the bullshit I'm currently facing down. But I don't know what to search for outside of "spy blackmail." So I search for that, and the first story it returns is about a spy who was blackmailed with racy photos and murdered by the KGB.

Not a comforting start to this search.

I check my e-mail to see what the new assignments are from Stanislav. It's a light couple of days, which is good. Again, he ends the message by asking me to stay on and offering to get my work visa straightened out. Even though I've heard it's a huge pain in the ass and takes longer than I'm allowed to be here, he insists he can get it taken care of quickly.

My enthusiasm for staying is suddenly a lot lower, unfortunately.

As I'm opening a new tab to search for flights, picking Tokyo to start, a brush of blonde hair floats across the window. I grab my laptop and ditch the half-empty coffee and duck outside, nearly slamming the door into a lean, young Middle Eastern guy with a top knot and some patchy facial hair. I apologize to him and he gives me a dirty look as I dash onto the sidewalk, where I see Samantha walking down the street with a bag of groceries.

Well shit, that was easier than I expected.

Except I have no idea what to do right now.

I can't follow her into her building. I mean, I can, but that's creepy, and there's an outside chance I'll get maced or kicked in the balls for the effort. Better she doesn't see me. So I stand there and watch her disappear inside.

After five minutes of watching the front of the building, I consider going back for another cup of coffee. I can't stand here. It's a quiet street and I'm staring at a building. It makes me wish I still smoked. At least then I'd have an excuse to be outside.

As I'm thinking I should go, the front door opens and Samantha comes out, headed in the direction of Wenceslas Square. She doesn't seem to notice me and I hang back. Another few blocks and it'll be so crowded that I can get closer.

So we walk, and I follow twenty to thirty paces behind her.

I try to figure out Samantha's deal. Something to pass the time. From the way she carries herself, from the neat way she's dressed, I bet she's polite. Probably has a cat, or at least shares a lot of cat pictures online. Drinks cider. Talks to her mom every day.

Character profiles are fun. Back when I was doing the amateur PI thing, I would sometimes have to follow people. Not a lot, but every now and again. Sometimes I would have to follow people and keep a log of where they went. I would create profiles for them in my head to see how much I got right about them if our paths actually crossed.

A lot of the time, I got pretty close. Some of the finer details I'd flub, but you meet enough people, you see patterns in their stride, the lines of their faces, the tone of their voice, their word choice.

The thing I don't like about this is there's a wide-eyed innocence radiating off Samantha. So I'm hoping that whatever goes down between Roman and me manages to stay clear of her.

By the time she stops, we're back near the apartment where Roman and his men jumped me. She turns down a side street and stops at a café. That's cover enough, so I follow her inside. It's crowded and she sits at a table so I do the same, taking a seat across the dim, noisy room.

This is the first time I've ever followed someone across half a city.

I hate to say it, but it's kind of fun.

Every time I think I'm going to get away from this kind of work, I end up doing it.

I should take that as a sign.

She orders some food and I do the same because I'm starving. I pick something that is mostly meat and potatoes and bread because everything in Prague is meat and potatoes and bread. Which is nice. I've spent the last year mostly around vegans and have some making up to do.

The food comes out quickly and I dig into it, keeping one eye on Samantha, who's reading a book with a title I can't make out.

Once I'm done with the food, I order a coffee and open my laptop, not wanting to be sitting here doing nothing. The Wi-Fi login is scratched on a blackboard behind the bar, so I hop on and as soon as I open my e-mail, a chat window pops up.

Bombay: Yo. What's up?

Bombay is my closest friend from back home. One of the few people besides my mom I miss on a routine basis. It's been a while since we spoke, so even though I feel like I should be paying attention to Samantha, I figure I owe it to him.

Me: Nothing much. Working.
Bombay: How's the other side of the world?
Me: Good. How are things there?
Bombay: Same. You're not missing much. That's a nice laptop.
Me: How do you know what kind of laptop I'm using? You're like 20,000 miles away.

Bombay: 4,000 miles. And I know what type of laptop you're using because you're shit at internet security and so is the coffee shop you're sitting in.

That's the other fun thing about Bombay. He works in IT and does some light hacking, which, given the things I tend to get caught up in, often comes in handy. Our friendship extends beyond that usefulness—we've been friends since grade school, actually—which is why I don't usually feel bad asking him to help me out with stuff.

Except for that time his apartment got trashed by someone looking for me. That wasn't so good.

Bombay: You must be making good money. That's an expensive rig.
Me: Someone left it behind in an apartment.
Bombay: So you stole it.
Me: It's not stealing. We tried for three weeks to get in contact with the person who left it. If they want it back, I'll hand it over. But until then, finders keepers. You'd be amazed at the kind of stuff people leave behind.
Bombay: Hold on . . .

The computer screen flashes and the mouse zooms around the computer, zipping through

51

folders. After a few minutes of this, the chat window flashes green.

> **Bombay:** There. I checked to make sure the person didn't leave behind any porn or personal information.
> **Me:** That's nice of you. Last time you did that you needed me to download a program and give you access.
> **Bombay:** Learned some new tricks. You'd be amazed at how vulnerable computers are. You don't want to fuck around on this stuff.
> **Bombay:** So when you coming home?
> **Me:** Not sure yet.
> **Bombay:** Everything okay?
> **Me:** Yeah. Why?
> **Bombay:** Seems like something is wrong. From your tone.
> **Me:** It's words on a screen. How is there a tone?
> **Bombay:** C'mon.

The other thing about Bombay is he knows me better than anyone, so if there's something to pick up on, he's the one to do it. Part of me wants to clue him in—I might need his help before this is over—but I also don't want to get him involved. Not on something this weird. Given that he's Muslim and works with computers, he's convinced he's being at least passively monitored. I wouldn't be shocked to find out that was true.

I'm trying to think of a good excuse that'll throw him off the scent when there's movement at the front of the café. A man enters who appears to be homeless, given the tattered state of his clothes and the sloppy beard. The hostess makes a face, like she's going to bounce him, but he looks around and zeroes in on Samantha, walks to her table, and leans in close to her so he can whisper something.

She doesn't recoil, doesn't turn up her nose. Just nods, hands him some money, and he walks away.

That's interesting.

Me: Everything will be fine. I have to run. Sorry.

An ellipses pops up under the message, to indicate Bombay is tapping out a response, but I don't wait for it. I leave some money on the table and when I'm sure Samantha is focused back on her book, I shove the laptop in my bag and duck out the door.

The homeless guy stops in a liquor store and comes out moments later with something in a brown paper bag, then walks a little to a public park off the Vltava. The wind is harsh and frigid coming off the water.

The man sits on a bench, takes a plastic flask bottle of vodka from the bag, then downs a good portion in one gulp. I had planned on taking this slow, but at the rate he's going, I don't know how much longer he's going to be useful. Within ten feet of him I can smell him. He smells like mildew. As I get closer, he tucks the bottle inside his coat, as though afraid for it.

"In that café, you spoke to a girl," I tell him.

He doesn't seem fazed by the fact that I know this. He nods and speaks in a hazy mumble. "*Dosti*. Pretty."

"What did you talk about?"

"I give message."

"What kind of message?"

He looks around. Doesn't say anything. I take the roll of money Kaz gave me from my pocket—a little annoyed I'm now spending my own money—and break it in half. More than I want to pay on something like this, but I've got plenty more stacks from Kaz stashed away.

And it works. His eyes go wide and I think there's a tear forming in one of them as he snatches the wad from my hand. He proceeds to count the money out, giggling as he does it.

"Tell me the message."

"Charles Bridge at four."

"Forget that you saw me," I tell the man, but

it's like he barely hears me. He's counting the money again. That plus the vodka, I bet he's going to forget anyway.

I head back toward the apartment, which is near enough to the Charles Bridge. It's probably one of the bigger landmarks in the city. Prague Castle complex and the Kafka Museum are on the other side. I always see signs for the Kafka Museum, but I've never been able to find it.

It's five now. I'm betting four means in the a.m.

So. Now I have plans for tonight.

This is suddenly starting to suck less. At least there's a path to a resolution.

As I'm turning the corner, I see a man with a top knot and some patchy facial hair. He seems to be looking at me but quickly turns and holds up his cell phone to his ear.

It takes me a couple of minutes to realize why I recognize him.

That guy was going into the coffee shop as I was coming out, back on Římská, and here he is, half a city away, trying real hard to not look suspicious.

FOUR

I turn, hoping he won't notice I noticed him.

He stays where he is on the other end of the block, urgently "talking" into his phone while intensely studying a brick wall. I pull out my phone and look at it so I have an excuse to be standing still, try to get a good look at him without making it obvious. He could be another skinny goofball with a stupid haircut—the top knot is all the rage right now, like suddenly we live in feudal Japan—but after a moment, I'm sure of it.

Same guy from the coffee place.

He's been following me for as long as I've been following Samantha. When I broke off, he stuck with me. The fact that he hasn't engaged makes me think he's supposed to keep an eye on me. I am not a huge fan of this. I could run over and beat the living fuck out of him until he tells me who he is and what he wants. It comes with the added bonus of working through some of the frustration I'm feeling right now. But I'm committed to living a wiser, less violent lifestyle.

So, first, I want to see if he keeps following me, rather than go after the homeless guy. There's a small bookstore-café combo nearby. I head for that, trying really hard not to glance behind me, but as I turn a corner, I manage to sneak a look back, and he's there, not too far away.

This is weird. I've gotten myself into some tight spots before. I've had guns pointed in my face. But I've always managed to extricate myself. Not always with an abundance of grace, but I've managed.

This is a whole different kind of game.

I've been chased. I've never been hunted.

The bookstore is crowded, which bodes well, and even better, there's an exit through the café that you can't see from the entrance. There's no way he can cover both, so if he really wants to keep an eye on me, he'll have to follow me inside. I stroll the shelves and after a few minutes of browsing, find something pretty cool: a story by Raymond Chandler where the prose is in English on the left, with a Czech translation on the right. It's a slim volume, pocket-sized, and I wish I'd found this two months ago. Maybe it would have helped with my Czech.

As I move to the counter to pay, I see Top Knot looking at a spinning rack of tourist books by the front entrance, making it a point to not look at me. After I've paid, I walk outside, making sure not to get too close. I try to figure out my next step because I would like very much for him not be following me anymore.

One of Crash Hop's buildings is only a few

blocks away. That could work; I can get in and he can't.

When I get there, I take the little fob out of my pocket and press it to the reader on the outside of the door. The lock clicks and I push it open. The hallway is long and narrow and smells like boiling meat, the subway tile lining the walls dirty and scuffed. There are four apartments on each floor. I think the Crash Hop apartment is on the third floor but I'm pretty sure it's occupied.

At the far end of the hallway, opposite the staircase, is a rounded mirror, positioned so you can see the hallway as you're coming down the stairs. I run over and crouch on the first landing and watch the tiny, distorted figure of Top Knot come up to the door and try to open it. I can just wait until he leaves.

But he's not going anywhere.

I can't tell what he's doing, but after a few moments, I hear the click of the door opening. I turn and rush up the stairs, trying my best to be quiet. The building is only five floors and the door leading to the roof doesn't have an alarm. Outside, it's cold, and there's a heavy blanket of gray thrown across the sky.

This works. I can climb across to the next building, take that staircase down, and be gone before he knows where I went. I'm feeling pretty good about it until I find the roof of the next building is about ten feet shorter than the one I'm on, and six feet across a chasm that drops straight down to the street below.

Ah fuck.

I have to figure Top Knot is on his way up here. Physics seems to be on my side since the roof is lower and therefore friendly to gravity, so before I have a chance to really mull over how stupid this is, I run and jump, the fear center of my brain shrieking at me.

My stomach tilts. Then I land hard on the next building, coming down on my knee. I fold and roll to disperse the impact, scramble around a large brick chimney. My heart is slamming into my chest, and over the sound of that I hear the door opening on the other roof.

I wonder if he thinks I'm dumb enough to make the jump.

There's a lot of scratching. He's walking around, exploring the roof. His footsteps draw closer, toward the edge closest to me. He stops there. I can feel it. He's looking this way.

After a few minutes, more scratching, and the door slams again.

When I look around the chimney, this roof and the building next door are empty. Just me up here.

This is an interesting development.

It could be Roman, sending someone to keep tabs on me. That would almost be preferable because then at least I'd know who I was dealing with.

Otherwise, what the fuck?

I crawl on my hands and knees over to the edge, to look down and see what it was that I missed. My head spins. It is a long way to the ground. I climb to my feet and look around. Bells clang somewhere in the distance. Orange roofs dusted with snow stretch to the horizon and it is beautiful up here and I cannot wait to leave.

I settle on an apartment nearby that I know is empty. It's on the smaller end, and very European—compact, modular, everything straight lines and with the feeling it's slightly flimsy. There are neon lights built into the tub, which makes me not want to use the tub, because I'm worried about what else it's been used for. I should tell Kaz about this place, though. He'd get a kick out of it.

I polish off the mediocre pad thai I picked up on the way over and call up the Charles Bridge on Google Maps on my laptop. There's not much to see. It's a bridge. I tell myself I'm going to come up with a plan, but there's not much to plan. It's a smash-and-grab job. I scare the shit out of the girl, get her to give me the thing, run like fuck in the other direction, hope Roman keeps his end of the bargain by returning my passport and disappearing from my life forever.

The idea of scaring Samantha makes me queasy. I'm not a bully. I'm the guy who stomps the ever-loving shit out of bullies.

But I remind myself of what Roman's implied: what she's doing is very bad.

Not that it's a huge comfort, because for all I know he could be full of shit.

Now that I've got a little distance from the nonsense this morning, I remember the little story Roman told and run a search for golems. Mostly out of curiosity because, of course, it turns up nothing of use. There is a famous work called *The Golem of Prague*, published by Judah Loew ben Bezalel, a rabbi from the sixteenth century. The golem was originally created to protect the Jewish ghettos from anti-Semitic attacks.

I like that interpretation better than Roman's.

Next up, I search for the address of the U.S. Embassy. I'd like to at least know where it is, in case this goes south. That's the search that makes me get up from the computer and go to the window and stare out it like there's some kind of answer out there in the sky and snow. But there's not.

Every single fiber of my being is telling me to run.

That it's a bluff, it has to be.

Nothing is worth what Roman threatened.

But instead of running, I sit and wait.

The alarm rings and I nearly bash my head on the ceiling as I jerk myself into a sitting position. Loft beds are dumb.

I check the clock to make sure of the time: 3 a.m. More than enough time for me to get dressed and maybe grab a cup of coffee somewhere—I have no idea what's even open right now—and make it to the Charles Bridge with about twenty minutes to spare.

On the way out, I find a Cossack hat someone left behind on the coat rack. I put it on and undo the big floppy ears and let them fall down at the side of my head. Most people are going to think I look like an asshole, but the hat is very warm, and I also don't care what most people think. Anyway, something that obscures my identity a bit is nice.

I dump my wallet and phone and keep the key fob and a few thousand dollars in crown. I figure it's better to not have identifying papers on me. Which might be a mistake, but I guess I'll find out.

Outside, I'm surprised to find there are still people milling about on the streets, despite the brutality of the wind. My head feels full of sticks and mud, so when I come across a late night store selling snacks and coffee, I am very pleased. I get the largest cup of Americano they've got and head onto the darkened streets, which get emptier and emptier as I make it toward the bridge. I step off to the side where I can finish my coffee in a pool of shadow, the massive complex of Prague Castle lit up gold and looming across the water.

No stars in the sky. Too many clouds.

As I watch the castle and the sky, my adrenaline revs up, making me feel light-headed.

This is stupid.

But it also feels comfortable. A little bit of my old life gleaming through the cracks.

Point me at a job, I get it done.

It makes me wonder: What if I did try to do this full time?

Not the spy thing. That's ridiculous. But the private investigator thing.

When you spend a lot of your time cleaning stray hairs off toilet seats and laundering used towels, you can't do much but think about a life where you're not doing those things.

Following people, finding stuff, getting information, it's something I have a knack for. I never really considered doing it above-board, like a real grown-up job. But eventually I'm going to need one of those. I don't want to reach the end of my life and find I'm living in a trash can.

More than that, I don't want to reach the end of my life and feel like I didn't actually live a life. Because what I'm doing right now isn't a life. It's the bare minimum of what's required to keep food in my stomach.

I wonder what private investigators actually make.

This is not a good time for introspection. There's work to be done.

A few minutes from four, I toss my cup into a trash bin and head onto the bridge. It's a hell of a thing to see during the day—crowded and lined with statues, it looks like the kind of place two warriors would do choreographed battle at the end of a Kung Fu movie. Specifically, a wuxia movie, where people float in the air and leap off blades of grass.

Right now, it's empty and slightly foreboding. Like Times Square emptied out. It doesn't look right.

The statues, all of them religious figures, take on a sinister hue in the dark. As I walk past them, it feels like they're accusing me of something, but isn't that the point of religious imagery?

About halfway down the bridge, there's a flash of movement but it's hard to make out in the darkness. I head for that. Try to calm the thunderstorm of fear and anticipation inside me. Focus on the task.

A few dozen yards out, I can see Samantha, wearing a long tan coat bunched up against the cold. Her blonde hair pulled back into a tight ponytail. White fuzzy earmuffs. She's standing under a statue of a cloaked figure with a large, gold cross.

There's about an inch of snow on the ground now, more floating in the air around me, and there's someone else on the bridge, coming from the other side.

Perfect. Maybe that's the person making the handoff to Samantha.

She's looking in the direction of the other person. There's something about her posture that feels a little off.

Like she's tense. Scared?

As I get closer, a couple of things happen at once.

Samantha's head snaps around and she looks at me and says, "Motherfucker . . ."

She's angry—and looks very much like she recognizes me—which should give me pause, except the other person has broken into a run. From further away, I thought he was wearing a hat, but it's actually a balaclava, obscuring everything but his eyes.

That plus the dark clothes paints a not-so-great picture.

The picture gets a little weirder when I realize he's carrying a shovel.

The man raises it, holding it like a baseball bat, aiming it for Samantha, and I yell, "Hey!"

Samantha ducks away and I dig in, slipping a little on the snow and then running hard at the guy with the shovel. It's all instinct and muscle memory. I know this isn't the gig, but I'm not going to stand by and watch her get hurt.

I brush past Samantha, making brief contact with her, and collide with the guy hard, moving inside his swing so he can't hit me with the shovel. We tumble to the cobblestones. The Cossack hat goes flying off my head.

We both get to our feet at the same time. The man takes a little hop forward and reaches back to swing the shovel, so I move close in again, close the arc so he can't get enough power behind it.

Except it's a feint.

He jabs me hard in the face with the handle and my vision explodes. So fast I barely see it happen. It's not even a full-on blow, but it's the hardest I've ever been hit.

The pain is immense.

Pressure point? Broken bone?

I take a few steps back, try to put some distance between us, but the man is behind me. Like he snapped his fingers and teleported. He slams the shovel into the back of my knee and I go down hard. The shovel then smacks me in the back of the head, sending my forehead into the stone wall separating us from the Vltava.

Fists plow into my body like a torrential downpour and my vision swims as I fall to the ground and the man is lifting the shovel over his head, the pointed end of the spade aimed at me. It's sharpened like an animal's tooth.

I throw my foot out, get a lucky shot, and nail him in the kneecap. Something crunches and I crab-walk backward, climb to my feet, preparing for whatever's next, knowing deep down that there's not much I can do.

I've been in a lot of fights.

Some I won, some I lost, but I always walked away.

This might be the one where I don't.

That thought is confirmed when the man comes at me and I throw a serious haymaker, putting my entire weight and hopes and dreams into the point of my fist, but it kisses cold air, like he was never in front of me, and suddenly his hand is on my wrist and he twists my arm behind me at such an angle that he can move me like a marionette.

He yells at me in Russian.

Except, it doesn't sound like a he.

It's a thick, heavy voice, but it sounds like a woman. Which makes me hesitate, because my brain is hard-wired to not hit women.

Turns out hesitating is a very bad idea, because she jabs me once, twice, three times in the side of the head, and yells at me again in Russian. She pushes me against the wall and places a knee in my back, so I'm looking out over the black water of the river.

"What?" I ask, blubbering, tasting blood in my mouth.

"Who are you?" she asks.

She flips me around and pushes the wooden handle of the shovel into my throat, my back arched over the stone wall, and I can't breathe.

"Who are you?" she asks, letting off the pressure on the handle a little.

"What . . ."

I'm pretty sure this is it. The moment I die.

Just before dawn, alone on a bridge in a beautiful city.

As my vision is going wonky, there's an explosion of light and someone yells, "*Policie!*"

The woman looks to the side and I seize on the moment of distraction, try to push her away and fail, but manage to hook a finger into the balaclava and rip it free. I get a look at her face. She's old. Well past fifty. Sharp and angular and there's an angry scar crossing her forehead and running down her cheek, like someone tried to carve her face off.

The scariest part is her eyes. They're chips of obsidian pressed into her face, small and hard and furious. She is, without a doubt, someone who is prepared to kill these cops, and me, and anyone else she feels like she needs to.

Well, fuck that.

I get my foot into her sternum and shove off hard enough to send me over the wall and tumbling toward the lapping waters of the Vltava.

FIVE

There are two good things about falling into a river in the middle of the winter when you've been beaten nearly to death.

One is that the cold hits you like a bolt of electricity, snapping every muscle to attention and waking you right the hell up.

Two is that the current drags you away from the person who wants to kill you.

The positive aspects end right there.

This is cold like I've never known cold. Cold down to the marrow of my bones. I may be awake, but within seconds I'm sluggish, my muscles freezing. I kick to the surface and when I get above water, even breathing is hard. My lungs are developing a layer of frost, like they've been sitting in the freezer too long.

The water tastes filthy in my mouth and I can't see anything and I've got a general fear of water. I'm dangling a foot over the precipice of panic. Need to focus on something else.

I wonder how clean the Vltava is, and how bad it is to be in here with so many open wounds. That doesn't help.

My vision clears enough to make out the bridge against the night sky, which I'm moving away from, quickly. I concentrate on not sinking with the combined weight of my boots and jacket, kick in the direction of the current because I would like to be further away from the lunatic with the shovel.

North. I think I'm going north. I look for Prague Castle to orient myself and confirm my direction. Keep my head above water. I'm closer to the east bank so I push for that. My arms feel like dead things tied to my body.

If I can make the bank, there are plenty of staircases and pathways around the water. I'll find something. Anything.

Maybe I'll live through this.

If not, hopefully the cold knocks me out before I realize I'm drowning.

I cough and my head dips below the black water. My body is growing harder, metallic and brittle, like if I push too hard, pieces are going to snap off.

I kick, concentrate on reaching the wall.

Even my thoughts are slowing down.

From the cold.

A low deck comes up. I grab that. Think I missed it. Realize my hand is hooked into a rope. I can't feel that I'm holding it. The current is dragging me and I reach out my other hand, pull, muscles screaming, scramble onto the deck.

Once I'm out of the water, on my back and staring into the sky, I feel very, very sleepy.

If I sleep, I'll die.

Have to keep telling myself that.

Because I'd really like to sleep.

A lot.

Climbing to my feet takes a couple of tries because my muscles feel like fully-frozen hamburger meat. Once I'm up, I can see where I am: a barge restaurant. Smoking deck or something. There's a set of glass doors leading inside to a darkened dining room. I pray that it's unlocked, find that it is. No one's trying to sneak in from the river. Either that or someone fucked up. Doesn't matter. This is good. My hand slips on the handle so I try to blow on my fingers. I'm shaking so hard I can't keep my hand in front of my mouth.

The dining room is quiet, the tables pushed off to one side and not set, the chairs askew. The walls are wood and there's an intricate, dormant chandelier hanging from the ceiling. I move for the kitchen, on the other side of the dining room. Practically fall into the stove and try to turn it on. Fire means heat. It doesn't work. Fucking fuck. Might be closed for the season.

I need to get out of these clothes. They're heavy and keeping the cold flush against my skin. I search the kitchen and find some chefs coats, but nothing else.

Better than nothing. I peel off my jacket and shirt, drop them to the floor, put on a few of the chefs coats, piling them up until they're thick.

The dry clothing feels wonderful against my skin, but it's not doing much for the cold. The boots and pants cancel that out.

I carry my coat, head up the stairs that lead to the entrance. This door is locked so I take a fire extinguisher off the wall, hoist it over my head, and bring it down hard on the handle. It breaks off. Once I'm outside, the air cuts at me like razor blades.

I don't know what to do.

Calling the police might not be the best way to handle this.

Neither is going to a hospital. I can imagine Roman becoming very upset to find out I did those things. I don't even know where the hospital is. I don't have any paperwork on me, or my phone. Not even my passport. I am soaked and probably close to succumbing to hypothermia.

I think about my mom. Wishing she was here.

That's how deep this goes.

Big, blooming fear, like a child waking from a nightmare, alone in the dark.

Warm clothes. I need heat and warm clothes. The apartment I left my stuff at is too far from here, but there's one closer, and all the apartments have first-aid kits. I can blast the heat and run a warm bath. Once I get warmed up, I can get in contact with Kaz.

The street outside the restaurant is empty so I

walk until I reach Křižovnická, a wide block with a tram line running down the middle. There are a few cars coasting down the street and one of them is a cab. I wave it down and the guy doesn't seem to notice that my pants are drenched and that I'm shaking. The apartment I'm aiming for is only a few blocks away, but I don't know that I'd make it on foot.

It takes me a second to get the door open because my fingers don't want to cooperate.

After I climb in, I give him the address and he looks back. I have no idea what I look like but I'm sure it's not good. He's hesitant, so I take out all the cash on me and hold it up, again with a great deal of effort and not much help from my hands. The sight of the cash is good enough for him because he drives.

"Can you turn up the heat?" I ask. "*Teplo. Teplo.*"

He fiddles with something on the console and there's a roar from the front. I feel nothing.

The drive is quick but it leaves me with time to wonder what the fuck is going on.

That wasn't a handoff. That was someone trying to kill Samantha Sobolik, and had I not showed up when I did, that's probably what would have happened.

Frankly, I'm not even sure how I'm alive.

Luck?

Also, why the shovel?

The cab coasts to the curb in front of the building and I climb out, tossing the money through the glass partition and onto the passenger seat. He picks it up and starts yelling something at me in Czech but I ignore it, half-walk half-stumble to the doorway, work around in my pocket for the key fob, which miraculously didn't fall out of my pocket in the river.

The door clicks open.

All I have to do is make it to the fourth floor.

By the second, I'm huffing and puffing so hard I don't think I'm going to make it.

By the third, I'm pretty sure I am nearly dead.

The building is quiet and empty so I strip off my pants and socks. By the time I get to the fourth floor, I'm down to my boxers, and I figure on taking a nap inside a warm shower.

I throw myself at the door, use the fob to open it. It clicks open and I fall inside.

The lights are on.

And there's a group of people here, like I walked into a dinner party.

Most of them are dressed, except for the naked couple having vigorous sex on the kitchen counter.

Oh right, this is the apartment I told Kaz he could use tonight.

A fact that is confirmed for me when Kaz steps out from behind a group of people holding cameras and lighting equipment.

"Ash?" he asks.

The girl twists around and looks at me, blue and shivering in my boxers. My face undoubtedly a mangled mess.

"Is he in the scene?" she asks in a heavy Eastern European accent. "I did not agree to that. It is going to cost extra."

"Could use some coffee . . ." I start.

And then I collapse.

I wake up to a bright light and a massive headache, like an elephant is standing on my forehead. There's a pile of heavy blankets thrown over me.

The rest comes to me in stages.

I'm dry.

I'm also naked.

The room is completely blank. A bed low to the floor, no closet. A small dresser in the corner. A lamp in the other corner. Daytime. Harsh morning light pushing through the blinds.

There's someone moving next to me.

It takes me a minute to recognize her. The girl from the kitchen. I think she's naked, too, curled up besides me, but then I feel the rasp of clothing against my skin.

I'm not numb anymore. I'm still cold but I've advanced from subzero death freeze to sort of chilly. It's an improvement, for sure.

I try to speak but have a hard time forming words.

She looks up at me. She has big brown eyes, her hair falling over them. Her skin so soft against mine, and after the events of last night, if I could put the headache aside, I would want to stay right here forever.

"You were incredible," she says.

"What?"

She sticks her fist out from under the blanket and bops it off my shoulder. "Kidding. You were very cold. The doctor said you need body heat. Body heat costs extra."

"What . . ."

"I will go get them," she says.

She slides out from under the covers and stands. She's wearing a tiny bra and tinier panties. She fixes her hair, pulling it back into a ponytail, which she secures with a band from around her wrist. She stands there for a moment, letting me get a good look, lingering like she's teasing me. I want to say something witty about whether the view costs extra, but I can't move the words from my brain to my mouth.

As she steps into the kitchen she says, "He is awake now."

After a moment, a man comes in. Black guy, skinny, with a shaved head and a heavy beard. He has a grave expression on his face, which is not encouraging. He takes out a small flashlight and shines it across my face. The light feels like the sun exploding in my eyeballs. I clamp my eyes shut, open them, then blink away the ghosts they left behind. When I can focus again, I see Kaz is standing over his shoulder.

"He has a concussion," the man says in a French accent, more to Kaz than me. "Ribs are badly bruised but I do not believe they are broken. There does not appear to be any internal bleeding. The hypothermia should be under control now, but I would leave him under the blankets for a little while longer."

I want to ask pointed questions about my current state of health but my synapses are firing too slowly.

"What about his nose?" Kaz asks. "His nose looks pretty fucked up."

"Yes, because it was broken," the French man says. "I set it on my initial examination."

Well, that explains the pain radiating from my face.

"Sir," the man says. "Can you tell me your name?"

"Ashley McKenna."

"And where are you?"

"Prague."

"What is the Czech name for Prague?"

"*Praha.*"

"You are American, yes?"

"Yes."

"Can you explain to me the exchange rate between the crown and the dollar?"

"Something like five cents on the dollar?"

The man nods and stands up, seemingly satisfied with my answer, even though that last one was a bit of a guess.

"Do I need to keep him awake?" Kaz asks the doctor.

"He should be fine," the man says. "The concussion is minor. Let him rest. If his speech becomes slurred or he complains of the pain growing worse, please call me immediately."

I attempt to slide myself into a sitting position and my entire torso hollers in protest, so I stay where I am. The man nods toward the floor next to the bed, where I find a blue plate with two white pills and a plastic yellow cup of water.

"Please take that in a little while," he says. "Tylenol. I can't give you anything stronger, I'm afraid. Please stick with acetaminophen. Ibuprofen and aspirin are dangerous to use when you have a concussion. Do you understand?"

"Can someone please tell me what the fuck is going on?"

Instead of answering me, the French man looks at Kaz. "He should rest. A few days in bed and no strenuous activity."

"Understood, Étienne," Kaz says, handing the man a tightly-packed roll of money. "Thank you, my friend."

"Happy to help," Étienne says before turning to me. "You are lucky to be alive. Another blow to the head before you are healed could prove to be fatal. You might want to think about the things you do in your spare time. This violence . . ." He surveys my face. "This is the kind of violence people go looking for."

"Fixing me up doesn't give you the right to be a judgmental asshole."

He does not smile at this, but Kaz does. Étienne leaves and Kaz crosses the room to me and sits cross-legged on the floor next to the bed, which brings him to eye level.

"My friend," he says. "What happened?"

"It's a long story," I tell him, leaning back into the pillow. "To be perfectly honest, given the implications, I don't know if it's safe to clue you in."

"*Pozhaluysta*," he says. "Please. Tell me."

"Before I do that, why were there people fucking in here?"

Kaz smiles. "You did not know I was a porn producer?"

"You never told me."

"You never asked."

"Fair."

"It is very popular genre here," he says, swelling with pride. "Pick-up porn. A man finds a girl on the street and offers successive amounts of money for her to do things until they are having sex. It is all scripted, of course, but to the viewer it is made to think the world is full of possibility."

"Sounds delightful."

"You have never seen them?"

I shake my head.

"I will send you links."

"Do you appear in any of them?"

"Not for a long time," he says. "Porn is a young man's game."

"Don't send me any of those."

He laughs. "Maybe I will put one in there, as a surprise. You will be amazed at my prowess. Now, tell me. How did you end up here freezing, naked, and like you have been beaten by an army of men?"

"You sure you want to know?"

He holds his hands up and waves them at me, like someone trying to get a dog to come closer. "I can handle it."

I walk him through what happened—the bridge, Samantha, the nut job with the shovel, the swim to shore. At the end I ask, "What do you think?"

He sits for a long time, staring at the wall, processing it. Finally, he says, "I think you are in a lot of trouble."

"Thanks. Who was the doctor?"

"He is a friend," Kaz says. "He owed me a favor. I tell you this." He pats his chest. "I know people."

"Well, good. I think it might be best to stay out of a hospital right now."

"That is correct." Kaz stands and looks around

the room. "We have cleaned up everything from the shoot."

"Sorry to fuck that up. I kind of forgot you guys were here."

"Is no problem. A little creative editing. They got right back to it after you passed out."

"That's weird."

"Is fine. I will show you final cut when it's done. Now, I am tired, so I will go to sleep on the couch."

"You don't need to stay," I tell him.

"Yes, I do," he says. "You are a fucking mess and someone should be here in case anything happens. Get some sleep, my friend. I will check on you in a little while, to make sure you are still alive."

That hits me square in the feelings. My throat gets a little thick. He has no reason to stay or to help me. And being this far away from home, it feels so much better to know there's someone in the other room.

"Thank you," I tell him. "I can't tell you how much I appreciate that."

"No worries, my friend. Your stuff is on the floor next to you."

I roll over as much as I can manage, see my backpack lying against the wall.

"How . . ."

"You asked for it," Kaz says. "I sent someone to the other apartment to retrieve it."

"I don't even remember doing that. You're pretty good to me."

"Because you have been good to me. It was no trouble. Now rest."

Kaz disappears and I lie there looking up at the ceiling. Roll over and take the aspirin, get most of the water down before I start coughing, hard enough that maybe I finally did crack a rib.

I have no idea what time it is, but the sun is coming in strong, so it's got to be, what, 7:30 in the morning? Eight?

Was it really four hours ago that I was on the bridge?

It doesn't feel like it. It feels like a month.

I roll over to my bag, pull it closer, find my phone sticking out of the front pocket. The battery is low. It's actually 9 a.m. Three missed calls from a number I don't recognize. I'm about to call it back when the phone vibrates in my hand.

I answer it, expecting to hear Roman on the other end, because at this point I have to suspect he knows the job went sour. But it's Stanislav, probably calling from one of the phones in the office rather than his cell.

"Mister Ashley!" he says in his big, booming, cartoon bear voice. "How are you?"

"Not great," I tell him. "Tripped and fell down some stairs."

"Ashley," he says, his voice taking on a tinge

of concern. "Did you have too much to drink?"

"Actually no," I tell him. "I slipped on a patch of ice."

"These sons of bitches, not clearing their walkways," he says. "I was calling to tell you that we have had some cancellations, so the next couple of days are light. Feel free to take a few days. Though I guess the timing was good, no? Now you can rest a little?"

"That's some perfect timing right there," I tell him. "Thank you, Stanislav."

"It is okay. You are good worker and I am happy to reward good worker. You do know you can continue to be good worker? I handle all the paperwork. All of it. Maybe even give you a permanent apartment."

"I think it's time to move on."

"Will you go home? If so, I hope you give my love to Lunette. Tell her that her cousins miss her, and she should come visit us sometime."

"Not sure where I'm headed, but I'll let you know soon."

"Okay, Mister Ashley," he says. "You get some rest. And you think about it anyway. In case you change your mind."

"Sure thing."

Stanislav clicks off and this is a relief, at least. I consider calling my mom next, to make sure she's okay, but New York is six hours behind Prague, which means it's . . . three in the morning? Math is not working so great for me right now. Feel like I'm pushing stones up a hill trying to think about numbers. I set my alarm for four hours from now. That'll be 7 a.m. for her, and she's an early riser.

As I'm rolling over, the phone rings again.

And of course, it's Roman on the other end.

"What happened?" he asks.

"Dunno," I tell him. "Some crazy person with a shovel tried to kill Samantha but decided to try to kill me instead. Beat me nearly to death. So, thanks for that, you fucking asshole."

There's a pause on the other end.

"A shovel?" he asks.

"Yes."

"Are you positive?"

"Yes."

He goes silent for a few moments, and I think we've been disconnected. Then he says. "Keep your phone on. I'm not done with you yet, little golem."

Click.

I put the phone down next to me and stare at the ceiling for a little while longer. Sleep tugs at me, and I don't bother to fight it.

"Hey."

The room is dark. I think someone said something, but waking up is like coming up from the waters of the Vltava. Deep and confusing and scary.

How is it dark out? How long was I asleep?

My alarm must have gone off. Did I sleep through it?

I try to get myself into a sitting position but there's a weight on the bed. Someone is sitting next to me.

"Kaz?" I ask.

There's a foot control for the lamp in the corner. I reach down for it, but before I can, it clicks and the light comes on. There's a small sneakered foot on it.

The sneaker is a grey Nike with a white swoosh.

It belongs to Samantha Sobolik, who is perched on the edge of the mattress, holding a small knife, the blade extended and resting against the leg of her jeans.

The blade is black, sucking up the light rather than reflecting it.

"Try again," she says.

SIX

The sight of Samantha Sobolik sitting there throws me a bit, and not because I'm tired and suffering from a minor brain injury.

No one in the world besides Kaz knows I'm here, and on top of that, she's holding herself completely different than she did yesterday.

The tasteful, bland outfit is gone, replaced by black jeans and a skintight black thermal shirt that accentuates her slight curves. Her hair is pulled back in a tight ponytail. Her demeanor is different, too. The flat look she's giving me makes me believe she'll use the knife.

She sounds American. There's a bit of Southern drawl slipping between her words but it's like smoke. I can't be sure.

I'm still naked. That's not making any of this better.

"How did . . ."

"I ask the questions, dummy," she says. "First and foremost, who are you and why were you following me?"

"You noticed I was following you?"

She arches an eyebrow and smirks. "I hope you do not do that shit professionally because you are terrible at it. I made you outside the coffee shop. You followed me across half the city and then you showed up on the bridge—what did you do, shake down the bum who passed on the message to me? That's how you found me?"

"I did."

"So you're only half a dummy. I ask again, who are you?"

My stomach grumbles. I haven't eaten or had anything to drink in too long and I can feel it. The surfaces of my mouth are sticking together. "Can I get up? Get a glass of water?"

"Talk first," she says, holding up the knife. "Water second, if I decide not to open your throat."

"My name is Ash McKenna," I tell her. "Yesterday, some asshole named Roman blackmailed me into doing a job for him. That job was to follow you and retrieve for him whatever you were supposed to get."

"Ash? Short for Ashley?"

"That's right."

"You have a girl's name."

"Thanks. No one's ever pointed that out before."

"So this guy tells you to do something and you listened to him? Do you do whatever people tell you to do? If I told you to take a running leap out that window over there, would you do it?"

"You have a knife. And he said he would go after my mom. I believe him."

She sighs. Stares off into the distance. "Okay. That's not nothing. So who was he?"

"He said he was from a government agency. He couldn't tell me which one, but said I wouldn't recognize the name."

She rolls her eyes. "There are no secret government agencies. That's fairytale Hollywood bullshit. There are seventeen U.S. agencies that do something akin to what a dummy like you might call spying, and they're all a matter of public record. If you come across an actual spy in real life, they're probably CIA, though I doubt he's CIA."

"Why?"

"Because I would know if he were CIA."

"Does that mean you're CIA?"

She doesn't acknowledge the question. The balance in my head shifts. From the concussion or the woman on my mattress with a knife, I'm not sure which.

"Hey, earth to dumbass," she says. "Did this Roman guy call you yet?"

"This morning. Said he's not done with me and he'll be in touch."

"Nothing else?"

"Nope."

"Do you draw? Can you draw a picture of him for me?"

"Not really."

"Then you're useless." She pulls up the leg of her jeans to reveal a black strap. She stashes the knife, tucks the hem down over it, and stands.

"You are very lucky to be alive. Crazy lucky. Lucky like you should play the lottery because the universe is very much in your favor right now. Get out of this town as quickly as possible. Because that guy on the bridge might be looking for you. And if I can find you, it won't be long before he does. He won't be as sweet as me."

"It's not a guy."

Samantha had turned halfway toward the door but when I say that, she freezes, one foot actually hanging in the air. She turns to me, her skin blanched, her eyes so wide I can see white all the way around the irises.

"What did you say?" she asks, her voice small and tight.

"I said it wasn't a guy. It was a lady. I saw her face before I went for a swim."

She inhales hard, looks around the room like a trapped animal, then falls to her knees beside the bed, grabbing my shoulders and pulling me close.

"Are you telling me the Chernya Dyra is a fucking *woman?*"

"I . . . guess?"

She falls back into a sitting position on the floor, her whole body sagging. She presses her thumb and forefinger into the bridge of her nose and closes her eyes.

"You saw her face," she says.

"Yes."

"She knows you saw her face?"

"Yes."

"Then I was wrong," she says, looking up at me. "I am very sorry to tell you this, but you're going to be dead soon."

She seems genuinely upset for me, and given her attitude up until this moment, the sudden change of heart opens a pit in my stomach. I'm suddenly not so hungry.

"Can you please explain to me what's happening?" I ask. "Please?"

After a few breaths, she looks up at me. "I want a cup of tea."

She gets up and walks out of the room. I climb out from under the covers and grab my bag, pull out a clean pair of boxers, then jeans and a t-shirt. Get dressed, taking care not to move too much. Moving hurts.

I head into the kitchen. There's a note on the counter from Kaz, scribbled on the back of a receipt. Says he checked on me and I seemed fine and he'd be back in the morning. It's almost midnight.

Samantha roots around in a drawer and finds a couple of teabags. She doesn't ask me if I want one, pulls two mugs out of the cupboard, and fills the electric kettle in the sink. I go to the front door to make sure it's locked. I know it is because that's how these fancy locks work. They automatically engage behind you. But it's nice to be sure.

Given the current state of affairs, I think it's good to stay on top of my surroundings.

I stop in the bathroom and cup my hands under the faucet, drink some water. Brush my teeth and take a piss, purposely avoiding the mirror. When I'm done, I find Samantha pouring boiling water into the mugs. I'm not a tea drinker but I feel like something hot would be nice right now. Hopefully this has some caffeine in it. Then it'll be a double win. I feel like I could sleep for another two days.

Samantha leans against the counter and holds the mug to her mouth, letting the hot water touch her lip. She doesn't drink, just tests the temperature as she gazes out the window, which looks through the courtyard and to the other side of the building.

"What exactly is a Chernya Drya?" I ask.

She places the mug on the counter next to her and says, "Do you know what a black hole is?"

"Vaguely. A collapsed star. So dense not even light can escape. Blah-blah-blah science."

"Yes, but the thing about black holes is you can't see them. A scientist can't point into the sky and say, 'That right there is a black hole.' They have to measure it by the way it warps the space around it." She picks up the mug again and holds it, her voice growing quiet. "By the destruction it causes."

"I do not like where this is headed."

"You shouldn't. Chernya Dyra is Russian for black hole. And until this morning I wasn't even sure he . . . she really existed. Most people think she's a myth. According to said myth, she's a former Spetsnaz operative gone free agent."

"Spetsnaz?"

"You really are pretty dumb, aren't you?"

"Clearly."

Samantha walks to the small table next to the window, sits down, hunches over the steaming tea, breathing it in. "It's a unit of the Russian Special Forces. Think of the biggest, baddest motherfucker you know. That person is a floppy little bitch in comparison to a Spetsnaz agent. A lot of their training involves a very real risk of death. If a recruit gets jammed up, they let him die, because that means he's not fit for the unit. One of their final tests is to find a pregnant cat, gut it, and count the kittens inside. It's meant to desensitize them to blood and gore."

"Holy fuck."

"Holy fuck is right. And if she's a woman . . ." Samantha laughs. "You ever hear that quote about Ginger Rogers? That she did everything Fred Astaire did, but backwards and in high heels? A female Spetsnaz agent would have to work ten times harder to prove her worth. She never would have made it through unless she was hard as a bucket of nails. No one knows anything about her, other than what they call her. You are probably one of the few people alive who has seen her face. You are very, very valuable. But that also means she's going to want to kill you."

"Do you really think that?"

Samantha takes a sip of tea, seems satisfied with the temperature. "Without any question or doubt."

I pick up my own mug and sip but find it's still too hot.

"How did you even get away from her?" Samantha asks.

"I can handle myself."

"Fuck you. You should be dead."

"I got in a few shots. The cops interrupted us. Distracted us long enough so that I got her mask off and then jumped into the river. What's with the shovel, by the way?"

"One of the primary tools of the Spetsnaz agent. It can be used for a whole shitload of things. Dig a ditch to avoid enemy fire. Dig deep enough and you can survive a tank rolling over you. You can cook food on it, you can build stuff with it, you can defend yourself with it. And you can kill with it."

I want to say this is silly, but there was a time in my life where I carried a weaponized umbrella—a steel rod with a kevlar canopy. It didn't raise eyebrows if I carried it on my belt and it could fuck shit up as well as it could protect me from the rain. I understand the usefulness of a weapon that can hide in plain sight, even if a shovel is a step stranger than an umbrella. She and I have that in common. An appreciation for multitaskers.

"If she's so dangerous, why are we still here?" I ask.

"She hasn't already killed you, so clearly she hasn't been able to find you," Samantha says. "Yet. I'm sure she's looking. We have to move someplace else. Soon."

"What do you mean 'we'?"

"Between this Roman thing and you seeing the Dyra's face, I think you should stick with me for a little while." She points a finger in the air. "Not that I am thrilled about this, because you are a stupid dumb idiot. But until such time that I deem you a danger to my own life, I think it might be best to stay close."

"And you trust me?"

"I trust that you are fucking terrified right now and that you'll do what you're told." She gets up, takes a step toward me. "I trust you to believe me when I say that if you fuck with me, I will reach into your asshole, grab the first thing I can get a grip on, and pull, very hard. Now get your shit together and let's get the fuck out of here."

"What if I say no?" I ask.

She smiles. Shakes her head. "Do whatever you want. You want to die? Go ahead."

I sit at the table. Fold my arms and put my head down. Breathe deep, exhale slowly.

Seems I've got three choices. Roman, Samantha, the Dyra. None of whom are particularly nice.

All of whom seem to be pretty cavalier about my continued survival.

The Dyra tried to kill me. Roman threatened to kill my mom. Samantha may be unpleasant but she hasn't actively tried to hurt me yet, she's just belittled me. My gut tells me to pick the fourth option, but since there doesn't seem to be a fourth option, there's only one choice to make.

"I need to call my mom first," I tell her.

"Oh my god, you giant baby. We don't have time."

"I am going to call my mom, and if you want to stop me, you are welcome. Care to give it a go?"

She stares sharp little points at me and breathes in deep three times before she says, "Five minutes." Then she sits back down with her tea.

As the phone rings, I nudge the door closed with my foot. My mom picks up on the second ring. "Ashley?"

She sounds tired. I'm worried that I woke her but remember it's just after dinnertime back home.

"Hey, Ma."

"Oh, honey, it's so nice to hear your voice."

"You, too."

"Is everything okay?"

"Yeah, just a little homesick. Figured I'd check in."

"You can come home, you know. You're welcome to stay here until you get settled."

"C'mon. I can't move back home."

She laughs a little. "What, you wouldn't be cool anymore if you lived with your mom?"

"No, I'm afraid I'm not cool enough for you."

"Sure. Early dinner, some Netflix, and in bed by ten. I am a woman on fire."

I want her to get out of town, maybe buy me some time if this goes sideways, but better if she thinks it's her own idea. My mom is too smart to not know something is up if I suggest it myself.

"Listen, I wanted to make sure you knew, I have to leave Prague soon, but I figure as long as I'm on this side of the world, I might as well poke around a little bit longer," I tell her.

"Where will you go next?"

"Not sure. Maybe Tokyo."

"You really should go to Ireland. See where our family came from."

"I'd rather do that with you."

She pauses. "It'd be nice to travel a little. It's been so long since I went anywhere."

"Well, why don't you, then?"

"What do you mean?"

"I mean get out and have a little fun. You're always saying you miss Aunt Ruth. Ever since Uncle Bryon died she's in that big empty house in Pennsylvania."

"I was hoping for something a little more exotic than Pennsylvania."

"Start with that. When I come home, we can

plan a trip to Ireland. See it together. Wouldn't that be fun?"

"It would . . ." Another pause. This one a little more precise. "Ashley, it's like you're trying to get me to leave. Don't say you're going to show up and surprise me. I'd like to know you're coming . . ."

There she goes. Still can't get a lie over my mom.

"I'm sorry, I'm not," I tell her. "But c'mon, I feel like a shitty son being all the way on the other side of the world, and I can't bear the idea of you being lonely. At very least, you and Ruth can make some margaritas and have a couple of days of fun."

"You're not a shitty son. You're mediocre, at worst."

"Hey."

"Kidding." She huffs, sending a little burst of static into the receiver. "You know what? I think I will go see Ruth."

"Good idea, Ma. I'll let you know as soon as I decide where I'm headed next."

"Okay. And, Ashley?"

"Yeah, Ma?"

"Stay safe."

"Got it. Love you."

"Love you, too."

Click.

"That was actually kind of clever," Samantha

says from the doorway, now wearing a dark coat that goes down to her knees and a dark purple scarf wrapped tightly around her neck. "You probably bought her a day or two in case this Roman fella does decide to go after her."

I sit on the edge of the bed, put my head in my hands, feel my stomach collapsing on itself. I want to puke. I want to scream. I want to cry. After losing my dad, I can't bear losing my mom. I can't. I wouldn't survive that.

"What if I'm dead?" I ask, looking up at Samantha. "Would she be safe then?"

Samantha purses her lips. She leans over and places the mug of tea on the floor and crosses the room toward me. She reaches out, and for a moment I think she's going to put her arm around me, but she sends the flat of her hand hurtling at my face. She connects hard enough to throw me back onto the mattress. It rings a bell under my skull that keeps ringing as I get myself into a sitting position.

"What the fuck did you do that for?" I ask. "I have a concussion."

Her voice takes on a high, mocking tone. "*Ooh, I have a concussion.* Don't be a pussy. You're no use to me or your mother that way. Now get up. And give me your phone."

I stand, pull it from my pocket, and hand it to her. "I don't like you very much."

"The feeling is mutual," she says, and she

wings the phone hard against the wall. It shatters in an explosion of plastic, the pieces skittering across the hardwood floor.

"Why did you do that?"

"Because as long as it's on, you may as well be wearing a big red neon sign that says, 'I am right here and also a giant dumbass'," she says. "Phones can be tracked. Welcome to the twenty-first century."

I step into the kitchen, grab a broom and dustbin from the closet, and go to clean up the shards.

Samantha asks, "Really?"

"This is my job."

"You're a janitor?"

"If you want to call it that."

It's quick work. I get the remains together and dump them in the trash under the sink.

We gather our stuff in the foyer. Sam has a designer backpack, gray cloth with a leather bottom. It looks heavy. She cinches it tight to her back. Mine, in comparison, looks like it was fished out of the trash—an olive green off-brand pack left behind in an apartment by someone who was done with it.

"So, you got any cool spy toys in that backpack of yours?" I ask.

"Shut up," she says. "Get dressed."

Kaz left my coat hanging on the towel radiator in the bathroom. It's dry but also a little stiff and smells funny. I'm going to need a new one. I reach into the pockets, out of habit, and come out with both my key fob and another small disc, the size of a dime. Samantha takes the disc out of my hand and sticks it in her pocket.

"Thanks," she says.

"What is that?"

"How do you think I found you? I slipped it into your coat on the bridge."

As I'm fastening the buttons on the jacket, there's a knock on the door. Samantha puts one hand on the back of my neck and the other on my mouth. Once she's sure I'm paying attention, she lets go and looks at me, pressing a finger to her lips and pointing at the peephole, gesturing that I should take a look.

It might be Kaz. He did say that he was coming back. I lean forward slowly and take a look, careful to not make a noise or throw light under the crack of the door that might indicate there's someone here.

It's empty hallway on the other side, and I wonder if maybe someone had the wrong door, but then a figure strolls past the peephole, his features fish-eyed. Looks like he's pacing back and forth.

In profile, I can't really tell who it is, but when the figure stops and leans forward, peering into the peephole like he knows I'm there, I recognize him as Top Knot.

SEVEN

Samantha steps back into the apartment and waves for me to follow her.

Once we're in the living room, she whispers, "Who the fuck is that?"

"I don't know who he is, but he was following me earlier."

"Are those locks secure?"

"He got through one like it. So did you, right? I guess they're not secure at all."

"I didn't come through the door."

She turns to the window and pushes it open. I already know what she's going for. The window leads out to the inner courtyard. There's no ledge and no fire escape, but there is an elevator tacked onto the outside of the building. It looks like a child's erector set, clearly added on long after the building was constructed, and long enough ago I prefer to take the stairs whenever I come by this apartment.

It's so close you can almost reach out and touch it.

And a few times in the past I thought it would be fun to scale the side of it and slip into the window. But I haven't done that because I am not a crazy person.

"Are you sure about this?" I ask. "It's two against one."

"Moscow rule," she says. "Pick the time and place for action."

And with that, she plants a foot on the windowsill, stands up, and steps forward into space, grabbing onto the outside of the elevator. She climbs up like it's no big deal. Like this is a normal thing for normal people to do.

There's a sound like metal rattling from the front of the apartment.

I could stay.

That guy isn't very big. I'm sure I could take him.

Or maybe not. I'm not running on a full tank right now. And anyway, apparently there is some kind of Russian super assassin trying to kill me. He can't be working for the Cherna Dyra because he was following me before I was on her radar.

But still, this is all bad.

If I'm going to take sides here, Samantha strikes me as a better bet than this guy. I don't really know what I'm basing that on. If I slip and fall out this window and splat on the concrete, I don't think she would give a shit.

The straps of my backpack are a little loose so I tighten them and climb onto the window ledge, look back into the apartment, and feel a little wave of nausea that, mercifully, passes quickly.

And I step over to the elevator.

As I do, the entire world spins sideways.

I reach for what I think is a metal pipe, but when I close my hand, there's nothing there. I fall forward into the empty space and my knee bangs into something. I throw my arms out, manage to hook them around a support beam. The metal is slick and cold and digs into my palms. I hang there for a moment, wait for my vision to steady.

Samantha is up at the top, already swinging her leg over.

It's not like I've got a fear of heights, but still, I don't look down. Jumping between buildings yesterday may have been dumb, but it was over in a second. My back is to the window and I hope this guy doesn't have a gun, coupled with any interest in shooting me. I steal a glance over my shoulder to make sure he's not in the window, but it's clear.

And I climb. Careful I don't knock my vision into a tailspin again.

Once I get to the top and make it over the ledge, I fall to my knees. Find myself out of breath. I give myself a moment and stand to find Samantha with her arms crossed and her lips pursed, like I was making her wait while I got dressed to go on a date.

"Can we go now?" she asks.

I look down into the apartment. The lights aren't on, and I can barely make out Top Knot at the window. He's looking up at the elevator.

Considering it. But he can't see us given where we are and the darkness of the night sky framing us. After a minute, he disappears into the apartment.

Samantha hits me on the shoulder, a little harder than she needs to. "C'mon, let's find a way down."

Once we're safely a few blocks away, power walking down an empty street, she stops and pulls me into a darkened doorway. We're in a deep pool of shadow that you could walk by and maybe not notice us.

"So he followed you earlier today?" she asks. "And you have no idea who he is?"

"Nope."

"I'm surprised you even noticed him."

"Hey. You know what? I get it. You're hardcore. But I've seen some shit, too. I walked away from a brawl with someone you're scared shitless of. So how about you cut me a little slack."

"No."

"What do you mean, no?"

"You tripped and stumbled out of the way of a speeding train," she says, her voice low. "You're circling the arena of a very deadly game right now, so you need to dissuade yourself of the notion that you've got what it takes to hang. You're a little league pitcher and this is the majors. You get stupid and you get yourself killed. Maybe me, too. Which is why you will shut the fuck up and do what I tell you. Understood?"

She raises an eyebrow at me, waiting, maybe goading me into saying something.

I kind of want to, but also I am pretty sure if I do, she will punch me in the face.

And I think I need her more than she needs me.

"So, what's it going to be, tough guy?" she asks. "In or out?"

"I haven't eaten since yesterday."

"I know a place near here. Do you like Indian?"

My stomach roars in recognition of the word and that's enough to get me to stay in her company.

The host is an overweight man in a half-tucked white shirt. He tries to seat us near the window but Samantha points to the line of booths in the back. He shrugs and pivots, leads us over to the one closest to the kitchen. He very clearly wants to look at my face but doesn't want to make it obvious, which makes me wonder how badly I've been beaten. I haven't even looked in a mirror yet, purposely avoiding it in the bathroom back at the apartment.

Samantha takes the gunslinger seat—back closest to the wall, facing the front door—and the host puts down the menus and walks off. There's one other couple on the far side of the restaurant and they seem to have no interest in us.

After a few minutes of awkward silence, the two of us scanning the menus, an emaciated waiter with a gleaming bald head comes out of the kitchen and takes our order. When he's out of earshot, I ask, "So is your real name Samantha?"

"Call me Sam."

"You didn't answer my question."

"It's the best you're going to get."

"Okay, Sam. What happened on the bridge?"

"That's none of your business."

We both stop as the waiter appears and pours glasses of water for us from a heavy pitcher, his hand shaking as he tries to keep it steady, splashing droplets of water on the white tablecloth. When he's gone, I say to Sam, "Seems dumb to meet in the middle of the night like that. During the day, there are thousands of people walking back and forth across that bridge. I would have done it during the day."

"I didn't set the parameters of the meeting."

"Okay, so you're there to get something. I'm coming from one direction. Crazy Russian killer lady is coming from the other. Neither of us is supposed to be there. So I guess the person you were supposed to meet never showed, or got scared off."

Sam looks at me and shrugs.

"So the thing you were supposed to receive must be pretty important if the Cherna Dyra wants it," I say. "I assume she doesn't come off the bench for just anything. She's not a market-rate goon."

Sam keeps staring at me, hard and flat.

"So it's big and important and probably related to Hemera Global," I tell her. "So if you're CIA and you're a spy, that's your cover. You're working at the bank because it's related to the job you're doing."

"What are you doing?" she asks.

"I'm bored. And you're a shitty conversationalist."

"I'm not here to entertain you."

"Fine." This is like talking to a brick wall. I get up and head for the bathroom. It's small and cold and sterile with white tile from the floor up to the ceiling. I stand in front of the mirror and put my hands on the sink and look.

I do not like what I see.

There's a piece of bloodstained tape over my nose and nasty bruises the color of eggplant bloomed around both eyes. I poke at the bruises and there isn't much give before my nerves wake up and make a ruckus. I am not at my prettiest. I wash my hands a few times, like that might help things, but it doesn't.

When I exit the bathroom, the waiter is walking to the table with a big stack of plates. I sit and he puts them down in front of us—tandoori chicken for her, lamb curry for me, a big pile of naan and a shared plate of rice.

"Oh, thank god," Sam says.

"What?"

"You can't talk if you're eating."

The two of us eat in silence. She must be hungry, too, because she's putting the food away fast and furious. She has a hell of an appetite for a small girl. I wouldn't be surprised to find out she ate a couple of bones in the course of destroying her chicken. She also reaches over and spears a piece of lamb off my plate and pops it in her mouth without asking or even acknowledging me.

This is the first thing she does that makes me attracted to her.

Which makes me think two things.

One, what the hell is wrong with me?

Two, best keep that to myself.

Halfway through my own plate, I get a little queasy. I know I'm hungry but my body doesn't want me to go much further. But I figure I need the energy, so I push a little bit past where I'm comfortable.

Once the plates are mostly clear and Sam is nibbling at a piece of naan, I ask, "So if the Chernya Dyra is coming to kill me, then why keep me around?"

She snaps back to attention. "What?"

"This woman is dangerous. You said that. You also said you were only keeping me around as long as I wasn't a danger to you. But I'm a big walking target right now. So why keep me around?"

"I've got a bad habit," she says, putting down the naan. "I move around a lot. I don't think there's any harm in acknowledging that. Do you know what the weirdest thing is that I carry with me everywhere?"

"What?"

"A Ziploc bag full of little shards of soap. You know those pieces that are too small to use once you've run the bar down? One day when I have some free time, I'll go online and figure out how to melt all those pieces into a new bar. Seems wasteful to throw them out. But I never find the time, so the bag gets bigger. Sometimes I dump out a few, but I can never toss the whole thing." She picks up the naan and takes a bite, chews a bit. She points the bread at me. "That's why you're here. You're a shard of soap. Possibly useful. If not, I'll toss you."

I stare at her. She smiles a little at this, but only because she senses a challenge. Which I offer when I tell her, "You think you're so fucking cool, don't you?"

"I do, yeah."

"You know what I think?"

We're interrupted by the waiter, who clears our plates and replaces them with little tin plates of ice cream—a single scoop in each one. I bet it's mango. It's always mango. I take a bite and confirm it is, and look up at Sam, who hasn't touched her ice cream. She's just looking at me.

I finish my ice cream and put down the spoon. "There's a lot about you I can't tell. Your accent makes me think you're American, from the South.

Not deep South. Maybe Virginia or Tennessee. The way you dress, the way you carry yourself, I got nothing. But this whole tough-girl routine, it's a defense mechanism. That's obvious. That's so obvious I don't deserve any credit. But I do think the reason is Ginger Rogers. About how the Chernya Dyra needed to be ten times tougher than the guys to be taken seriously. You've got to constantly prove your worth. The fact that you're so aggressive about it means you're still trying to prove yourself."

Sam's expression doesn't change, but a storm cloud passes over her face. She holds my eyes for a couple of seconds and looks down at her ice cream, picks up the spoon, and takes a bite.

When she looks back up, the cloud is gone.

That's what I thought.

After we're done, Sam takes out her phone and taps at the face of it. I take that as an opportunity to check my laptop. I need to make contact with my mom to let her know my phone is out of commission. I send her an email, telling her I dropped it in a toilet, but I'm not in a rush to buy another since I might be going to a new country soon.

I write a note to Kaz, too, minus the toilet excuse, just so he knows I'm alive and knows not to go back to the apartment.

Once I've got the emails off, Samantha whistles at me and I look up and she's handing me a small plastic phone.

"A burner," she says. "Just in case. There's only one number programmed into it. Mine. You tell anyone else the number and I'll cut you into little pieces, like soap."

"You're pretty paranoid."

"Paranoid is a virtue in this game."

"You're full of little gems, aren't you?"

She exhales and takes the laptop away from me, places it on the table in front of her, pokes at the keyboard, and hands it back. It's open to a Wikipedia page. There's a list she's highlighted with the cursor.

Assume nothing.

Never go against your gut.

Everyone is potentially under opposition control.

Don't look back; you are never completely alone.

Go with the flow, blend in.

Vary your pattern and stay within your cover.

Lull them into a sense of complacency.

Don't harass the opposition.

Pick the time and place for action.

Keep your options open.

"The Moscow rules," she says.

"Right," I tell her. "You said something about them in the apartment. What are they, exactly?"

"Rules of thumb said to be developed in Moscow during the Cold War, when literally every single person you met stood a fifty-fifty shot of being a spy," she says. "Memorize them. Practical for anything."

I look up at her and she shakes her head in disbelief and raises her hand to the computer monitor.

"I said memorize them."

I read them over a couple of times and then look up, but Sam isn't looking at me. She's looking across the room, at the host, who is at the stand by the front door and writing something down.

"What?" I ask.

"The guy at the front took a call and glanced our way."

"Could be someone was asking if there were any free seats."

"No, he looked at us."

"No one knows we're here."

"Do you have a phone?" she asks. "Another one, besides the one I gave you?"

"Nope."

"Anything else . . ." She stops herself. "Damn it. Do you have anything on that laptop that's really important? Like end of the world if you lose it important?"

"Not really."

"Good. Not that I really cared anyway." She stands up, picks up her half-empty glass of water, and pours it over the laptop. For a few seconds nothing happens, and then it sputters and the screen wavers and blacks out. She picks it up and cracks it in half backwards over her knee, little pieces of plastic shooting into the air. The host really is looking at us now.

"Hey!"

"Shut up and get your things," she says. "We have to go."

EIGHT

Sam's shoulders are bunched up and her hands are shoved deep into the pockets of her coat. I have to jog to keep up. We pass small groups of people standing outside bars, but otherwise it's late and quiet, and I wonder if she's overreacting.

At the same time, I'm out of my depth, so I figure it best to follow.

After a few blocks, she turns to me, makes sure there's no one within earshot, and asks, "When you said that asshole was following you—he followed you from the coffee shop across the street from my building, right? So I've been compromised, too?"

"Presumably."

"Well, shit. We need to get someplace safe."

"Wait, you noticed me and not him?"

"He's better than you, apparently."

I take the metal disc out of my pocket and hold it up. "I have access to a ton of apartments."

"Right, because you're a janitor."

"I'm not a janitor."

"The people following us know where you work. They're probably going to assume you're hiding out in one of those apartments. They might just go door to door until they find us."

"What about my friend Kaz? He has no ties to me."

Sam stares off into the distance, like she's trying to see through some fog. "That could work. It's not ideal, but it's better than sleeping outside or trying to find a hotel. Too many eyes at hotels. Okay, we'll find a payphone. You can call up your friend."

"I don't have his number."

"What do you mean you don't have his number? What kind of friend is he?"

"His number was programmed into my phone, which you destroyed," I tell her. "Give me your phone and let me e-mail him."

"No go," she says. "Too risky. You don't know where he lives?"

"I've never been to his place. But if Pats is still open, he's probably there."

"Okay, that's the next stop then . . ."

Sam stops talking. She's looking over my shoulder, at three people who are speed-walking down the block toward us.

The one leading the pack is Top Knot.

"C'mon," she says. "Now."

She leads me around the corner and takes off at a full sprint. I follow, my head throbbing and my stomach full of too much Indian food. We duck down an alley and approach a group of people smoking outside a black metal door dug into a corner, behind a dumpster.

Sam pulls the door open and we step into a small, dark room. The walls are painted black.

There's a man, also in black, standing behind a podium, which is painted black. He's tall, built like a grizzly bear, his face so full of piercings he's probably generating a magnetic field.

He barely looks at us and mumbles something and Sam takes out a stack of bills and puts them on the podium. He holds up a stamp and taps it against the back of our hands, leaving a little black star behind.

Sam steps around him, to a door in the wall I didn't realize was there. When she opens it, a wave of techno music crashes into us. She looks at me and says, "Try to keep up, sweet pea."

We dive into a room that's packed with people, the air heavy with humidity and heat generated by moving bodies. I can't make out the boundaries of the room. It reeks of sweat and pot and stale beer. Sam pushes through the sea of glistening, gyrating bodies. The music is so loud it's making my teeth vibrate.

One room ends at a doorway and another one begins past it. This place is like a beehive. Lots of small rooms connected by portals and small staircases. There are giant holes in the walls, broken furniture like the place was decorated by dumpster divers. I've heard of these. Ruin bars. They're more common in Budapest. They're called that because they're set up in industrial spaces on the cheap. Everything is scavenged. A lot of times they're not even operating with a real license, they coast until the authorities bust them up.

It reminds me a lot of Apocalypse Lounge, the bar back home that meant the world to me and closed down as I was leaving New York. It was the same ethos—who gives a fuck about refinery and décor and clean bathrooms when there are drinks to be had?

Sam knows where she's headed so I keep an eye out for her. Sometimes I lose her so I push forward a little harder until I manage to find her again. We seem to be moving away from the music.

We end up in a bar area where the crowd is thinner. It's cooler here but the air still feels wet. People are hoisting drinks in red plastic party cups. Sam turns, waves at me, and points to a door. On the other side is a flimsy metal staircase, and we go down a level, our feet echoing in the narrow corridor.

The next doorway leads to a similar setup of catacombs, but the vibe down here is much quieter. There are fewer people. The walls are made of stone and it's possible to talk over the music. Little bar areas are carved into alcoves, assembled from the dregs of failed liquor stores.

I follow Sam through a series of rooms until we reach one that's empty. Broken chairs and trash bags in the corner, a rough linoleum floor, and a door at the other end. A single bare bulb lights the room in a harsh white. She runs to the door and throws her shoulder into it but it doesn't budge. I come up alongside her. She punches it and kicks it and yells, "Motherfuck."

"What?"

"This used to open into the basement of the building next door. They must have sealed it."

"Okay, but do you really think those assholes followed us all the way down here?"

As if on cue, there's a scrape from the front of the room.

We both turn and find Top Knot, flanked by two guys. Both of them Middle Eastern, wearing jeans and leather jackets. And young. They're too excited to be here, too happy they're about to be in a fight. They don't seem like the kind of people who've yet learned the unpredictability of violence. So none of them strike me as actual, legitimate threats.

But still, it's three against two, I'm all fucked up, and Sam weighs about as much as my left thigh.

Top Knot says something in a language I don't recognize. I step in front of Sam and put my arm across her, hoping I can be lucky for a second time in two days. If I move quickly, aim for takedown shots like throats and knees, we might make it through this.

"Stay behind me," I tell Sam.

Sam bats my arm away and strides past me

as she drops her bag and jacket on the floor.

"That's the first funny thing you've said," she says. "Stay put."

"Wait . . ."

But she's not listening. She walks across the room toward the three of them and I'm about to charge forward to back her up when she breaks into a run.

She reaches down into a corner, comes up with a discarded beer bottle, and wings it at the face of the guy furthest from her. It explodes and he screams. The other two guys look at the guy instead of Sam, which is a mistake, because she jumps, kicks off the wall, and lands a flying punch to the thug closest to her, focusing the entire weight of her body into the blow.

He goes down like a sack of bricks. It's so quick, so vicious, that Top Knot stands there in shock, his face slack.

Also a mistake.

Sam moves like a viper. Like this is a martial arts battle that's been blocked and choreographed and rehearsed, but no one clued him in.

She throws her foot behind Top Knot's knee and he drops in a kneeling position. Her other knee comes up and she drives it into his face. His head snaps back. He hits the floor and I can hear it bounce from across the room.

She turns to the guy she hit with the beer bottle, who is now coming at her, his face weeping blood. He wraps his arms around her, squeezing and lifting her off her feet at the same time. She throws her head forward and catches him on the nose, then slams her fist down like a hammer on his thigh. He lets go, stumbling back, holding his face, blood seeping between his fingers.

Once she's got her bearings, she throws her foot into his nuts. She catches him true and square. It hurts to watch. He goes down and a quick jab to the throat puts him out of commission.

By the time I make it there, the fight is over.

The thug she hit with the flying wall punch is trying to get up, so I put my foot into the crook between his shoulder and neck and shove him to the ground. Top Knot is reaching into his pocket for something but Sam stomps down hard on his wrist. There's a crunch and he screams.

"Now it's time to go," she says, and she takes off back into the bowels of the club without even making sure that I'm behind her.

Outside, Sam takes off at a brisk walk. A few blocks later, slightly out of breath, I ask her, "What was that?"

"What was what?"

"You tore those guys apart like it was nothing."

"A combination of krav maga and kenpo," she says. "Plus growing up with two older brothers and a handsy uncle. Thanks for not getting in my way."

"I could have helped."

"I don't need your help," she says. "Now, how do we find this Kaz guy?"

I point in the general direction of Pats. "This way."

We walk in silence for a couple of blocks. Finally, I ask, "So who do you think they were?"

"No idea. Doesn't matter now, though, does it?"

"You're not worried there might be some more people following us?"

"Doubtful. But I've got my eye out."

"You haven't looked behind us."

"I don't have to," she says. "There are reflective surfaces everywhere. Sound carries. The streetlights cast shadows. Following people and catching tails isn't just about getting from point A to point B. It's also about looking like you're not trying to follow someone or catch a tail."

"Is that a little piece of spy wisdom?"

"It's whatever you want it to be."

A little more silence. Empty streets lit yellow by the streetlights. A homeless man comes toward us and before he can open his mouth to ask, Sam takes out a few bills and hands them over without breaking stride. We turn the corner and for a second I think we're lost, but then I see a bookstore that looks familiar, so we keep on going.

"So what kinds of cool spy toys do you have?" I ask. "Gadgets and stuff?"

"You watch too many movies."

"Nothing? Not even a gun?"

"You know what kind of shit I'd be in if I got bagged by the cops with a gun on me? This gig isn't all shootouts and fights. It's barely those things. I've never even fired a gun at anyone before."

"I'm no fan of guns. But it still seems a little surprising."

"Guns are only useful if you need one. I don't generally need one."

Even if I didn't witness her beat the shit out of three guys, each of them twice her size, the amount of confidence she builds into that statement makes me believe her.

Pats is half full. There are a lot of people outside and at the surrounding bars so that makes me feel good. Just to be around people.

Kaz is sitting at the bar. Another stroke of good fortune. I slide up alongside him.

"My friend," he says, patting me on the back. "You are still alive." He notices Sam and nods toward her. "Your friend is very pretty." He offers his hand. "I am Kazimir Lyovin."

She doesn't smile, doesn't reach for his hand.

"She bites," I tell him.

Kaz nods and retracts his hand. He catches on pretty quickly that this isn't a social call. "Understood. What do you need, my friend?"

• • •

I don't even know where to start with Kaz's apartment.

There's nothing unique about the building. If anything, it looks pretty understated compared to a lot of other apartments around here. We take the elevator to the top floor. It's like every elevator in this city. Too small, the three of us so close together we might be legally married in some cultures. The elevator is slow and shakes and I think there is a very real chance we are about to plummet to our deaths, but then the doors open.

The three of us spill into a blank hallway, with one door at the far end. I'm not expecting much, having gotten used to the European style of apartments: small, somewhat modern, lots of Ikea furniture, not a ton of personality, but comfortable enough. Like living inside a catalogue you flip through at the doctor's office.

When Kaz opens the door and beckons us inside, the first thing that strikes me is the size. The living room is bigger than most of the entire apartments I work in. And it goes on from there. A bathroom and kitchen and long hallway with multiple doors beyond. It must take up the entire top floor of the building.

The next thing I realize is that it's the most Russian place I've ever been.

I'm not overly familiar with the Russian design aesthetic, but having spent some time down in Brighton Beach and Coney Island, I know it can be a little ostentatious. I don't know why. A rebuke against the blandness of communism, maybe. The Russians seem to like things such as neon and chandeliers and candelabras and cluttered architectural flourishes.

This place is like a Russian fever dream.

It has all of those things and more. For starters, everything is gilded on the borders. The corners of the furniture and the baseboards and the edges of the ceiling. The curtains are gilded. The black border around the massive flat screen TV bolted to the wall is fucking gilded.

"My friends, welcome," Kaz says, tossing his heavy green coat and hat onto a chair next to the door. He strips off his shirt, too until he's in his jeans and boots, and immediately I realize why. It's boiling in the apartment. I drop my jacket, too, as does Sam.

"This place looks like if Liberace was getting married to a Russian czar," Sam says.

"Exactly what I was going for," Kaz says, dropping onto the couch and picking up an open bottle of wine off the coffee table. He takes a swig and holds it toward us. Sam grabs the bottle and takes a deep pull without wiping off the rim. She holds it toward me but I wave her off.

She shrugs. "More for me."

"This one, she likes to drink."

"Don't call me 'this one', asshole."

"A girl doesn't usually speak in such a manner."

"Don't call me girl, either," she says, putting the bottle of wine back on the glass surface of the coffee table with a sharp clink. "I'm a grown-ass woman."

"Indeed you are," he says. "So, what's the plan, you two? Have some drinks? Should I call some people over? We throw a little party?"

"No," I tell him. "Sleep. Sleep is the plan. Also, if you can scare me up a new jacket. Mine smells like the Vltava."

"Do you want me to make you an American Thanksgiving dinner, too?"

"No, but I wouldn't object to being tucked in."

He points over his shoulder. "There are empty bedrooms. Down the hall. Take one, take two, whatever. Please excuse the presence of marital aids. I sometimes use them for shooting."

"Shooting?" Sam asks.

"Kaz is a porn producer," I tell her.

"Lovely," she says.

I can see on Kaz's face: he's about to make a joke. Something about how she's welcome to audition. He glances at me and I shake my head. He gets it. That the joke would be immediately followed by the removal of his tongue.

With the promise of a bed, exhaustion hits me hard. I excuse myself and head for the back, stopping into the bathroom so I can rub some toothpaste in my mouth.

The edges of the mirror, of course, are gilded.

Somewhere in this world is a person who manufactures gold leaf, and that person is very rich thanks to Kaz.

The room I pick is small and sparse, next to the bathroom. There's a small bed in the corner and a pile of books. Three walls are painted white, and the far wall is exposed brick. No marital aids. There's a small window covered in tin foil, for which I am thankful, because even when the sun comes up in a few hours, it'll be dead dark in here. With any luck I'll get a good few hours of sleep in.

I click off the light, fall onto the bed.

Stare at the ceiling.

Of course, sleep doesn't come easily.

Instead I lie awake and wonder about what the fuck I am doing.

When I wake up, my head is pounding and I don't know if it's the concussion, or my sleep schedule veering off course, or the caffeine deficit. Could be all of the above. I dig out my toothbrush so I can give my teeth a proper cleaning.

A shower would be nice. I haven't taken one since my little swim and I can smell myself. What I smell is not nice. Like a stagnant puddle on a warm day.

I pull the bandage off the bridge of my nose, wincing as it protests and yanks at the cut underneath. There are still deep black bruises around my eyes, the cut on my nose mottled and black. When I strip off my shirt, I find half my torso is varying shades of purple and yellow and some colors I don't even have names for. Every move I make sends dull aches through my body.

Once the water is nice and hot, I climb in and let it beat down on me as I assess the situation.

Which is: I am super fucked.

And yet, there's something oddly comfortable about it.

Maybe I'm having a stroke. There's a bubble somewhere in my brain about to burst and therefore I am incapable of rational thought. But the more I think about it, the more I think that this is my thing.

I've made peace with the fact that I can't lead a normal life. I'm a magnet for stuff like this, because when bad things happen, someone needs to step up, and I can take the punishment. It makes me feel alive. Like I'm doing something worth doing.

Maybe I have an addictive personality. I kicked drugs, kicked smoking, kicked binge drinking. Something's got to take the place of my vices.

The only thing I'm sure of is that being here, doing something, it's made me feel more at peace, more galvanized, since I moved to Prague.

At least now there's some momentum.

Once I've exhausted the supply of hot water,

I dry off carefully, not wanting to put too much pressure on anything. I get dressed and find Sam is sitting on the couch, her legs up on the coffee table, a steaming cup of coffee to her left. She's balancing a laptop on her legs, clicking away.

"Is there more coffee?" I ask.

"Kitchen," she says without looking up.

The kitchen matches up with the rest of the place. The fridge is gilded. There's an American-style drip coffee maker, which is rare in these parts. Everything is Americano—espresso cut with water. Called Americano because the GIs in World War II couldn't handle the strong flavor of espresso, so it needed to be watered down for them.

Truthfully, I can't handle it either. Espresso is always too bitter for me, and god forbid I have to add milk or sugar. I want coffee, not a milkshake. So it's nice to have some regular old patriotic drip right now.

Back in the living room, I take the seat on the other side of the table and test the coffee but it's too hot. Being up and moving around has cleared my head out a little. But there's still this odd, alien feel to my skull.

Still not at full steam. Maybe three-quarters steam.

"Kaz had to go," Sam says. "Porn stuff. He's nice though."

"I'm glad you're capable of liking somebody. What's the plan for today, then?"

Sam closes the laptop and picks up her coffee, staring at me. After a long sip she says, "Turns out you're more useful than I would have expected."

"How's that?"

"I have a handler," she says. "Fuller. I can't get in touch with him. The only reason for that is he's been compromised. Captured or dead. I need to find out which and track down where he was staying so I can go through his stuff. Here's the problem: I don't know where he was staying."

"So we have to figure that out."

"I think I might have. Not exactly where, but how to find it. And coincidence of coincidences, I found some correspondence that indicates he was using that place where you work as a janitor."

"Crash Hop. And I'm not a janitor."

"Don't care," she says, downing the last of her coffee. "Get your shoes on."

NINE

We cut through Reigrovy Sady Park, walk a sloping path, and come along a rolling hill that leads down to a series of buildings that looks out over a vista of the city. Sky a brilliant blue, the orange rooftops dusted with snow like a dessert that's just been sugared, and for a moment I am very sad I'll be leaving this city.

Then I remember it's full of people who want to do me harm.

"Let's go, princess," Sam says.

Present company maybe included.

I button up my jacket against the bracing air. The fabric is a little stiff and it's going to take some work to loosen up. I figured Kaz would give me a cast-off coat but this is brand-new. Heavy black wool with red trim around the collar. He also gave me a pair of black boots with steel toes that are both comfortable and fashionable.

The outfit, along with the sunglasses that are cutting down on the glare of the sun and making my head hurt less, make it look like I'm way too into *The Matrix*. But this is Eastern Europe so maybe that makes me cool.

Sam steps off the path, headed for a copse of trees. I follow along and we duck into the brush. Once we're far enough from the roadway that we can't see it, she sets down her duffel bag and hands me the contents: a bundle of sweaters.

"Pad yourself," she says. "You need to look like a fatty."

"Why?"

"Because it's not enough to change some clothes. We need to change your physical appearance to such a degree that anyone watching will skim right over you."

"Where'd you even get these?"

"Kaz's closet."

"He's going to be annoyed."

"Don't care."

I pull up my fleece and tie the sweaters around my mid-section, bunching them up around my stomach.

When I turn to Sam she's fitting a black wig over her head, before placing a knit cap on top of it. She puts on a big pair of sunglasses, and pulls the collar of her sweater forward and sticks wads of tissue down her bra. When she's done, her respectable cleavage now looks far ampler, and everything taken together is enough to make me not recognize her unless I knew her pretty well.

When we're both finished, she nods. "You look appropriately fat."

"Thanks. Why can't we walk in? I work there. We could sit at a computer and have everything we need in two minutes."

"Two reasons," she says. She sticks one gloved

finger into the air. "First, that place is almost definitely under surveillance." She holds up finger number two. "Second, I don't want anyone to know we're there. Because if someone can remember us, someone else can confirm it. And I don't care if the people in that office know you and want to protect you. Shove a kitchen knife under a fingernail and loyalty goes out the window pretty quick. Do I need to speak slower?"

"You do not."

"Good. Let's go."

We trudge toward the building, which is on the other side of the park and a few blocks past. The sweaters are bunched up and uncomfortable but at least they're keeping me warm. The wind is picking up and it's not in a nice mood.

"You don't need to be such a dick," I tell her.

"I think I do."

"I get it. You're good at this and you look at me and you see an amateur. That's fine. I've never claimed to be a pro at anything other than drinking. I've made some mistakes, but I have done some good, too."

"Have you now?" she asks. "I thought you were a janitor."

"People used to call me a private investigator," I tell her. "I didn't always call myself that but that's what I was doing. Odd jobs, helping people out."

"Were you licensed?" she asks. "Or were you playing make-believe?"

"That's . . . I wouldn't put it like that."

"How would you put it?"

"I like to help people."

"Why?"

"The satisfaction of knowing I did the right thing."

"Fuck satisfaction," she says. "Everyone does everything for one of two reasons. To make money or to get laid."

We stop at the corner of the street and wait for traffic to slow enough so we can cross. The sunlight has reduced lingering snow to dank puddles and dirty slush. "So then what are you in for?" I ask. "The money or the fucking?"

"I've got my reasons," she says, not looking at me.

"Oh, so your high and mighty skepticism falls apart with the slightest bit of scrutiny," I tell her. "You are so full of shit."

"I don't care what you think."

Her voice is thin and harsh and I don't figure on pushing any more right now. We turn the corner and find the building we're looking for and Sam asks, "Fourth floor, right? Is there a bathroom? A broom closet?"

I think for a minute. Remember when I was there last. "A bathroom, yeah. Other end of the hall. Unisex."

"Good. We get in, pull the alarm, hide in the bathroom. When it clears out, I go into the office."

"And then what? We're probably not going to have very long."

"We don't need long. You stay in the bathroom. Wait five minutes after the alarm gets shut off and leave. Meet me back in the park where we changed. Same spot."

"Maybe we should sneak in at night. This building can't be that secure."

"I don't want to wait that long."

We reach the building and pass through an ornate set of double doors. When they close behind us, it's dark, light streaming from dingy frosted windows. There's a wide staircase leading up to a landing, and a bank of elevators. The place looks abandoned until a man shuffles across the landing using a mop handle to push a bucket on wheels. Sam shoves me into the corner, slightly out of view, but the man doesn't look in our direction. When he's gone, we climb the staircase, my boots squeaking on the waxed floors. Sam tenses at the noise and has a look on her face like she wants to slap me, but mercifully doesn't. I walk toward the elevator but she pats me on the shoulder and nods toward the stairs.

The fourth floor has carpeting, which muffles my footsteps. I do like she says and head toward the bathroom.

There's a long line of offices here, and only one of them is Crash Hop. I already told Sam what it looked like inside. Small, a few desks and a back room, mostly in disarray. Two computers. The one closest to the door is the one used by the receptionist, a sweet woman from Ghana named Abénna.

She's the only permanent staffer. Stanislav is there sometimes but mostly in the field. I have a master key, apartments are stocked with supplies, and a guy finds where I'm staying and drops my pay off in an envelope. I haven't had to come into the office in the two months I've been here, so I assume it's like that for the other employees.

As we make our way down the hall, I'm thinking we've got things set up pretty sweet. The bathroom at the end of the hallway clearly isn't occupied, the door slightly ajar and the light off.

Right next to the door is a little pull fire alarm.

It couldn't be more perfect.

We're within five feet of the Crash Hop door when it swings out and Stanislav lunges into the hallway.

I say Stanislav lunges because a man of his size can't do much else than heave himself forward to achieve locomotion. The dude is big. Unhealthy big. But he seems at peace with himself. He's wearing the same thing he's worn the few times I've met him—a nice dress shirt and fine black pants and a pair of well-worn but clean sneakers.

The remaining wisps of his black hair combed over his shining head in a desperate refusal to surrender. He's wearing a heavy coat, so he must be leaving.

This is exactly what we didn't want.

And it's pretty damn awkward to have to explain away several things, like my beaten-to-shit face, and why I've got sweaters stuffed underneath my shirt, and why I'm even here in the first place.

I pause, like I've got to come up with some on-the-spot excuse, but Stanislav doesn't stop. His eyes slide off me and onto Sam's tits for a second. Then he smiles and nods and says, *"Prominte."*

We both move to either side of the hallway, pressing ourselves against the walls, and he walks past.

Sam looks at me and I see one eyebrow raise past the boundary of her glasses. I nod to confirm her suspicion, and we keep walking. By the time we reach the bathroom, the hallway is clear, Stanislav having reached the elevator, so we both duck inside. It's a small space. Someone missed the toilet by a wide margin and left it to dry. It doesn't smell nice. Sam takes off her sunglasses.

"I can't believe that worked," I tell her.

"I'm not surprised. Changing someone's gait or physical appearance is one thing. You've got a built-in disguise."

"What's that?"

"Your face," she says. "You are very unpleasant to look at right now. People are going to actively not want to look at you."

"Whatever works."

Sam opens the bathroom door, reaches out, flips the alarm, and pushes me against the wall. A bell rings in the distance, a white light flashing in time with it. She leaves the door slightly ajar, presumably so anyone who walks by will assume it's empty and doesn't check it for stragglers.

Out in the hall I can hear a succession of doors opening and closing, and footsteps receding down the hall. Sam reaches into the pocket of her jeans and pulls out something that she holds in a closed fist. After a moment she peeks out, goes all the way around the door, and disappears.

I pull out my phone and check. Wait for the time to pass. When it gets up to four minutes, I peek around the door. Find a middle-aged guy in cowboy boots and a long black coat. Close-cropped hair and a face carved out of ice. He's holding something in his hand that I think is a cell phone but then realize is a small handgun.

Ah, fuck.

I push open the bathroom door before I even realize what I'm doing. For a second I wonder how I can be so stupid and impulsive, but the man moves the gun behind his leg, so from my vantage point I can't see it. He must think I'm a random worker from the building.

Which gives me the advantage.

I come out of the bathroom, acting as naturally as I can, stride down the hall like now I'm evacuating along with everyone else. Halfway between us, there's a flashing light set high on the wall. The alarm has stopped but the light is still flashing. Our footsteps are lost on the threadbare industrial carpet.

He smiles and nods at me as I get close, lingering a little too long on my face, like he wants what he's doing to seem natural. Concentrating real hard on making me think everything is okay. But I get what Sam was talking about.

Moments like this make me miss my umbrella. It made me feel more confident about going up against someone with a gun. Not that it was foolproof, or bulletproof, but it seemed to level the playing field a bit.

Right now, I've got nothing. And I'm a little nauseous, and every time I take a step forward and put my foot down, I feel like I'm going to tumble forward.

As we move alongside each other, the man sidesteps out of my way, turning slightly toward me, rotating his hand behind him so I won't see the gun.

When I'm perfectly perpendicular to him, I throw my hand into his throat as hard as I can, using the momentum first to crush his windpipe, and then to push him into the wall. He tries to bring the gun up but I grab it with my left hand, keep it pointed at the floor.

I'm pushing down so I've got all the leverage. I don't let off his throat, either. He coughs and chokes, his face growing red. Tries to pull my hand away with his free hand, but can't, so he throws a few punches into my midsection. The sweaters absorb the blows.

I brace myself, expecting him to fire, but he doesn't. I think my hand is blocking him from pulling the trigger. He reaches back to swing at my head, so I move in closer, preventing him from getting a solid shot.

Just as it looks like he's about to pass out, I let off on his throat a little and throw my knee into his stomach as hard as I can, nearly puking from the exertion. His grip loosens on the gun as he folds to the floor. I take it from him, stash it in the inside pocket of my jacket. Reach for the Crash Hop door, push it open, but find there's no one inside.

Could Sam have already been in and out?

The mystery man is writhing on the floor, coughing, trying to say something. Instead of letting him, I throw my foot into his stomach so hard it knocks him back into the wall, and run down the hallway, toward the exit.

Safely concealed in the copse, I strip off my jacket and realize I still have the guy's gun, which does not make me feel great, but I don't want to toss it. What if a kid finds it? I hang the jacket over a branch, pull off my fleece, and dump the sweaters. I'm sweating now and the cold air feels nice.

Once I'm recombobulated, I step onto the path, looking in the direction of where we came from, expecting to see Sam. But all there is to see is an empty pathway. She couldn't have gotten compromised. I got that asshole before he got to her. She was barely in there.

What if she didn't go in? What if this was a ploy to distract me?

I have no idea why she would do that, but what else is there?

If she's gone, I've got nothing. The best I can figure is go back to one of the apartments and wait for Roman to find me so I can let him know what I know, which is nearly nothing, and hope that's enough to get him to let me off the hook and leave my mom alone.

I take the burner Sam gave me out of my pocket. No texts, no calls. Navigate to the only number inside that's saved and dial. I count off fifteen rings before I hang up.

There are footsteps out on the path. I peek out and see a young couple walking hand in hand.

How long should I wait here? I wish Sam had given me some kind of guideline. Like if she didn't show up in ten minutes, to run like hell.

She could have taken the long way around, but if she got a little held up, why isn't she calling me?

I do not like any of this, on any level.

Moscow rules. *Never go against your gut.*

My gut says run.

I step out of the safety of trees and there's a crunch to my left. Sam is standing there, staring at me. Like she was the one waiting for me.

"Giving up on me already?" she asks.

"What took you so long?"

"There was a complication," she says.

"Tell me about it. Some guy with a gun was coming after you."

"What?"

I hold out the coat, which is ridiculous because it's not like she can see the gun in the pocket. "Some dude, with a gun. I stopped him. I have the gun. You are welcome."

"Wait . . . that doesn't make any sense."

"What was the complication?"

"There was already a trace on the computer," she says. "Someone got to it before I did. Which makes me a little nervous. I mean . . . they can't be this far ahead of me."

She looks at the ground, and then at me, and her eyes narrow.

"Are you playing me?" she asks.

"What? No."

Sam nods, bites her lip, and strides toward me. Moving like a viper again. Her limbs flick and then she's on top of me and I feel something cold pressed against my throat. The knife with the black blade.

"I ask again, are you playing me?" she whispers.

I keep my head up and speak slowly. "I just stopped someone from killing you."

"You could be lying. You've got a mom to protect. Mama's boy. Are you playing me, mama's boy?"

"You tell me."

She tenses her arm and I feel something sharp, then warm. She looks me deep in the eye, like she's trying to see the colors of my optic nerve, and for a second I think she's going to open my throat.

But she backs off.

I reach up and touch my throat and my finger comes back with a dot of red.

"Really?" I ask.

"C'mon. We've got work to do."

She takes a few steps. Realizes I'm not following her. Stops and turns.

"Who are you?" I ask. "Who do you work for?"

"You wouldn't believe me if I told you."

"That's not an answer."

"I don't care."

She turns around and walks. I know it's stupid of me to follow, but I really don't see any other moves on the board. I hold my hand to the nick on my throat, in case it's still bleeding.

The man sitting at the window is wearing a pair of headphones so big I'm sure the back of the store could blow and he wouldn't notice. The café is busy and the space between the tables is narrow. This might actually look legit.

I weave through like I'm headed for the counter, but stumble and knock his espresso into his lap.

He leaps to his feet and yells, more from surprise than anything. It was halfway drunk and looked like it had been sitting there for a while so I got the sense it wasn't too hot. I reach down to grab the cup and pull a wad of paper towels off the table across from us.

"*Prominte, prominte,*" I tell him, handing him the napkins and moving my body to shield his view from what I hope will be Sam taking his laptop. I feel a little bad about this, but the guy has money. Designer glasses, expensive boots, a fine leather bag, and noise-canceling headphones. Sam has been wanting to pull this move for six blocks now but I told her we're not taking anything from anyone who can't seem to afford a replacement.

And here we find ourselves.

"No trouble," the man says in a British accent. I'm pretty sure that translates to "Fuck you and die in a fire" in the Queen's English.

The man takes the wad of napkins and dabs at the front of his pants. There are only a few drops of espresso on them.

Once he's settled, I look down and see his laptop is gone, and Sam is nowhere in sight, so I head to the counter and buy a coffee, because turning around and running immediately after a show like that would end with someone chasing after me.

Another point where Sam and I diverge. She told me to hoof it out the second I could. I argue that there's no sense in making it look like I'm guilty. What if there's a cop in the vicinity and the guy points me out?

The man realizes his laptop is missing, yells in frustration, and runs to the front to look around. He doesn't seem to regard me at all, even though he knows I'm still there, so my plan worked.

After a moment, he comes up to me.

"I think someone made off with my laptop," he says. "Did you see anyone?"

"I saw a guy lingering near the front. Skinny guy, tattoos, looked like a junkie. I'm sorry, man. Now I feel like this is my fault."

"Not your fault it was taken," he says, like he blames me entirely for the laptop being taken. He heads back toward the front to pack up his stuff and look for the imaginary thief.

I take my coffee and leave a big tip in the jar, out of guilt, and head to the bar a few blocks away where we're supposed to meet. When I find Sam, she's tucked into a booth in the back, where you can't see her from the street. She's got a drained half-pint glass in front of her and she's clicking away at the laptop, her face illuminated by the blue glow.

She doesn't look up when I sit across from her on the scarred wooden bench.

"Want a beer?" she asks.

"Better not."

She looks up at me and rolls her eyes. "What's the matter, not a big drinker?"

"Used to be too big."

"What was your poison?"

"Jameson. Though a few months ago I was mainlining plastic jug whiskey I got from a wholesale distributor. Nothing says rock bottom like plastic jug whiskey."

She betrays the slightest hint of a smile, which feels like real progress, but doesn't stop typing. "So what happened?"

"I was self-medicating," I tell her. "A bad thing happened. It was messing with my head. Drinking made it easier to sleep. When the supply got cut off, I caught a case of the DTs. Which was bad enough. But I was living in a bus in the middle of the woods, and that's a weird place to have the DTs."

"What was the bad thing?"

I put my hands flat on the table. Think about whether I should keep this to myself. Then figure she's heard worse. "Killed someone. Accidently but a little on purpose. He was very bad so I don't think it was entirely wrong . . . but . . . yeah."

"It's not fun, is it?" she asks.

"What?"

"Killing someone. I'll tell you what: It's good that you suffered. Means you still have a soul." She looks down at the laptop and mutters under her breath, "That must be nice."

I can see pages of her life flipping past me. There is so much in that statement, so much more than anything she's told me up until now.

I'm about to ask her to elaborate when an old man comes over, wiping his hands with a towel, and asks if I want a beer. I decline and ask for ice water. He looks at me much the way Sam looks at me most of the time and wanders off. I get the sense I am not getting my water.

"So what happened at Crash Hop?" I ask.

"Put a remote wireless transmitter on the tower," she says. "Lets me log on and do whatever I want without anyone noticing."

"Do we have to go back and get it?"

"Once I'm done, I send a command that fries and erases it," she says. "By the time they find it, if they find it, it'll be a useless piece of plastic."

"I knew it."

"What?"

"You totally have cool spy gear."

"Shut up. You can buy them off the internet."

"And you said there was already one in there?"

"In the USB port. Not happy about that. It means someone is monitoring that computer.

It could be completely unrelated to everything we're doing here, but it's safer to pretend like it's related."

"Moscow rule," I tell her. "Everyone is potentially under opposition control."

"Gold star for you."

She finishes typing, takes a deep breath, goes to take a sip of the beer, and finds that it's empty.

"Well," she says. "I'm in. All their records for the last six months. Now I have to figure out his alias."

"You don't know what it is?"

"He switches them up a lot."

"Okay, so, do you know any of his other aliases? Maybe there's a connection between them. Like baseball players or movie characters or something."

"The last one he used that I know about was John Jones. And once he used Barry Allen."

"Let me see the computer."

She turns it toward me and I click around a bit in the customer database, focusing on recent rentals. It doesn't take long to find at all. I highlight the entry and turn it around.

"Hal Jordan," I tell her. "That's the one."

"How can you be sure?" she asks, actually a little impressed.

"Your handler has a thing for comic books. John Jones is the Martian Manhunter. Barry Allen is the Flash. Hal Jordan is the Green Lantern. He's working his way through the Justice League." I pump my fist. "Boom."

"You fucking nerd. Let's go."

I stand and a small wave of dizziness hits me. My head feels like there's loud music playing against my skull. "That address is a good half hour walk from here. Should we cab it? Get on the train?"

"We walk."

"Do we have to?"

"Public transportation has cameras and cab drivers have memories."

"Fine."

As we head outside, there's another light snow falling. It's always snowing a tiny bit, but never a whole lot. As we walk, I ask, "So where are you from, originally?"

She doesn't answer. I thought I had detected a crack in her façade but I guess we're back to not being friends. She walks quickly, not pausing, not seeming to care whether I'm able to keep up. I duck and weave through the crowd, try my best to match her pace.

When we reach the building, which is further from the river than I've been, I pull out my key and Sam says, "Those things can probably be tracked. There's got to be a log or something. Put it away for now."

"How are we going to get in?"

148

Without slowing down or answering, she heads to the door and pulls out a small piece of metal that's dull and hammered flat, along with another slim, longer piece with a slightly curved end. She inserts them into the lock and within a few moments the door clicks open.

"That's so awesome," I tell her.

"It's a valuable skill."

"Can you teach me to do that?"

She looks at me for a moment and says, "Maybe later."

We climb the three floors to the apartment. There are four other doors in the hallway. As soon as we make it up to the top, I can tell we're not going to like what's behind the door. There's a faint but unmistakable smell of rot.

She makes short work of the door and as soon as it cracks, the stench hits us like an open hand. A full dumpster on a hot summer day.

There's a narrow hallway that opens up to a living room. A small couch and a coffee table and a flatscreen television mounted on the wall, and in the center of it all, a man splayed out on the floor wearing only boxers, lying in a black pool of blood. The nexus point of which is a jagged gash in his neck.

TEN

Best I can tell, Fuller was in his foties. Maybe he was in his fifties and took care of himself. His skin is a shade somewhere between blue and gray. The hue grows darker closer to the floor, where the blood has stopped flowing and settled. He has no tattoos, and his hair is unkempt, but he looks like the kind of person who kept it kempt. Despite the horror of it, he has the kind of face that makes it easy to imagine him as fun to talk to at parties.

There's a deep spray of dried, brown blood on the wall next to him, a flourish against the tacky and evaporating pool underneath him. There are some flies crawling across the body, lingering in the wound on his throat, but no maggots. I think that means the body is reasonably fresh. The smell in the room is so thick I can taste it on my tongue.

The last time I saw a dead body, a few months ago, down in the woods in Georgia, which right now feels like a million years ago, I had a much more visceral reaction.

It's a little easier now. Not to say it's easy. I knew nothing about this man but still I feel a little chasm open up in the center of me. Dead in real life doesn't look like dead in the movies. Dead in the movies is serene. In real life it looks like a perversion of nature, the way the whole body collapses in on itself. The way you can tell something is missing by looking at it.

It's sad. It's sad when anyone dies. Someone somewhere in this world loved him, and that person will be very sad to find that he's gone.

When I look to my left, I find the person who loved him.

Sam's eyes are rimmed red and she's fighting back tears. Not well. Her left hand is bound in a tight fist, which she's pressing into her leg. Her other hand, also in a fist, is pressed against her lips, like he's trying to prevent something from escaping her mouth. Usually, the way she stands is like she's ready to spring at you, but now she looks like a coat left to hang on the wall.

"Are you okay?" I ask, immediately realizing that's a stupid question.

She doesn't say anything. Doesn't even register I said it. Just continues staring at the body. Given her habit of outsized reactions, I figure it best to leave her there for a few moments to process things. There's a small hand towel on the couch so I use that to flip the latch on the window and get a little air into the apartment. I step into the kitchen and root around, using the towel to open and close drawers, until I find what I'm looking for: a half-empty bag of ground coffee. I dump it into a dented, scarred frying pan on the stove and turn on the electric burner. There's a scratch behind me and I turn to find Sam standing in the doorway, like she's waiting for me to invite her in.

"What are you doing?" she asks.

"Covers up the smell," I tell her. "Cop told me that once. They do it at crime scenes. Figured you'd want to have a look around. If we're going to be here a bit."

"You keep moving stuff around like that, you'll make it obvious people were in here after the victim died."

Her voice is cold and her eyes are still a little red but they grow hard again. I want to ask her again if she's okay—given she's referring to Fuller as "the victim," clearly not—but instead I tell her, "We may as well look for what we can. No one's found him yet."

She opens her mouth to say something but stops and inhales, looks down at the floor.

"What do you need?" I ask.

"Anything weird or out of place," she says.

She turns into the living room. I walk the edges of the room, using the towel to move things. It looks the same as all the Crash Hop apartments. Sparsely but tastefully furnished. Nothing that's too expensive. The occasional piece of detritus left behind by guests. Receipts and books and a blank book of matches and a white ceramic mug on the counter stained brown with the remains of coffee.

The bedroom is at the back of the apartment. There's a small dresser, which turns out to be empty, a roller suitcase in the corner, and a nightstand next to the bed. The bed is unmade, and on the nightstand there's a bottle of lube and a box of condoms, both unopened. Next to that is a small yellow bottle with a plastic wrap seal. I pick it up with the towel and turn it over.

Alkyl nitrites, also known as poppers. A sex aid popular in the gay community.

Footsteps behind me. Sam asks, "Anything?"

"He was expecting to get laid," I tell her. "Everything's out and ready to go, but he didn't use any of it."

"I can work with that," she says. "We have to find his laptop or his phone. If the victim was having someone over, they'd be well hidden."

She moves to the kitchen without another word.

Given her reaction, I thought she might be in love with him. Maybe she was, even though he was gay. Maybe he was bisexual, or was a straight guy who liked poppers. Maybe she didn't know, although that would surprise me. Could be he was a father figure. Like a mentor.

Whatever it is, she's riven.

There's no closet in the bedroom. It's practically a bare room. No vents, either. I walk around and tap my foot on the floor. Hardwood, but it's a cheap faux laminate, so there are no loose boards to hide things under. I hear Sam open the bathroom door, and then the ceramic clunk of the toilet tank.

In the kitchen there are plenty of hiding spaces, but I think about what she said. Well hidden. Cabinets are out. That's too easy. I check the fridge, then lean against the wall and peek behind it. Nothing. There's a vent down near the floor that doesn't look big enough to hold a laptop but I take out a butter knife and unscrew it to be sure. Only dust.

As I'm screwing the vent back in, I look along the floor. There's the stove and the dishwasher, separated by a row of cabinets. I look inside the appliances, for fun, and when I close the door of the stove, notice some scrapes in the floor, like it had been moved. Maybe recently, judging from the stray flecks that come up on my finger when I touch the gouges.

The pan with the coffee grounds is sizzling and smoking. The apartment smells better. At least in here. Burnt coffee is preferable to dead body. I turn off the pan and move it to the back of the stove, grip the sides and pull. I manage to slide it out far enough I can see behind.

And, bingo.

A small laptop bag. I pull it out, wipe down where I touched the stove, and slide it back into place.

"Sam," I say.

I put the computer case on the counter.

"Good," she says, nodding.

She opens the bag and takes out a small laptop and a smartphone, putting them both on the counter next to each other. Next up: chargers, a handful of passports from various countries, and a thick stack of hundred dollar bills, tied with a purple rubber band.

Finally, a postcard.

She turns it over in her hand. The picture on the back shows the Eiffel Tower at night. It's worn, like it's been taken in and out of pockets for years. There's a shiny piece of tape mending a tear down one side. Handwriting, too. Faded. Sam reads it over, nods, and puts the postcard in her pocket.

She opens the laptop, and positioned underneath the keyboard are two track pads—one right underneath the space bar, and a smaller one off to the right. She presses her thumb to the one that's off-center and says, "Fingers crossed."

After a moment, she smiles. Fingerprint scanner, I guess. She looks up and sees I'm watching. "Keep looking."

She types on the laptop as I move to the living room. I avoid the body the best I can but feel compelled to at least give it a once over when I'm done with everything else.

I crouch down close to it, covering my nose and breathing through my mouth. The eyes are looking up at the ceiling, cloudy and unfocused.

It makes me think of how every movie with a dead body has a scene where someone solemnly places their hand on the face of the deceased to close their eyes. Give them a little dignity by making it look like they're sleeping.

There's nothing dignifying about this.

And I figure it's best to not touch a dead body.

The way he looks is doing something to me. It's not him being dead. It's him being dead in this place. This blank space. My life lately has been an assortment of apartments like this—white, inoffensive, easily mistakable for each other. Worst of all, cold. Like dying in purgatory. Alone and afraid with nothing to comfort you. Where do you even go from a place like this?

"Ash," Sam calls from the kitchen.

She turns the laptop toward me as I walk in. It shows the picture of a handsome man standing against a brick wall. Young, very trendy, which I can tell because the sleeves of his sport jacket are pushed up and he's wearing a scarf wrapped a hundred times around his neck. He has a shaved head and a five-o'clock shadow that's rolling over toward six. Standing next to a canvas covered in trippy, multi-colored boxes.

"Evzen Doskocil," she says. "Local artist. Kind of a big deal. Based on the nature of their conversation, I think this is who the victim was waiting for. So we find him and we talk to him."

"How do we do that?"

She closes the laptop. "Therein lies the problem. Remember the Moscow rules?"

"Which one?"

"Assume everyone is under opposition control. I don't know if he's in on it or if he got strong-armed into doing something he didn't want to do. But he's been active on both Facebook and a gay hookup app in the past twenty-four hours so he's not trying to hide. I think it's time to honeypot."

"What's honeypot?"

"Seduce the target to get them to give up information."

"How are you going to do that if he's gay?"

She smiles, and the way she smiles, like she's about to have a laugh at my expense, makes my stomach sink a little.

"First," she says, "I don't do that. It's demeaning. Second, I think you're a little more his type."

I've been meaning to make it out to the Kafka Museum and I wish it were under different circumstances. It's the weirdest museum I've ever been to. The place is less a museum and more of a surreal, shadow-drenched art installation. The room I'm in is almost completely dark. The exhibits float in pools of harsh, jaundiced light. Demented circus music plays over the loudspeakers and is occasionally interrupted by the cawing of crows.

It feels a little like an analogy for my life right now.

I find a quiet alcove and turn toward the wall. "Are you sure he's here?"

Sam's voice buzzes in my ear. Once again, a cool piece of spy tech she pretends is something you can buy at Sharper Image. The two-way earpiece looks like the nib of a pencil eraser, and it doesn't feel like I'm wearing anything at all.

"Yes," she says. "He just checked in on Facebook. Shut up."

"I don't think this is a good idea."

"Shut up."

"I'm not uncomfortable with the fact that he's gay. It's fine that he's gay. I have gay friends. But what if he knows I'm *not* gay?"

"Pretend he's a chick."

"It's not that easy. Like, what if he makes a move on me and I flinch?"

"Don't flinch."

"Right, but what if I do? Like, unintentionally?"

"Shut up and make him think you want to fuck him."

Sigh.

The place isn't very big and it doesn't take long to find him. He's standing over a glass case, looking down at a series of old, yellowed pages, resting on dark felt. As I draw closer, I can see they contain writing in tight cursive and a few have doodles. Little stick figures that seem to be trapped in the crushing mediocrity of their lives, or afflicted with a severe case of nihilism.

I get close to him, but not too close. He's wearing a heavy topcoat similar to mine, nearly buttoned up to the throat, barely showing off a bright yellow scarf.

"Hi," I say to him.

He looks up at me and regards me like a cat meeting a new person. He's extremely handsome. Almost depressingly so. Like it would make you feel bad to stand next to him in a bar.

"Hello," he says, then gets a good look at my face and frowns. "Got in a fight, did you?"

"You should see the other guy," I tell him. "Barely a scratch. It wasn't my finest moment. So . . . do you come here often?"

Sam buzzes in my ear. "Are you kidding me?"

"Just . . . you know . . . are you a big Kafka fan?" I ask.

"Well, he was one of the great writers," Evzen says, like I am a not very smart person, which might be true.

"Where should I start?" I ask. "What should I read first?"

"*The Metamorphosis* is probably the most accessible," he says, perking up a little, if only because now he gets to show off. "But if you really want to understand the man and his work, stick with the short stories. 'A Hunger Artist' is my favorite."

159

"Thanks for the recommendation."

"You are . . . not from around here," he says.

"Right. I'm from . . ."

He puts his hand up. "Let me guess. New York?"

"Nice catch."

This makes me cringe. God, I suck at flirting.

"Are you enjoying your time in Prague?" he asks.

"Immensely," I tell him. "Though I don't know much about it."

"Are you here on business or pleasure?"

"Sometimes I can't tell the difference," I say, trying to sound suave, and then realizing that means absolutely nothing, and also how much of an asshole I must look like when chatting up strange women.

Evzen nods like he's humoring me and says, "Well, I hope you're able to discern the difference. This is a wonderful city, regardless of your intention."

"Listen, I'm trying to meet some new people. It's . . . a little lonely being in a new place like this. Would you be interested in getting a drink?"

"Thank you, but no," he says, offering me his hand. I take it and we shake. He gives me a short, tight smile, and turns to leave.

Well, don't I feel like an asshole.

Just because he's gay doesn't mean I'm his type. Which is still a little dispiriting, no matter how you slice it. Getting shot down is getting shot down. I tell myself it's because I'm not at my prettiest.

Sam yells in my ear, "Don't lose him, you dummy."

Maybe if I can't appeal to Evzen's taste in men, I can appeal to his ego. I call after him. "It's just, you're the painter, correct? Evzen Doskocil? I'm a big fan of your work. I'd love to bend your ear a little."

He turns and smiles a bit. "You know my work."

"I'm a painter, too."

"What medium?"

I give a cursory answer. "Watercolor."

He rolls his eyes. "I don't know how I could possibly help you, but if you're buying . . ."

"I'm buying."

"Good job, honeypot," Sam says. "Now bring him to me."

By the time we get outside and make it down a few blocks toward this bar I claim I really like, it becomes abundantly clear that I know nothing about painting.

I bullshit as much as I can and try to get him to talk more about himself, but he seems interested in learning about my work. What are my subjects? Do I try to sell my paintings? Have I ever tried to get into a gallery? I play along, make sure to sound like a hobbyist who's breaking in, and therefore has no excuse to know anything.

When he asks me about my favorite brand of watercolor, I tell him I pick up whatever's available, which offends him on a deep and personal level.

I'm almost worried I've lost him when Sam appears out of the doorway of the building we picked, grabs him by the collar, and pulls him through. I double check behind us to make sure the street is clear and follow them inside.

It's a bare brick room with a dusty floor. The place is under construction, but given the layer of debris on the tarp in the corner, no one is in any rush. Evzen struggles as Sam drags him over to the wall, then throws him against it hard enough to knock the wind out of him. Before he has time to orient himself, she snaps a handcuff around one wrist, and the other goes onto a thin pipe running from the floor to the ceiling.

"Who are you?" he asks.

Sam flicks out the same knife she held to my throat earlier. She holds the point toward Evzen's eye and he stops struggling, moving back so he's flush against the wall.

"You do not speak unless I tell you to respond. Otherwise, we play a little game, which I like to call 'which of your eyes is the dominant one.' The way we play it is, I carve one out and you tell me if I was right. Do you understand?"

He nods.

"Within the last twenty-four hours you scheduled a liaison with a man," she says. "Mid-forties, fit, graying hair. Do you remember?"

He stares with wide, terrified eyes.

"You can answer. Do you remember?"

"Yes. I mean . . . no . . ."

"Which is it? Yes or no?"

"I didn't arrange it," he says. "A man came to me. To my home. He called himself Mr. X. He had two other men with him. He told me I had to do a thing for him, and if I didn't do it, he'd . . . he'd tell someone something I didn't want them to know."

Sam glances at me over her shoulder, and I know the question she wants to ask is, 'Was that Roman?' I nod to her and she turns back.

"What then?" she asks.

"I agreed. I'm sorry. I agreed. They gave me the phone and told me to arrange a meeting and get his address. It took two minutes."

"So you did it and, what? They just left?"

"They just left."

Sam puts the knife a little closer to his eye. "You're not lying to me?"

He spits and sputters. "No, I swear. I promise. I didn't even go to the apartment. I never even met him."

She stares at him for a moment, inspecting different parts of his face. After a few moments, she nods, clicks the knife closed, and slips it into her pocket.

As she turns to me to say something, the door swings open and Top Knot and the two guys she beat down the other night come rushing in. Top Knot's forearm is wrapped in a thick cast, and the guy she hit with the beer bottle has a constellation of small white bandages covering his face.

"Are you fucking kidding me?" Sam asks.

Three more guys follow in after.

None of them look particularly happy to see us.

"I guess not," she says.

ELEVEN

The scent of blood is in the air and we haven't even gotten started yet. This is not a good sign. The six guys across from us are full up on youthful anticipation. Six against two isn't great odds, even given Sam's ninja-like abilities. So, I figure on maybe diffusing the situation a little.

"Listen, so, who the fuck are you clowns, anyway?" I ask.

Sam scrunches up her mouth, annoyed. The idiots look confused, like they don't understand why I'm not more worried.

Top Knot raises his voice and says, "We are pledged to the Islamic State. Praise be to Allah, who commands us to be just, and permits us to retaliate against our oppressors in kind."

And this is where stuff gets a little hazy.

Here's the thing: my dad was a New York City firefighter and died on 9/11. He wasn't supposed to work that day. Left my mom standing at the kitchen counter and me in bed, home sick from school. They never found his body. The thinking goes he got too high up in the building, so that he could evacuate the people who were trapped inside.

These are not the men who killed my dad.

But they subscribe to the same newsletter.

Hearing it sets off a bomb deep inside me, the fire of it consuming me. It's like I'm hovering above my body, watching as I move from one to another, throwing punches so hard it feels like my arm is going to rip off and the bones in my fist are going to shatter.

It's barely even a fight. They seem to get it within a few moments, because by the time I get to the third guy, his eyes are so wide with fear I would not be shocked to find he pissed himself.

I'm operating on another level of awareness.

When I drive my fist into his face, I feel his teeth shift against my knuckles. The air fills with the smell of pennies as his blood aerosolizes.

And when I get my bearings back, I'm standing over Top Knot, holding him by the collar of his leather jacket—which I'm pretty sure makes him a shitty Muslim—and it takes a lot of effort to not rip his fucking head off and puke down his neck hole.

Breathe.

Control your anger before it controls you.

He's covering his face now, sobbing.

Before I can make a bad choice, someone grabs my arm. I turn and Sam is holding me. "Holy shit, dude, calm down."

"I am calm."

"You were screaming."

"No, I wasn't."

"Yes, you were," says Evzen, who is now

crouching and cowering against the brick wall, still handcuffed to the pipe.

"Well . . . sorry," I tell Sam.

"Let's keep one of these dummies conscious long enough to figure out who sent them."

I let go of Top Knot and he falls to the floor. He scrambles away but doesn't do a great job. His face is brushed with blood. I should be more worried about this. Maybe.

Sam nudges me aside and puts her foot on his throat.

"What's your name?" she asks.

He chokes and spits. "Fuck you."

She puts a little pressure on the foot. He gasps and wheezes, his face growing red. She pulls out the knife, flicks out the blade, and holds it up. "First off, if you're not Toshiro Mifune, you should not have a top knot. It's really not working for you. Second, normally I'd go off on some elaborate threat to scare you into complying, but I don't even have to do that right now, do I?" She nods toward me. "I'll just turn this asshole loose on you. By the time he's done, there'll be nothing left."

"I said I was calm," I tell her.

"You're not helping," she says.

She lets off on the pressure and Top Knot takes a huge gasp of air and sputters, a little blood coming out with it.

"Now, name," she says.

"Raahil," he says.

One of the guys lying on the floor is trying to get up. I throw my foot into his stomach and he folds into himself, moaning.

"Raahil," she says. "Who sent you?"

"Fuck you," he says.

Sam sighs, leans down, and throws her fist into his face, bouncing his head off the floor. He groans and she says, "C'mon, you guys love to brag. Who are you with, at least?"

"Ansar al-Islam."

She applies a little more pressure to his neck, to hold him in place. "No, you're not."

"What do you know, you fucking whore?"

Sam doesn't react to the insult. She just looks confused, and applies more pressure to Raahil's throat to keep him in place.

"What does that mean?" I ask.

"Ansar al-Islam was an insurgent Sunni group in Iraq and Syria," she says. "Active during the '03 invasion. But they were supposed to have merged with ISIL and disbanded a few years ago. I heard there were splinter groups that rejected the merger. But then again, there are so many terrorist groups out there, sometimes these dummies will pick a name off a list that sounds cool." She looks down at Raahil. "Hey, so why are you following me?"

"Orders," he says.

"Who's orders?" she asks.

"They'll kill me."

"I'll kill you. And I'll take my time. But if you tell me, you might have a chance at running."

"They'll find me."

"Hey," I tell him. "I thought there was glory in death?"

Raahil glances at me but doesn't say anything. I lean down to him.

"Or does all your fucking bluster and doctrine disappear when you realize there is a very real chance you're about to die?" I ask. "You really want that, I'd be happy to oblige. You wouldn't be the first person I've killed. But I'm trying to walk down a straighter path. So how about you cooperate and we all go our separate ways?"

I stand back up. His face softens and twists. He's considering it.

Just when he's ready to speak, the door opens.

Pug and Hulk come in.

"Come on!" Sam yells.

For a moment we all stand there staring at each other. Like it's an awkward party and nobody knows what to say to each other. When they draw their guns, though, everyone moves quickly.

Sam dives for the other side of the room.

In the small space, the sound of gunshots is deafening. Huge explosions that bounce off the brick walls, mixed in with the spray of red stone and plaster. I run, too, following Sam, but by the time I get into the next room, she's already lost in the labyrinth of the building, so I pick a direction and go.

There's a web of empty rooms until finally I get to a dead end. But there is a window. I grab a can of paint off the floor, swing it hard. The glass shatters and I grip the sleeve of my jacket, use the thick fabric to clear shards off the windowpane, and hit the street.

There's a restaurant across the way with a small crowd of people outside smoking cigarettes. I wave to them. "*Prominte.*"

And I run.

Sam must have taken a different door, headed deeper into the building. Hopefully, she got away. I don't know how Pug and Hulk showed up, nor do I have any idea why they suddenly seem keen on killing me. There's not a whole lot about this I understand right now.

I turn over my shoulder and see Hulk down at the end of the block. He's not holding his gun but he's moving at me a lot quicker than I would have guessed a guy his size could. When I turn a corner, I break into a hard sprint, pain pulsing under my forehead, and see a red sign for a bookstore. Shakespeare & Synové.

I glance over my shoulder and Hulk hasn't turned the corner yet. This might work.

Inside, I'm blasted by warm air. The air is heavy with the musty smell of old books. I head toward the back, find a spiral staircase leading down, which brings me into a stone-floored basement. There's a little more room down here, and a few people browsing, but no one pays me any attention. I head for the back, where it looks like there might be some daylight, and come up on the last thing I want to see.

A big bay window overlooking a canal that must branch off the Vltava.

I look into the lapping water. There doesn't seem to be another way out down here. I contemplate a plunge. The window is locked. I pick up the closest book. *Anna Karenina* by Leo Tolstoy. A thousand pages of Russian aristocrats pretending to be French. That'll work.

Except, I really don't want to go for another swim. In part because I really like my new coat, but also, it was really unpleasant the first time.

Fuck it. I'll sit down here in a corner. Hulk probably ran past this place anyway. I doubt he even saw me go in.

So, of course, when I turn around, he's standing there.

He opens his jacket to show me the handle of his gun, sticking out of the front of his pants.

"Roman would like to see you," he says in a heavy Czech accent.

We walk in silence for a couple of blocks. When it's clear he's not going to inquire about my day, I ask him, "Did you guys get the girl?"

"No."

"What about the other guys there? What happened to them?"

"They are all dead now."

"Everyone? Even the guy who was handcuffed."

"No. Him we let go."

"Are you lying to me?"

"No."

"I don't believe you."

He smiles a little. "I do not care."

After a little while walking, I ask, "What's your name?"

"I don't know that I should tell you my name."

"C'mon. After all we've been through."

He doesn't say anything.

"Who the fuck am I going to tell?" I ask.

"Vilém," he says.

"Well, Vilém, I wish I could say it was nice to meet you."

"Same."

There's something about him I like. A weariness at the frenzy of all this. Like he's over it. It makes me think in another life we could have sat down and gotten a drink. That would have been nice. But now he's in a position where he has to deliver me somewhere and if I refuse to go, he'll probably shoot me in the head.

Funny how the world works.

We reach a restaurant and I can tell it's fancy

because there are white curtains in the window. Vilém nods toward it. "Inside."

"All right, then. See you around."

He turns and heads back the way we came. I find the restaurant is empty and, indeed, very fancy. White tablecloths, intricate chandleries. A well-stocked bar with no one behind it. Dim light trickles in through the front windows. It looks empty, until there's a flash of movement across the way, against the far wall.

Seated at a table, facing the door, is Roman, in a white shirt and black tie. The tie is tucked in between the buttons of his shirt. I make my way over and sit across from him. He's chewing as I sit. He puts down his knife and fork, holds up a finger, finishes what's in his mouth. He takes a sip of wine and pulls the napkin off his lap to dab at his lips.

On the plate in front of me is a freshly-cooked steak.

"You look like you've had quite the adventure," he says, surveying my face.

"Sure. An adventure. Let's call it that, and not the clusterfuck you thrust me into the middle of."

He nods toward the steak. "I guessed medium-rare. You strike me as a medium-rare kind of guy."

I pick up my knife and fork, hover over the plate.

"Do you think it's poisoned?" he asks.

"Is it?"

"If I wanted you dead, you would be dead," he says. "Would you like a glass of wine? The wine is not poisoned either. I'd tell you the name but I doubt it'll mean much to you. It's very expensive. Compliments this cut very well."

"Water is fine."

"Well then," he says, gesturing to my plate with his fork. "You're probably hungry."

We eat in silence. The restaurant has a funereal quality. No sound coming from the kitchen. The steak, though, is real good. Perfectly cooked, still hot. Probably the best steak I've ever had. At least I'm getting a meal out of this.

Once Roman is finished, he sets his plate aside and folds his hands in front of him.

"A lot has happened," he says. "To be honest, I'm a little disappointed. You didn't go back to the apartment. You dumped your phone and your laptop. Are you hiding from me, little golem?"

"Nope," I tell him. "That was all Sam's idea."

"Please, take me through what's happened since we first met."

I finish the last bite of my steak and take a sip from the glass of water sitting in front of my plate. I run him through the bullet points of everything since he left me. I don't know if any of the information is worth protecting.

At this point, I might as well play ball.

When I'm done, he nods a few times, chewing it all over.

"Ansar al-Islam doesn't make a lot of sense," he says. "I knew there was some kind of terrorist connection here. But they haven't been active for a few years now."

"That's what Sam said."

"Interesting. She knows her history. But this Chernya Dyra. You said she's Spetsnaz? I've never heard of her."

I remember back to when I told him about the shovel on the phone, and way it gave him pause. It seemed very much like he knew what I was talking about. Maybe he's lying to fuck with me? Fine. I'll play along.

"Apparently that's the point," I tell him. "She's bad news. She fucked me up pretty good. I got the living shit beat out of me. All because of your stupid fucking game."

He bristles. "First, language. Second, how was I to predict that would happen?"

"Do I get a pass on this job now? Can I go home?"

"Oh, no, definitely not. Samantha Sobolik is keeping you around. I don't know why. But you're going to stick with her and find out."

My stomach sinks a little. "Why?"

"You're expendable and resourceful. Those are two valuable qualities."

"You're a dick."

He shrugs, takes another sip of wine.

"I also don't believe you work for the government."

175

"Why's that?"

"You said you're from some branch I never heard of," I tell him. "Sam says there's no secret branch of spies in the U.S. government."

"And you believed her?"

"The burden of proof is on you."

He smiles, empties the glass, and places it back down on the table, not letting go of the stem. "Here's the truth about your new friend. She works for Hemera Global. I know this. That bank is doing a very bad thing that's somehow related to, presumably, Ansar al-Islam. So that makes her complicit with jihadists. How does it feel, to know that?"

"You're telling me she's a spy who works for a bank that works for terrorists?"

"I never said she was a spy. You did. And you'd be surprised to find out about the kind of people banks employee these days."

"You're lying."

"How so?"

"Those Ansar al-Islam goofballs chased us down. If she's in league with them, why would they do that?"

"You really don't understand how any of this works, do you?"

"Try me. I can be clever if I think real hard."

"There is a piece of information," he says, playing with his silverware, lining it up next to his plate. "It is a very valuable piece of information.

It's the thing that will tie a lot of disparate elements together. To some, it is worth a great deal of money. To others, it could do a great deal of damage to some wealthy people. The value is so great, nothing else really matters. It's every man for himself right now."

"If this is such a big deal, why even get me involved?" I ask. "I thought the whole point of using me on this was because it wasn't worth a more valuable asset."

"That's when I though the job was easy. Now I'm finding how much it's not easy."

"Well, then handle it your-fucking-self," I tell him, pushing my seat back and standing. "Thanks for the steak."

Roman reaches into his coat and I think he's going to come out with a gun. Instead, he puts a phone on the table.

"Please sit," he says.

I stand there, contemplating whether I should break the wine glass next to my plate and shove the stem into his neck.

"Sit," he says.

I do. He picks up the phone and clicks it a few times. Stops, waits, and then the phone buzzes. He hits a button and turns it around so I can see. There's a harsh shadow, so it's a little hard to make out, but after a moment the image comes into focus: a copy of the *New York Post*. The phone is focused on the date.

Today.

The view on the phone swings away from the paper and settles on my mom's house.

I nearly puke up the steak.

"My colleague tells me that your mother isn't home," Roman says. "Hasn't been since last night. I'm beginning to suspect you tipped her off. Very smart. You must understand, the best you've done is save yourself a little time. That is all."

I want to speak but find I can't.

"Tell me again what you said in that apartment," he says, smiling, flashing those teeth. "Something about a bell that can't be unrung? You're a . . . what was it . . . 'born and bred New Yorker with anger management issues'? I allowed you the indulgence, but going forward there will be no further disrespect. You will do what I tell you until you are done, or your mother will die. It won't take long to find her. Understand me."

My skin burns.

The first man I killed, that was an accident.

I'm at the point where I'd take joy in killing this smug asshole.

My mouth feels like sandpaper. I take a sip of water and it doesn't help.

He doesn't take his eyes off me. I take a few breaths, calm down. I need to be calm about this. If he's not going to let off, my only hope at this point is Sam. So I need more information.

178

Something that'll please her. Something that'll make her feel indebted to me.

I need her. Otherwise, I'm alone on this.

"Why did you kill Sam's handler?" I ask.

"That man? Fuller? He was not a good man."

"So who was he?"

"An independent contractor," he says. "We're not sure exactly who. But we're working on it. The apartment was cleared out when we found him. No laptop, no phone, nothing."

Score one for the close eye. Though Roman scores a point too, because I feel myself smile a little when he says this. He notices.

"You found something," he says.

"His body."

"And his laptop? His phone?"

"Nope."

Roman stares at me for a moment, then lets it pass, says, "Sam gave you a burner, I presume?"

"She did."

"Give it to me."

I hand it over to him. He takes it and clicks around on it, then types in something and hands it back.

"I have the number now," he says. "If you lose this phone or it's destroyed, I give my colleague the order to kill your mother."

"What if she takes this one from me?" I ask.

"Don't let her."

"She likes to swap out burners."

"Don't. Let. Her," he says, enunciating each word.

"What kind of guarantee do I have that you won't send your men after us and start shooting again?"

"I wasn't shooting at you, golem. I was trying to separate you two in a compelling way so that we could talk. Do you really think my men have such bad aim? I understand it was a small room."

Good point.

"Now run along," he says. "Get back to work. And when she gets that piece of information she's looking for, I don't care what you have to do. You get it for me. The terms still stand. Do that, and you're free of me."

I stand, salute him, and say, "Fuck you, you fucking fuck."

Then I leave.

I wander a few blocks until I see the twin spires of a church jutting into the sky. The phone buzzes in my pocket. Presumably Sam. I don't answer. I need a minute.

The church is a basic Gothic-style church. Still pretty nice, though, as churches go. I wander inside to find only two other people, kneeling in silent prayer toward the front. I guess this one isn't one of the tourist-attracting churches. Not like St. Vitus, up in Prague Castle, where the queue of visitors means sometimes it takes up to ten minutes just to get through the doors.

From the trappings it appears Roman Catholic. A sign near the door says: Church of Saint Ludmila. I pick a pew closer to the back and sit, take in the surroundings. The design work on the stained glass behind the altar is incredible.

Focus on that.

Not on the pit of acid in my stomach.

This is falling apart and I don't know what to do. The best I've got is to stick with Sam. But I'm not sure I can trust her—that turn in the park was as unpredictable as it was terrifying.

What else can I do?

Move forward. That's the best I can come up with.

That's my fault, really. When I left New York, I thought maybe I didn't deserve to live there anymore. The truth was I was running away from my problems. I ran and ran until I backed myself into a corner.

This happened because of the choices I made.

After this, I need to make a change.

Still not sure what that is, but I need to make it regardless.

The phone buzzes again. I leave the church and answer.

"Where are you?" Sam asks.

I walk a little bit until I find a red street sign tacked onto the side of a building. "Sleszkà."

"Ditch that burner. It's probably compromised.

Then meet me at Kaz's apartment. We're about to take a little trip. I hope you like trains."

Click.

I hold out the phone. Consider winging it into the wall. But I can't.

Destroying the phone would protect Sam and me but put my mom in danger. My priority here isn't even in question. Especially because I'm starting to wonder, between Roman and Sam, who's lying to me and who's telling the truth.

Unless they're both lying.

The phone is at half battery. I click the ringer all the way down until it's silent, make sure the vibrate feature is off, stick it in the inside pocket of my coat, and walk.

TWELVE

The front door of Kaz's apartment is unlocked. Sam is sitting on the couch, looking at the door, like she knew I'd walk through at that exact moment. Her face is a smooth stretch of stone.

The phone beats like a heart in my pocket. I take off my jacket, hang it up, sit on the wingback chair across from the couch.

She doesn't say anything.

"Who's Toshiro Mifune?" I ask.

"Are you serious? *Seven Samurai*? *Yojimbo*?"

"Haven't seen them."

"You make me sad," she says. "Did you trash the phone like I asked?"

"Tossed it in the Vltava."

"So where the hell were you?"

I consider lying to her, but my dinner date doesn't seem important enough to hold back. Plus, the more lies I stack, the sooner the whole thing will topple.

"Roman treated me to a steak," I tell her.

She nods. "What did you two talk about?"

"Can I get a drink first?"

"What are you, a child? Do you need a nap, too?"

I don't bother with arguing, just head into the kitchen. There's a fresh pot of coffee on the counter, which makes me happy. I dig around in the cupboards until I find a mug, which has a 1950s pinup girl on the side. I head into the living room, sit on my chair. Settle in and blow the steam curling off the top of the mug.

"Well?" Sam asks.

I touch the rim of the mug to my lips and the coffee is too hot. I hold it in my lap. "He was familiar with Ansar al-Islam. He doesn't know who Chernya Dyra is but I think he's lying. He says you work for Hermera Global and the information you're looking for is about a very bad thing the bank did. He still insists he's a secret government agent. If you think I'm valuable enough to keep around, there's got to be a reason, and he wants it to play out. He also has a man outside my mom's house. She's not there, but it's only a matter of time before he finds her."

She doesn't say anything and that annoys me.

I take the coffee cup and try again. It scorches my mouth a little, but not enough to make me back off. "Where's Kaz?"

"Here, my friend," he calls, emerging from the hallway in jeans but barefoot and shirtless, rubbing a towel against his wet hair. I find it a little surprising that he doesn't have any tattoos. None that I can see, at least.

"Listen, I was thinking maybe we ought to leave," I tell him, then turn to Sam. "I don't want to endanger him by being here. And clearly these assholes have been able to find us . . ."

Sam clears her throat. "I don't think that's necessary. I cleared my phone. No trace. Smashed the laptop we snagged at the coffee shop. The key fob you have doesn't broadcast a signal so it can't be that. As long as you ditched the burner, we should be okay."

Well, there's that.

"Right," I tell her. "But someone has to know we're here . . ."

"Hey," Kaz says. His tone is sharp and a little angry. He's looking at Sam. "May I have an opportunity to contribute?"

Sam points to him. "Go for Kaz."

"Do *you* really believe you are safe here?" he asks Sam.

"If I didn't believe it, I wouldn't be here," Sam says. "And to sweeten the pot, I'll toss you some cash at the end of all of this, okay? Say . . . two grand? Euro?"

Kaz thinks about this for a minute. "Five."

Sam frowns. "Three."

"Deal," Kaz says.

Sam looks at me. "See? Problem solved."

Kaz walks out of the room with a look of satisfaction on his face. Once his bedroom door closes, Sam looks at me and says, "I could have done five if he really wanted."

"How charitable. Are we really safe here?"

"I'm not an idiot."

"I didn't say you were."

"Then stop implying it."

She picks up her phone and clicks away at the face of it.

"So what's the plan now?" I ask.

"We're taking a train ride," she says without looking at me.

"Where to?"

"Kraków?"

"In Poland?"

"Is there another Kraków nearby?"

"Why?"

"My contact, the guy I was supposed to meet with on the bridge. He's skittish about meeting me here. Which, given the super assassin after us, is fair. We meet tomorrow at Wawel Castle. So get yourself packed."

"How am I going to get on a train? Roman has my passport."

"Border checks aren't that tough between the Czech Republic and Poland. I mean, traditionally you'd show the conductor your passport, but I'll get that taken care of. We're leaving in two hours. I'd like to get there early, get some food, make sure we aren't being followed. I booked a sleeper car for the two of us. We'll arrive in Kraków tomorrow morning."

I pick up the coffee, take a long sip. I've been meaning to travel in the region but never got around to it. I'm comfortable here. Though maybe complacent is a better word.

"Sneaking me over borders now," I tell her. "That's a bit much for a plaything. Which is all I am to you assholes."

"Don't lump me and Roman together," she says. "For the record, I don't work for Herema Global. That was a cover. And I haven't lied to you yet, unless you count omissions, which I don't. This Roman guy is not some secret covert agent."

"Why should I trust you over him?"

"I'm nicer."

That makes me laugh out loud. "No, you are fucking not."

"Have I threatened to kill your mother?"

Pause. "No."

"Exactly. Now shut up. Go get dressed. Take a shower if you want. And man up while you're at it."

I've been able to weather Sam's insults, but that one sets me off, like a pot boiling over. I jump to my feet and yell, "I get that you're a super fucking badass. Congratulations. I'm no fucking slouch. If you want me to follow you on this, you are going to show me a modicum of goddamn respect."

As soon as the words leave my mouth, I feel like I maybe went a little overboard.

She doesn't move, doesn't flinch. She stares at

me for a long, hard moment, and then smiles and nods. "Okay."

The tension dissipates like smoke on a breeze. "Okay?"

"I told you to man up. You manned up. I'm going to lie down until you're ready to go."

Sam gets up and heads toward the bedrooms, leaving me alone in the living room.

Well. Maybe I should have gotten torqued off sooner.

Sam steps back into view. "Hey, what's your mother's name?"

"Theresa. Why?"

"Curious."

She disappears again.

Once Sam's door closes, I go to the room I've been staying in to get my pack and a fresh pair of clothes. I'm down to one clean t-shirt and the pair of jeans I'm wearing, plus a black fleece that Kaz gave me. I grab all my dirty clothes and go hunting for a washing machine, find it in a cabinet in the corner of the kitchen. I strip down to my boxers, load everything up, and start the cycle, then head for the shower.

Before I get into the bathroom, I realize my secret phone will die pretty soon, and I won't be able to top it off in front of Sam. So I take it out of my coat, wrap it in my t-shirt, find a charger in the kitchen, and plug it into the outlet next to the mirror in the bathroom.

Look in the mirror. The dark circles around my eyes are varying degrees of purple and yellow.

I let the water get hot, the room filling with steam until the mirror is fogged up, and pull off my boxers. Stand there and put my hands on the sink. My head is feeling a little better. A little more like my own skull, and not like pieces of broken wood nailed together. But I wish I could lie down, sleep for a hundred years.

As I'm about to climb into the shower, there's a knock at the door.

"Ash?"

It's Kaz. I crack open the door and peek out. He pushes in, so I pick a towel off the rack and wrap it around my waist. He looks at my battered torso and grimaces. "My friend, you look terrible."

"Thanks. What's with the naked rendezvous?"

Kaz speaks in a low tone, like he's nervous someone is listening. "I just . . . want to make sure you are okay. I know you are in tight spot. Do you know what you are doing?"

"Are you kidding? I have no idea what I'm doing. At all. Whatsoever."

"I think you should be careful around this girl. I'm not sure I trust her."

"You gave her clearance to use this place as a base of operations."

"I trust her self-interest," he says. "And I trust money. I do not trust her to protect you."

"Priority number one is my mom. Two is

you. Three is me. Four is everyone else."

"Okay, good," he says. "I am late for an appointment so I must be leaving you. But you will call me directly if you need anything, yes? Do not forget. I know people. I can help. Safe passage. Money. Weapons. You name it."

He stresses the word "weapons."

It's a little adorable, the way he says it. I know guys like Kaz. They all think they're on top of the place they live. I used to be like that, until I didn't live anywhere anymore.

I stick out my hand. "Thanks."

He shrugs and leans in to hug me. His grip is tight, and a little too long, and finally I have to tell him, "I thought you said you didn't star in porn films anymore. This is starting to feel like the start of one."

He pulls back and smiles. "Be safe, my friend."

When Kaz is gone, I drop the towel and climb into the shower. I'm stuck on a question: who's playing with me, and how do I make sure that person doesn't intend to dispose of me when this is all finished?

Sam and Roman can't both be on the side of angels.

Moscow rule. *Assume nothing*.

That's really the best I can come up with.

Hlavní Nádraží train station looks like a dreary shopping mall. Given how nice everything else in this town is, I am both surprised and disappointed. There are two levels of stores, a mix of general purpose and food stuffs, and ticket counters and kiosks and all the other things you'd expect in a train station.

The sun is setting behind us as we enter the station, a warm gust of air pushing away the cold and enveloping us. For the first time since we left the apartment, Sam speaks. "We should get some food. What are you in the mood for?"

"Dealer's choice," I tell her. "I'm not picky. Nothing with olives, though."

"Got it. I'll see if I can find us some wraps. Extra olives on yours."

"Thanks."

Across the way there's a bookstore that takes up two levels in the center of the station. "I'll be in there," I tell her. "You want a magazine or something?"

"Nope."

We part ways and I step through the door of the bookshop. I figure there is no way on this green planet I'm going to sleep well on the train and I should get something to read. There are plenty of English titles available, which is encouraging. Halfway here, I realized I left my Raymond Chandler book at Kaz's apartment. I didn't think it was worth bringing my bag on what is ultimately a quick trip back and forth.

Nothing grabs my attention on the displays up

front, so I wander the stacks, looking over my shoulder occasionally. I touch the outside of my coat to confirm the phone is still there. I hope it doesn't go out of range. I hope it works in Poland.

At the crime and mystery section there's a display with multiple copies of *Murder on the Orient Express* by Agatha Christie. That seems like a safe bet. I flip through to make sure it's in English and bring it to the cashier. As I'm paying, Sam enters. She notices me looking at her and smiles.

"You're paying attention to your surroundings," she says. "That's good."

"I try."

Something crinkles in her hand. I look down and she's got a Burger King bag clutched tight in her fist.

"Are you kidding?" I ask.

"What?"

I accept the change from the cashier, a young girl with pink hair and a pink lotus flower tattooed on her neck. "*Dekuji,*" I tell her.

"You're welcome," she says in an Australian accent.

Sam and I step out into the main part of the terminal and she asks, "Seriously, what's wrong with the King?"

"I don't even eat that shit when I'm home. Here we are in one of the oldest and prettiest cities in the world and we're going to eat American fast food?"

She sits on an empty bench and I sit next to her. She takes out a burger and hands it to me. "First, you're welcome. Second, it's nice to get a taste of home. Third, the line was shortest. I picked up some water, too, for the train."

I put down my new book and unwrap the burger. Take a bite. I'm not a fast food guy but I do have to admit the taste of it brings back a rush of something familiar. It's nice, if I ignore how it's going to gum up my arteries.

"Where is home, exactly?" I ask.

"None of your business."

"I'm from Staten Island."

"Okay."

"See? It's easy to share."

She thinks for a moment. "I'm from here."

"I feel like that's not true."

"I don't care."

Sam devours her burger in the time it takes to get through half of mine, and then rips open the bag to reveal two big containers of fries. She puts the bag on the bench between us and picks at them as she looks around the terminal.

"Do you know what the trick is to catching a tail?" she asks.

"No," I mumble through the last of the burger.

"Shoes."

"Shoes?"

She nods. "Some guy is following you, right?

There are quick and dirty ways to alter your appearance enough that you might miss them. We went over some of that in the park. Could be as simple as a wig or a fake mustache. A reversible jacket. A backpack with a different shirt inside. Something you change in and out of quickly. Get what I mean? Shoes are too much to carry. No one ever swaps out their shoes. If you suspect you're being followed, pay attention to shoes."

"Interesting," I tell her, shoving a handful of fries into my mouth.

"Here's another good one," she says. "When you want to send someone information, don't e-mail it. Instead, open a dummy e-mail account, save the information as a draft, and then give the person the account login. It's easy to track where an e-mail was sent from. Not so easy to track where you logged in."

I take out a handful of fries. "That's good advice. Why are you giving it to me?"

"Thought you might like to learn something," she says. "I have a gift for you, too. Something I picked up after we got separated today. It'll help pass the time."

"What is it?"

"I'll give it to you on the train."

"Do I have a brain tumor or something?"

"What does that mean?"

"You are suddenly being very nice to me and it makes me wonder if I'm dying."

A brief, pained smile flashes across her face. She looks different. Like when I first saw her coming out of her building. "I've been riding you pretty hard. I know that. But you're not completely useless. This whole thing . . . it's spiraling out of control. And now I'm alone. Before, I could trust that Fuller would swoop in and help when I needed it. Now I don't even have that." She pauses, looks down at her hands. "It's nice to have some backup."

Part of me wants to rib her for this, the way she's been relentlessly fucking with me. But there's a vulnerability that's so bald it almost scares me, so I let her have the moment.

"I'd take anything you're willing to teach," I tell her.

"Why?"

"I'm still trying to figure out what I want to be when I grow up," I tell her. "Maybe I'll be a spy."

"You don't want to do this job."

"Why?"

"For a hundred reasons. A million. But most of all because you've got someone somewhere in this world who loves you. And you love that person. And you can't love someone or be loved and do this."

"That's a grim assessment of things."

Sam looks up at the board looming over us, watching the numbers click over. "C'mon," she says. "Our train is here."

"You're being evasive," I tell her.

"Shut up, you girl. If it'll make you happy, we can braid each other's hair once we're settled on the train."

"There's my Sammy," I tell her.

She ignores me and stalks away. I follow and we pass crowds of surly locals and confused tourists and backpackers and wandering families. I look to see who might be looking at us, keeping an eye on their shoes.

We get to a concourse—a long, wide hallway with staircases shooting off it, leading up to the platforms. We find the platform we need and I can feel the cold on my skin before we even get to the top. It's snowing again. The ground is covered with a dusting where there aren't overhangs to provide cover.

In front of us is a large, belching train, blue and red and old. The paint scratched and scored, like a child's toy that's been treated roughly. I'm not sure where we board but Sam walks with purpose so I follow her, the crowd thinning until it's the two of us, our shoes crunching in the thin layer of snow.

At the last car she climbs aboard and stamps her feet to clear snow off her Nikes. It's pleasantly warm inside. There's a bathroom to the left, and in front of us a narrow corridor, leading toward the front of the train. Maroon carpeting and wood paneling. It looks like someone's basement.

Smells about the same, too. Dank. There's an old, heavyset man in a porter uniform at the end. He looks down the corridor at us and nods, then leans back in the open door, to some conversation going on in another room.

We walk the row to the fourth door and Sam opens it. There are three bunks on the left wall, each one creating a dark little alcove that looks like a coffin. The right side of the compartment is so narrow I have to walk sideways. There's a luggage rack running along the top, a window at the far end with some cheap curtains, a table and a mirror bolted into the corner underneath. Sam immediately opens the mirror, finds a plug, and sets up her phone and charger. Then she swings her backpack onto the luggage rack. I take off my jacket and put it next to her backpack, careful to fold it so the phone doesn't fall out, and far enough away she doesn't jostle it when she goes to get her bag.

The two of us can't help but be in each other's space. Standing this close to her, it's hard to not think about how slight she feels. And yet, there's a very good chance she could break me in two.

She looks up at me and says, "I'll sort out tickets and stuff with the conductor."

She pushes past me like a cat, her body contorting to slip through the slim space, and exits the room. I kick my boots into the corner, then climb into the bottom bunk and find that even though I'm six feet tall, it's not terribly uncomfortable. My feet barely miss the far wall. There's a nice full pillow and sheets and a little reading light, plus a couple of mesh storage pockets, like on the back of airplane seats.

Sam comes back in, closes the door, and slides the metal latch to lock it. There's a ladder for the top bunk hanging from the luggage rack but she doesn't use it, grabs her bag and climbs like a spider onto her bunk. She doesn't say anything and the train isn't moving and I have no idea how long this is going to take, so I take out my book, flick on the reading light, and get ready to start the first chapter.

"You ready for your gift?" she asks.

I slide the book into the corner. "Sure."

Something hard hits me in the thigh, just missing my crotch. I yell out and fold inward. Sam hops off the bunk and pulls down a seat that's bolted into the wall, the spring mechanism creaking.

"Did I hit you in the nuts?" she asks.

"No."

"Then I missed."

"You are not a nice person."

"Shut up and open it."

I swing my legs off and feel around until I find the package. Our knees nesting like spokes of a zipper. It's a small envelope, folded up and taped over. I open it and find a padlock. It's clear plastic

198

so I can see all the guts inside. There's also a small plastic package, holding an assortment of long, flat pieces of metal.

"You got me a lock pick set?" I ask.

"You said you wanted to learn," she says, taking it out of my hand. From the small pouch she extracts a piece of metal in the shape of a Z, but the middle is straight, rather than slanted. "This is a tension wrench. The rest are picks with a variety of different ends, but you'll find the only one you ever need is this one." She fishes out a pick with a slightly curved end and holds it up to me. I take it and turn it over in my hand. The metal is thin but rigid. Makes all those movies where people pick locks with paperclips seem far-fetched.

She puts down the envelope on the sink and picks up the lock and shows me the mechanics of it, explaining how the pins are at different heights and you have to line them up so they're flush and that makes the mechanism turn. Then she picks up the tension wrench and runs me through it, applying a little pressure with one hand, using the pick to move the pins into position with the other, the lock nestled in her palm. Within seconds the lock pops.

She hands it back to me. "Think you can do it?"

I take it from her and close the clasp, then insert the tension wrench like she showed. I go to work with the pick. Since it's my first time and I feel her watching me, the pressure makes it feel like I'm doing this with oven mitts. I get one or two of the pins, but by the time I get toward the back, the ones I moved slide back into place.

"Here," she says, taking my hands, holding them steady.

Her hands are small and warm. She guides my fingers, taking over for me, using them to make the pins move. The way she touches me is a way I haven't been touched in a while. Making a move on her makes me fear for my life. But given our proximity, it's hard to not think about it.

When I look up, I realize she has green eyes. I haven't noticed the color of her eyes before.

We're so close right now, and that intimacy takes down the brick wall that's been separating us. I wonder if she's thinking the same thing. And there's a faraway look in her eyes, like maybe she is. The two of us hold each other's gazes for a moment. She opens her mouth, like she wants to say something, and closes it again.

"What?" I ask.

"You're not my type," she says, her voice soft. A little more of that Southern accent peeking through.

"What's your type?"

"Not you."

"Okay."

"I'm sorry," she says.

"Don't apologize."

I pull my hands away and go back to trying, because I want to learn how and also I don't want to look at her right now. I'm not upset, just embarrassed.

After a minute or so, I get all the pins aligned and the tension wrench slips, turning the tumbler. The lock pops open. I look up and Sam is smiling. "See? Not completely useless. It's harder on older locks. This is like riding a bike with training wheels on both ends. When you get good at it, try doing it with your eyes closed. When you can do it quickly with your eyes closed, consider yourself graduated."

She doesn't wait for me to say anything, just swings herself up and onto the bunk. I don't hear anything else from her. It's like she disappeared and I'm alone in the compartment. I play with the lock for a little while, locking it and unlocking it, trying to ignore the burn of rejection.

I don't even know what my intention was there. But right now all I want in this world is for her to come down here and lie next to me. I don't even want anything to happen. It'd be nice to feel someone close.

And I want to say this to her but I can't bring myself to say it, so I concentrate on the lock.

I practice until I can open the lock in a couple of seconds. So I do what Sam suggested, close my eyes and try to visualize the movements. It is suddenly a million times harder. After a little while, I give up, take some comfort that I made at least some progress.

"Hey, you said you got us some waters?" I ask.

"Oh, right," she says.

A bottle appears. I grab it and find the cap has already been loosened. "Did you drink out of this?"

"Sorry, I only got one."

"Want it back?"

"All yours. Hey, Florida is nice this time of year, right?"

"Presumably. I've never been during the winter but have to figure the weather is mild. Why?"

"Curious."

"That's a weird thing to be curious about."

Silence from the top bunk.

I take a gulp and stick the bottle into the mesh pocket on the wall next to me and pick up the book. Best case scenario, it's awesome and keeps me riveted throughout the trip so that I'm entertained, because there's literally nothing else to do besides play with the lock. Worst case, the book is boring as shit and puts me to sleep. Maybe that's best case. I don't even know. I take another sip of water and ask, "How long is this train ride anyway?"

The words feel like marshmallows in my mouth.

Something is wrong. It takes a second for me to realize what it is: drugs. I know drugs. I used to do them all the time. I know when there's something in my system that shouldn't be there.

"Eight hours, without delays, and there'll probably be delays," Sam says. "There are always delays."

She hangs upside down from the bunk, her blonde hair cascading around her.

"I wouldn't worry too much about that, though," she says.

"Did you give me something?"

"Yup," she says. "Sweet dreams."

I try to say something but my mouth won't work. Try to lift my arms but they feel disconnected from my body. I want to scream but instead darkness creeps in on the edges of my vision, swallowing me.

THIRTEEN

Waking up is like going over the first dip of a rollercoaster. Sudden and a little frightening. The sunlight cutting through the curtain and the thunderous rattle of the train overwhelm my senses. It takes a few moments for things to get down to a bearable level.

When it does, I take stock of where I am. Inside the sleeper car. The train is moving. I have no idea where we are.

I slide off the bunk and pull myself to standing in the narrow space and find the bed above me is empty. The sheets and blankets are folded and neatly put back, like Sam hadn't even slept on them.

So I'm alone on the train, without my passport, or a lot of spending money, or a cell phone I can actually use. I look out the window but can't tell anything about where we are. Snow-covered fields as far as I can see, like we're traveling through a canvas that hasn't been filled in yet.

This is fucking great.

I slide open the door and check the hallway. No one on either side. I consider fishing the phone out of my jacket because at least that will tell me what time it is, when I notice something metal and gleaming, poking out from under Sam's pillow.

204

That knife she pulled on me and Evzen.

I take it and flick out the blade. It's short and looks sharp enough to cut through the wall of the train. Sam's bag and coat are still on the rack, so she must be in the bathroom or looking for food.

Either way, when she comes back, I'm going to be ready.

Maybe she found the phone, or she knows I kept it. Maybe there's some other reason for her to drug me. Either way, I'm getting off this train, going back to Prague, and figuring out how to deal with Roman. There has to be a way. Something else I can offer him. Some way I can convince him to find another golem and leave me the hell alone.

I back up into the room and wait. After a few moments, the door opens and I hold the knife down by my side, out of view. Sam is wearing a white undershirt, jeans, and her gray Nike sneakers. She looks me up and down and nods. "Good timing, sleepyhead. We're almost there."

She enters the room and shuts the door, and as she's turned slightly and looking away from me, I bring the knife up, placing it flat against her cheek. She freezes but doesn't say anything, just waits for me to speak.

"Why did you drug me?" I ask.

Her voice is level, unconcerned. "You understand I could take that and gut you before you even realize the stupidity of this decision."

"Why did you drug me?"

"Sleeping on trains sucks. I thought you'd like to get a full night's rest. Anyway, you need it, considering how hard you got knocked around the other night."

I press the knife a little, forming a tiny groove in her skin with the blade. Not enough to break it. Enough to let her know I don't believe her.

"What did you think? That I wanted to have my way with you while you were unconscious? Look, I'm not going to lie to you." She raises an eyebrow. "I might have."

"Why not tell me, then?"

"Because you're a pain in the ass. I'm going to give you a pass on this, on the condition you fold up that knife and calmly hand it to me right now. You do anything other than that, and we're going to have a real problem. In the form of you exiting this train immediately. We're moving pretty fast."

Breathe.

I fold up the knife and hand it to her.

She smiles, accepts it, and places it in the coin pocket of her jeans.

"What did you give me?" I ask.

"Something you've never heard of. Provides a nice restful sleep without any fuzzy feeling the next day. Admit it, you feel pretty good right now."

She's right. I feel like I slept for four days. I've had dark, blackout sleeps like that before.

They come from one of two things: alcohol or Benadryl. Problem is, with both of those things, you come out on the other end hung over or with a head full of cotton. Right now I feel like I could run a marathon while solving complex math equations. And I'm terrible at math. This is the best I've felt since my meeting with Chernya Dyra.

"You should have told me," I tell her. "I have a concussion. The drugs could have made it worse."

"Yeah, well, they didn't. If anything, the sleep probably helped. Now get your stuff together. We arrive in Kraków in a few minutes."

She exits the car. I didn't bother to bring anything so all I have to do is pull on my boots and check the pockets inside the bunk to make sure I didn't leave anything behind. I shrug into my coat, stash the book and the lock pick set, making sure the lump of the phone is still there. I exit the car and Sam is looking out the window.

"Hitting the bathroom," I tell her.

"Enjoy," she says without looking at me.

Inside, after getting myself situated, an unfortunately-timed burst of frigid air teaches me the toilets work by opening a latch that dumps everything onto the tracks.

An announcement comes over the loudspeaker, garbled so I can't understand it. The train slows down and I find Sam waiting for me outside the door, coat on and backpack slung over her shoulder.

"Let's go," she says.

We post up by the door as the train pulls into the station. When it finally stops, we climb off and follow signs through concrete corridors and wind up inside a shopping mall. Are all train stations in Eastern Europe like this? We exchange confused glances, then shrugs, and go hunting for daylight. We pass an ATM and Sam stops.

"Hold up," she says. "Don't have any złoty."

As she pokes at the ATM, I look around and see a massive clock that says it's 10 a.m. We should have arrived in Kraków hours ago.

"Train got delayed?" I asked.

"We were sitting on a track waiting for a connection from Budapest," she says. "Aren't you glad you were sleeping for that?"

"What did you do to pass the time?"

"I told you. Sexually assaulted you."

"That's not funny."

"It is a little bit funny, because now you're wondering if maybe I did," she says.

After extracting a handful of colorful bills, she looks around, nods, and walks toward the exit.

If Prague is ancient, Kraków may as well be prehistoric. The feeling of going from Prague to here is like going from Manhattan to Queens. Not as dense, more native. The buildings are smaller but no less intricate.

I know a little about Kraków. I know it escaped the worst of the aerial bombings in World War II, so a lot of the architecture is pre-war. I know I'm supposed to be nice to the pigeons because local legend says they're really knights who were trapped in that form by a witch. I know Auschwitz is nearby. Being this close to the blackest mark on human history makes me feel compelled to see it, to pay my respects, but I suspect Sam will not be down for sightseeing.

The taxi driver lets us off at the bottom of a road running next to a long brick wall. It's cold but not too cold. The snow is thick, somewhere between six inches and a foot. I'm glad I have a sturdy pair of boots. We follow footpaths carved out by the flow of pedestrian traffic.

It's a long walk up the road, following alongside the wall, the incline leading us above the city. The path leads to a large open field covered in snow and ringed by ancient, ornate buildings that are so fancy I imagine we aren't allowed to go inside them. The tallest is a cathedral, the green spires flecked with white peeking up into the gray sky.

"What now?" I ask.

"Still early," Sam says. "We wait."

"Can we go inside the church?"

Sam looks at her phone. "Fine."

There's a long, winding path carved in the snow that leads to the front of the cathedral. There are tourists taking pictures, looking up at the tight collection of buildings. At the entrance, we join the slow queue of people waiting to get inside. We pass a sign that says the cathedral dates back to the fourteenth century. The Royal Archcathedral Basilica of Saints Stanislaus and Wenceslaus on the Wawel Hill. I suspect neither of them are the patron saint of brevity.

It takes a few minutes of shuffling along with the crowd, and we find ourselves inside a vast chamber flanked by tapestries and leading to a gilded altar that makes me think of Kaz's apartment, except with less of a porn vibe. The space is filled with the low hum of prayer and hushed conversation. There are people snapping pictures, or kneeled in pews. I walk toward a section of pews that are empty and sit, happy to be warm and to have something to look at.

Sam sits next to me. "Didn't take you for a member of the god squad."

"I'm not. I like churches."

"Why?"

I have to think about that for a second. I have yet to explain it to anyone. It's one of those things that makes sense in my head but the meaning gets lost on the way to my mouth. After a few moments, I tell her, "Legacy."

"Legacy?"

"I've just been thinking a lot lately about that. What I'm doing with my life. What I'm leaving behind when I'm gone. And look at this place. It's been here for, what, something like seven hundred years? It's not even that it's old. It got built back before electricity. Before they had anything that would have made the job the slightest bit easy. And here it is. It's . . . incredible. It's nice to sit in a quiet place and look at a mark someone left on the world."

Sam nods slowly. Digesting it.

"What's the matter?" I ask. "No witty comeback? You're not going to make fun of me?"

"You think you're the first person to ever have a deep thought?"

We sit there for a little while, taking in our surroundings.

Sam takes her phone, looks at it, puts it inside her coat.

"Why do you do it?" I ask.

"Do what?"

"This job. This thing you do. Be a spy, or whatever you want to call it?"

"It's the only thing I'm good at."

The answer comes too quickly. It's practiced.

It's also bullshit.

"Seriously," I tell her.

She breathes in sharply through her nose, lets the air hiss out of her. Takes another breath. Folds her hands in her lap, then twists her fingers to crack her knuckles. "Inertia. One thing led to another thing led to another thing. That's how I got here. One day it'll kill me, like it did Fuller. That's the job. I'll go to my grave alone but I'll know I tipped the scales a little bit in the right direction."

"You don't have to be alone, you know."

"You're alone," she says.

"That's a matter of circumstance. And for a long time I thought I needed to be. I shut myself away. Turns out the best thing I ever did was learn to talk about the way I felt. I know that might be a little touchy-feely for you, but it helped."

In my peripheral vision, Sam's face softens. For a moment I think I've gotten past the façade. Then she purses her lips. "You and I don't do the same thing. Not even in the same league."

"First, it's not a contest. And second, I think we do. Because what I'm doing is what I think is right. It might not be the legal thing and it might not be the smart thing, but it's the thing I know in my heart needs to get done. If the path is tough, fine, I can handle it. Because in the end, that's the legacy I hope to leave behind. That I made someone else's life better. Doesn't mean I need to suffer in the process."

She looks at me. Opens her mouth. Begins to speak.

Stops. Takes her vibrating phone out of her pocket.

"That's weird," she says.

"What?"

"Got a text. My contact is here. The message says: *St. George's enemy?*"

"Your contact likes riddles."

"I keep telling him this phone is secure and he doesn't need to do it. He's a little . . . strange."

An old man in a navy vest is walking down the aisle toward us. Tall, long hair tied back in a ponytail, with a friendly smile and a bushy mustache. He's got on a nametag that says: Alesky. I've seen enough tour guides to know he's a tour guide.

"Excuse me, sir," I say, getting up from the pew. "What can you tell me about dragons?"

The man smiles, like he was expecting this question. "Have you not heard the dragon legend of Kraków?"

"We have not, but would like very much to hear it," Sam says in a sudden and effortless French accent.

"Would you like me to show you the way to the dragon's lair?" he asks.

"Please," Sam says.

We follow alongside the man as he leads us outside the church, back into the biting air, and across the property. We stick to the paths, walking slowly.

"So," I tell him. "Dragons." The man smiles. "The earliest telling of the story dates back to the thirteenth century. The dragon first appeared during the reign of King Krakus, and required weekly offerings of cattle. This was, as you can imagine, a bit of trouble for the townsfolk." He laughs and it sounds like a rattle in his chest. "So Krakus asked his two sons, Lech and Krakus II, to intervene. They fed the dragon a calfskin stuffed with sulfur, which felled the beast. Lech was a jealous boy, and decided he wanted the credit, so he killed his brother and blamed the dragon. Lech later became king. But the secret got out and he was exiled from the country. This city is named after the brave and innocent Krakus."

"That's quite a story," I tell him.

"It is not the only one," Alesky says. "There is another interpretation, from the fifteenth century. Very similar to the first, but it is the one I prefer. The dragon was terrorizing the town, but instead of cattle, it ate young maidens. Fearing for his daughter's safety, the king offered her hand in marriage to whoever could defeat the dragon. So a cobbler's apprentice named Skuba stuffed a lamb with sulphur. The dragon ate it and became so thirsty it drank from the Vistula until it exploded."

"Sulphur, it would seem, is the preferred method for combatting dragons," I tell him.

"In this part of the world, yes," Alesky says.

"Why do you prefer the second version?"

Alesky smiles again. It's a warm smile. "Less villainy."

"What does the dragon stand for?" Sam asks.

"The origins are actually thought to predate Christianity. Some historians believe the dragon was symbolic of the Avars, a nomadic tribe of barbarians who lived on this hill, sometime around the sixth century."

"And what do you believe?" I ask.

"That the world is a scary place," Alesky says. "And sometimes we need reassurances that monsters can be defeated."

We approach a wall overlooking a bluff with the city stretched out beneath us, rooftops and trees heavy with snow, sparkling in the sun breaking through the cloud cover. The city looks every bit as magical as the stories make it sound. I wish there were more time to explore. My own fault for waiting until circumstances forced me here.

Alesky leads us to an alcove, with a staircase leading down, fronted by a turnstile. He gives us a wave and says, "Enjoy your trip into the dragon's lair."

Sam and I thank him and he walks away.

"That was weird," Sam says.

"Are you kidding me? That was awesome."

"Of course you're impressed, you nerd."

We make our way through the turnstile and down a set of narrow stone stairs, until we get to

215

a cave that feels a little more like a movie set. It's well-lit by pot lights. The rock is fake. Fiberglass maybe? No dragon, sadly. I start walking but Sam says, "Stop." She leans against the wall and nods for me to lean next to her.

"Two minutes," she says. After a moment, she asks, "Can you tell me why?"

I look around at the space. Back up the staircase. "Because if someone were following us, they'd have to come down this staircase. There's no other way inside. And we're down at ground level. Two minutes isn't long enough for someone to get all the way around the complex to meet us on the other side."

"Very good," she says.

We stand there, watching the tourists taking pictures of fake stone walls.

Finally, Sam says, "C'mon."

We make our way through the cave, checking into the various alcoves, none of which lead anywhere, until we get to the exit. We step outside and find the dragon. A stone sculpture that's got to be fifteen feet, maybe twenty feet high. I look up at it as people take pictures, and after a few moments, it belches a bouquet of fire. I can feel the warmth of it on my skin.

"Sam?"

We both turn to find a nervous little black guy with large eyes and a young face. He could be fifteen or thirty. He's wearing a red wool hat with a poof at the top. The collar of his heavy black overcoat is flipped up so that from the side you couldn't make out his face.

"Jeremiah?" Sam asks.

The man nods but doesn't say anything. He just looks at me like I'm a black bear reared up on its hind legs. Sam says, "Don't worry, he's cool. I mean, not cool, but he's not going to mess things up for us."

"Okay," he says, eyes darting back and forth between us. "We need to go."

He doesn't say anything about my fucked-up face, which is nice. He turns and walks without making sure we're following.

We pass through narrow streets and small crowds of people, but otherwise, this town is quiet. Whenever we stop, so that Sam can look around and make sure we're not being tailed, I stop and look at the buildings, and every time, I'm sad when we start walking again.

Eventually, we reach a town square. This one is different from the Wawel Castle complex. No green space, but there's a fountain and a big hall in the middle, ringed on the edges by restaurants that look like tourist traps.

The square is filled with holiday booths. Getting close to Christmas now. As we cut through the thick crowd of shoppers, we pass vendors selling warmed wine from clay pots and pierogis from giant cast iron pans. And tons of colorful, handmade crafts. We pass a blacksmith in a white t-shirt stained with soot, standing over a fire where he's heating horseshoes and hammering initials into them.

As we reach the edge of the square, I find a booth that's selling handmade Christmas ornaments. My mom has a thing for Christmas ornaments and if I'm not going to make it home for the holiday, I should at least have something to send her. I tell Sam and Jeremiah to stop. The two of them do and turn, like there might be something wrong. Both of them seem annoyed to find me picking through ornaments. It doesn't take long to find something I think my mom will like. A bell shaped like a dragon, carved out of wood. It's small and intricate and beautiful. There's an old Polish woman behind the counter. I ask her how much and she says something in Polish.

I'm about to ask her again when Sam is standing over my shoulder, holding out a ten złoty note. The woman takes it and smiles, wraps the ornaments very carefully in tissue paper, and places it in a small bag. My understanding is that Czech and Polish are kind of similar so I tell her, "*Dekuji*."

She smiles and nods.

As we turn away, I tell Sam, "That was very nice of you."

"I'm not a monster," she says.

"Debatable," I tell her.

Jeremiah is hopping on his toes, looking around. "Maybe let's go now, please?"

He leads us to a pub on the other side of the square, walking quickly, making a beeline for a booth toward the back where we can't be seen from the entrance. But there's a mirror above us that gives us a view of who's coming and going.

We hang our coats on the hook on the wall and sit. The first thing I see on the menu is pierogis and I feel it would be stupid to come to Poland and not order some, so when the waiter comes over, I ask for a plate of them, plus a roasted pork knuckle. Sam orders a pork knuckle. Jeremiah orders bigos, a hunter stew. We get waters all around because it's early and I don't think any of us are in a drinking mood.

When the waiter is gone and there's no one within earshot, Jeremiah looks at me and says, "You were on the bridge."

"I was. Sorry about that."

"Why were you on the bridge?"

Sam interjects. "It's a long story and you don't need to worry about it. It worked out in our favor because someone very dangerous was also on that bridge and if he hadn't been there to get in the way, things could have ended very badly for both of us."

"Okay." Jeremiah reaches under the table and pulls something out of his pocket. He puts his closed fist on the table and looks back and forth between us.

He opens his fist and removes it, revealing a red plastic flash drive, which Sam quickly takes and puts in her pocket.

"You know the risk I'm taking," he says to Sam.

"I know. Is it password protected?"

"Yes."

"What's the password?"

"Back in Prague. Once you're safely back there, I'll tell you where it's hidden."

"You can't tell it to me?"

"It's an alphanumeric string that's twenty-five characters long. Randomly generated and I purposely didn't memorize it. Safety measure. You'll want to move quickly. It won't last long where it is."

The waiter comes back and puts our food down. Yup, tourist trap. Only tourist traps move food out this quickly. Still, it is incredible to look at. The pierogis are hot, but I pop one into my mouth. It's warm and buttery and delicious. The other two don't seem very interested in their food. I cram another into my mouth before I'm even done with the first.

"Where should I start?" Jeremiah asks.

"Explain it to me like I'm an idiot." Sam smirks, cocks her thumb at me. "Better yet, explain it like you're trying to explain it to him."

"Hey," I tell her.

Jeremiah ignores me. "Okay. So. Okay." He looks around, lowers his voice. "Remember a few years ago, when gas was up over four dollars a gallon?"

Sam nods.

"In order to bring the price down, a bunch of banks invested in drilling projects. Expensive drilling projects. Tons and tons of money got invested in this. Ramp up production so that the world supply could be replenished, right? It worked. Gas is a lot cheaper. The problem is, it worked too well."

"The market isn't flush, it's flooded," Sam says.

"Exactly. Supply is far outstripping demand. A barrel is under thirty dollars right now. Oil companies are going bankrupt." He flares out his fingers. "Kaput. Tens of thousands of people are losing their jobs. Some banks are counting loses in the billions. That's billions with a B. And it's only going to get worse. Analysts predict it could be under twenty a barrel within the next six months. That's a doomsday scenario. Investment bankers jumping out of windows scenario. Money that'll never come back. You follow me so far?"

Sam nods. I rip off a big piece of pork knuckle and stick it in my mouth. It's so good I want to cry. The bartender comes over to check on us and we all smile at him until he walks away.

"So," Jeremiah says. "The only way people are getting their money back is if prices go back up. Way, way up. For prices to go back up, one of two things needs to happen: demand needs to outstrip supply, which probably isn't going to happen any time soon because there's so much, or something has to jam up the works so new oil isn't being produced as quickly."

"Okay . . ." Sam says.

"And you know where many of the oil markets are?"

"The Middle East. So . . . wait." Sam's face drops. "No."

The look on her face makes the food I ate roil in my gut.

"Hemera Global is funding a terrorist group called Ansar al-Islam. They're making a hard push into Iraq and Afghanistan in the hopes they'll destabilize the market."

After he says this, you could about hear a pin drop between the three of us.

I've stopped mid-chew with a wad of potato in my mouth. I forget it's there long enough that I nearly choke, then have trouble swallowing because my mouth has run dry. I take a big swig of water to get it down.

"Are you kidding me?" Sam asks.

"I wish I were," Jeremiah says. "I found it by accident. There was a fault in their security I was trying to fix and I stumbled across it. They know I have it. Everything you need to prove it is on that drive. The evidence is very explicit."

"This is . . . this is . . ."

"I know," Jeremiah says.

He pulls his bowl toward him and takes a bite of the stew as Sam nibbles at a pierogi from my plate. I push my food away. I'm not hungry anymore.

FOURTEEN

Sam and Jeremiah talk more. I sit and listen. There's not much for me to contribute. Some of it is technical or refers to stuff I don't understand. After a little while, I poke at my food, less out of hunger and more so I have something to do with my hands.

After a few moments, Jeremiah says, "Please excuse me. I must use the restroom. As they say, no job is finished until the paperwork is done." He gets up and heads toward the bathrooms.

"Weird guy," I tell Sam.

"Yeah," she says, not looking at me.

That's all we can muster at the moment.

The idea is horrifying: a U.S. bank backing terrorists for financial gain. It's also not terribly hard to believe. Banks have done some craven things. Just a few years ago they willfully wrecked the housing market and destroyed the livelihood of millions in pursuit of profit.

It makes me upset and angry and confused and a whole lot of other emotions I don't even know how to process.

But it also makes me happy.

Because I will gladly play a roll in exposing this.

Whatever the risk.

So much of the last few days has been about surviving. Sorting out who to trust. Wondering about the decisions I've made that led me to this point.

And now I have a goal. Something worth fighting for.

Bad guys who need stopping.

That's all I ever really need.

"Ash?" Sam asks.

I snap back to the table. "Yeah."

"We have to go."

I turn to Jeremiah and he's hovering at the edge of the table. Sam and I stand and we get into our coats and Sam places down a wad of cash. She turns and shakes Jeremiah's hand. "You did good. You'll text me tomorrow with the information?"

"Yes," Jeremiah says. "Like I said, move quickly, okay? And after this, no contact, no nothing. I disappear."

"You're doing a good thing."

"Don't waste it."

He turns toward me, nods, and leaves the restaurant. We stand there for a moment, watching the door swing shut behind him, cutting off the white light from outside, until Sam says, "This is pretty fucked up."

"Yeah, it is," I tell her.

We exit the restaurant. The wind has picked up and it claws at us. Sam steps away, dials a number, and launches into a conversation in what

I think is Polish. I huddle next to the building, away from the wind coming off the river, look longingly at the guy across the street smoking a cigarette.

Sam hangs up the phone and steps toward me. "Got us on a train that's leaving later tonight."

"So what do we do until then?"

"I don't know. I hate being out in the open like this. I'd rather be hunkered down somewhere. Maybe a bookstore, or a library?"

"I've got a better idea," I tell her. "Give me the phone."

She hesitates for a moment and hands it over. I go to dial the Crash Hop office, and remember it's being monitored. Probably better to call Stanislav's cell, and luckily, that one I remember.

"Stanny?" I ask.

"Mister Ashley," he says. I can hear the smile in his voice. "How are you feeling?"

"Still a little run down, but coming along. Listen, I have something I need to tell you . . ."

He sighs. "You are leaving me. I know this is coming . . ."

"Now, wait, that's not it. I mean, yeah, I'm sorry to say that I am. I think it's time to move on . . ."

"It is fine," he says. "I can give you more work if you like. Or else you can come by and pick up the last of your pay. I will take you out to a restaurant I know. It is a very good restaurant.

You were a good worker. My way of saying thank you."

"I would like that," I tell him. "But first, I have a favor to ask."

"Anything," he says.

"So, funny story. I met a girl . . ."

At this, Sam rolls her eyes.

"And let me guess," Stanislav says. "You are looking for someplace with a little . . . privacy."

"Yes, but there's a wrinkle," I tell him. "We're in Kraków."

"Kraków! When did this happen?"

"Spur of the moment decision. She wanted pierogis so we got on the train last night. We're coming back today. But now we're both a little wiped out and, truthfully, need a place to warm up for a little bit."

"Say no more," he says. "We have a few apartments there. Let me check." Computer keys clack through the phone. After a moment, he says, "We have one open right now. It is on Rzeszowska, off of Starowiślna. That is in Kazimierz, the Jewish district. North of the river. Building number five, top floor."

I repeat all of that out loud the best that I can, gumming the words. Sam nods to indicate that she got it.

"Great, will my key work here?" I ask.

"It should," Stanislav says, his voice dropping. "We had an . . . issue with another apartment.

Police investigation. For safety's sake, we changed the relay on the master keys. They should all be reset by now. Yours should work. If it does not, call me."

I guess they found Fuller.

"Thanks for the hookup, Stanislav."

"Promise me that you will come see me before you go," he says.

"I promise."

"And make sure to change the sheets if, you know . . ."

"Got it."

Click.

Sam takes the phone from my hand and taps at the screen. After a moment, she says, "Found it. Not far."

The building is a five-story walkup without an elevator. We climb to the top, each landing dirtier than the one below it. On the final floor there's a steel door and a dusty rainbow couch outside. I hold the fob up to the door and it clicks open.

The apartment is sparse and clean, though the shape of it is odd. The ceiling is peaked, and so low at either end I would have to stoop down to keep from hitting my head. There's a room in the corner behind a sliding glass door with a skylight and some lawn furniture. It looks like a balcony but is actually enclosed.

Off to the left is a bedroom with two beds. There's no couch, just a table and some chairs near the stove. It looks like new and not terribly mindful construction. Probably added on to the building recently. That said, it's warm and cozy and nice enough to keep us occupied until we have to hit the train station.

We drop our coats on the chair closest to the door. Sam disappears into the bathroom. The door is frosted glass, which seems a little ridiculous in terms of privacy. I can see the vague outline of her as she sits on the toilet.

I take the opportunity to peek at the phone in my pocket.

It's nearly dead.

That's not good.

Also not good: I left the charger back in Prague.

It made sense at the time. A low-tech phone like this will usually hold a charge for a few days. Must have been the train. It probably wore itself down searching for a signal as we dropped in and out of range of cell towers.

Sam is still on the toilet. I step to the galley kitchen, which runs along the far wall of the apartment. Checking drawers. There's an unofficial rule at Crash Hop that if you find a charger, you chuck it in a drawer. The person who left it will come back for it, but more likely, the next guest in line will find a use for it.

Most of the drawers are empty, or full of a hodge-podge of silverware. Nothing matches. Blunt, dull items scavenged from who knows where.

By the fifth drawer I am getting very worried.

Because only two more to go, and I can hear the clank of the toilet seat, the spinning of the toilet paper roll.

In the sixth drawer I find a tangle of chargers. A half dozen, all wrapped up around each other and impossible to sort without a lot of time and patience. Neither of which I have. The inputs are all different. I flip through them and try to find a connecter that'll fit the phone, my hands slipping, plastic scratching against plastic as everything seems a little too big or too small.

My heart jabs my ribcage.

The toilet flushes.

I wonder if Sam will stab me when she sees I kept the phone.

Probably.

Score. I find one that works and trail the wire back until I find what I think is the right plug, stick it into the wall outlet next to an unplugged blender and coffee maker. Nothing happens.

Fuck. Wrong plug.

Try the next. Nothing.

On the third one, the screen lights up green. I push the rat's nest of wires against the wall as the bathroom door opens behind me. I move the coffee maker and blender to block them.

"What are you doing?" Sam asks.

"Looking for something to eat," I tell her.

She pauses. I don't turn to her so I can't tell

how she's looking at me. I can't hear anything so I don't think she's crossing the room to me. My body has to be blocking her view but there's something about the gap in the air between us that makes the skin on my neck tight.

"Can you make me a cup of tea?" she asks. "Is there tea?"

My body relaxes.

"Sure."

She steps into the sunroom. I exhale. Put on the electric kettle. Turn. She can't see me from her vantage point. I check under the sink, see there's an outlet down there. Hooray for shoddy construction. Stash the chargers, make sure the phone is still charging, and go about pouring two cups of tea.

Once they're done, I carry the steaming mugs into the sunroom. It's right on the border of uncomfortably warm, which is a nice respite from the weather outside. I place the mugs down and sit across from her. She says, "It's nice in here."

"I wish there were a couch. I'd take a nap."

"Shame," she says. She picks up her spoon and swirls it around the mug of tea but she doesn't take her eyes off me. She's got that flat lizard look again.

The same one I recognize from the park.

When her hand is free, she reaches underneath the table, into her jeans, and places the folded knife next to the glass. It makes a heavy clacking sound on the glass table.

I sit up a little straighter, my breath caught in my chest.

I'm sweating. I'd like to say it's the heat of the room, but I doubt it.

"So, how long?" she asks.

I take a sip of tea, careful to keep my hand from shaking. "How long what?"

"How long before were you going to wait before telling me you didn't destroy the phone like I asked?"

I reach for my mug and pick it up, but don't feel very confident I can maintain a grip on it. Put it back down.

"It's complicated," I tell her.

"Let me guess," she says. "Roman is tracking it. So he knows where we are?"

"He does."

Her voice is quiet. Almost sad. "And why didn't you feel fit to share this information with me?"

"You know why."

"Your mom." She nods, like this a fair answer, and I wonder maybe if I'm off the hook. But with that look on her face, I'm not taking any chances. "You should have told me. I would have been less angry about this whole thing if you'd been up front with me about it."

"When did you find it?"

"I knew you were lying when you came back," she says.

"That's why you drugged me, right?" I ask. "You didn't want me to see that you searched my coat."

"It was also so you'd get a good night's sleep," she said. "I wasn't lying about that. If I weren't on the clock, I would have taken a little nip myself. Those trains are a pain to sleep on. But, yes."

"So. Where does that leave us?"

Sam waits a moment. Runs a hand along the back of her neck and looks down at the knife. "I'm not sure. Part of me figures I should slit your throat, leave you here, and be done with all of this. I don't know. Is there anything else you haven't told me? Any other secrets you're keeping? Tell me now. Choose what you say carefully. I'll know if you're lying."

"There's nothing else," I tell her.

After a moment, she nods. "I guess I can understand the impulse. I mean, it's your mother. Personally, if it were my mom, I'd leave her to whoever this Roman joker is, but you seem to actually *like* your mom."

"I do."

"That must be nice."

"It is. And it's not."

"Why's that?"

"Because she's leverage, and it's all my fault."

We sit in silence for a few moments. Sipping our waters in the white haze of light coming down through the frosted glass above our heads. It's getting too hot. I pull the fleece over my head and place it on the chair next to me.

"So you're not going to slit my throat?" I ask.

"Not at this very moment, but I'm leaving my options open."

"That's encouraging, I guess."

"What was the end game here?" Sam asks. "Were you going to fuck me over?"

"I wasn't quite sure how to handle it," I tell her. "I'm used to improvising. I figured the most important thing was to see this through. But now we're at a place where this information really needs to get out. And I get the sense that Roman is trying to hide it. That's not acceptable."

"So?"

"So I'm all in. I'm going to help you see this through the best that I can."

"Why?"

"Because it's the right thing to do."

"You might get killed."

"You can get killed doing a lot of things. You can get killed crossing the street."

"You are more likely to get killed doing something like this."

"I'd rather do something than nothing."

She nods, seemingly satisfied.

"So we get back to Prague," she says. "We

get the password. The question is how we handle Roman. We could tell him to meet you someplace, and when he shows up, I'll open his dumb throat."

"You'd do that for me?"

"You lied to me, which pisses me off, but you're putting yourself out there and trying to help, which I can respect. So, sure. Wouldn't be the first."

"Problem," I tell her. "He travels with two men, and they have guns. That's a little different than beating on a roomful of goofy kids playing at being terrorists."

"You mean those two dummies who ambushed us when we had Evzen?"

"That's them."

She sucks on her cheek, thinking. "That's tough. They're not rocket scientists but they're also not complete idiots. We're going to need to make sure that whatever meeting point we set up is very favorable to us and very unfavorable to them. We have some time to think about it."

"Good. Which leaves us with the problem of Chernya Dyra."

"That's the real issue. Because I'm sure she still wants to kill you."

"Please don't say it like that."

Sam takes a deep breath, eases down into the chair to get comfortable. "Look, if she's coming after you, that puts us at an advantage. We know she's coming after you. She doesn't have the element of surprise. With any luck, I'll clear her off the field, too. That one's going to be a lot harder. But it's going to be worth it."

When she says this, she smiles. A soft smile that makes it look like she's imagining something happy and wistful.

It's weird at first, but then I get why.

The realization feels like something cold and sharp twisting under my ribs.

"That's it, isn't it?" I ask. "Why you kept me around."

"What?"

"You want to bag her and you're using me as bait."

"I don't know what you're talking about."

She says it like she knows exactly what I mean.

"Ginger Rogers," I say. "You take down big game, you build yourself a rep."

She breathes in and out a few times and says, "The thought had crossed my mind."

"Well, fucking thanks for that."

"This scenario ends with me saving your ass," she says. "Just because it benefits me, too, doesn't make it a bad plan."

"It would have been nice to know."

"It would have been nice to know about the phone," she says.

"Touché."

She stands, throws back the last of her tea, and

sets the mug down, clicking it hard on the table. She takes the knife and sticks it back in her jeans. "I'm going to take a nap. You going to be okay, sweet pea?"

"Yeah. Fine. Just . . . I like how we're talking to each other like adults here. We should try to keep that going."

"Oh, shut up, you girl," she says before turning to the bedroom and closing the door behind her.

I try to read my book but after a few pages don't feel like it, so I click on the television. *Three Days of the Condor* is on, which feels oddly prescient. The American dialogue is muted low and someone who is half asleep and has never felt a real emotion is very quietly reading the dubbed lines in Polish. Sometimes it's like he actually dozes off, and the actors go on for a minute and then there's a frantic rush to catch up.

I don't understand Polish but I find this mesmerizing.

So much that I nearly miss the scratching sound coming from the front door.

At first I think it's the movie. A sound so soft it's buried under the dialogue.

But given the orientation of the television, I'm practically sitting next to the door, and when I look over, I can see the doorknob give a slight jiggle, like someone is testing to make sure the lock is engaged.

No one should know we're here.

Except.

Fuck.

The key fob. Someone was monitoring the Crash Hop systems.

Whoever's doing that might know I checked into this apartment.

And while it could be a simple mistake, a neighbor looking to borrow something, a solicitor, anything—I'm pretty sure that's not what this is.

So, so stupid.

I get out of the chair, keeping quiet, grab the cell phone from under the sink, and step softly to the bedroom. As soon as I pass over the threshold, from the wood floor onto the carpet, Sam bolts up. She's a light sleeper. And she's still dressed, which is a smart move given the circumstances. I put my finger to my lips and, with my free hand, point toward the door. She nods, grabs her bag, and we move into the living room.

There's no movement, no sound from the door. We shrug into our coats and Sam pulls on her backpack, cinching the straps, and pulls out a pen. Which is an odd choice, but better than empty handed, I guess.

She looks around until she realizes there's a framed print hanging on the wall across from the door. It's reflective enough that we can see our own outlines, ghosts against a tasteful field of wildflowers. She pushes me back against the wall of the living room, so whoever is coming through the door won't see us, but we'll be able to seem them. She leans close to my ear and whispers so quiet I can barely make it out. Sounds like: "Close your eyes."

The door clicks and whines open.

We look at the print and it's hard to make out details but there's a figure moving toward us. Sam looks up at me, nods, and I do what she says. The last thing I see is Sam bringing the crook of her elbow up to cover her face and wonder if I should do the same, but it's too late.

There's a clicking sound and an incredible flash of blinding light cuts through my eyelids. So bright it burns.

As the white light fades, there's a gunshot and a scream.

I open my eyes and can't see anything but blue and shifting light. I don't know where the gunshot came from, but I'm pretty sure the scream came from Sam.

FIFTEEN

By the time we reach the landing, my vision is returning. I can make out shapes and borders, but it's like I'm looking through the haze of a snowstorm. Someone is leading me by the arm and I hope it's Sam. My foot kisses air and I topple forward into empty space, reach out and catch myself on a railing.

The stairs come into focus. Sam is next to me. Her face is twisted up in pain. She growls at me through gritted teeth. "C'mon."

We take the stairs so fast it's like our feet are barely touching them. We burst outside and it's overcast. Sam doesn't wait for me. She takes off running and I labor to keep up.

"The phone," she yells over her shoulder. "Get rid of the phone."

"I don't think it's the phone. Crash Hop . . ."

Sam interrupts, her voice labored. "I don't care. Do it."

I take the phone out of my pocket as we turn the corner and ring up the number Roman put in. He answers immediately.

"How are you, my little golem?" he asks.

"Remember the assassin I mentioned? She's on our ass. I need to ditch this phone. Meet me tomorrow night at eight in the apartment where we first met."

"Are you . . ."

"No time for a counter offer. Bring takeout. We might be hungry. Also, fuck you."

I hang up and toss the phone against the wall, plastic clattering to the ground behind us. After a few blocks, properly turned around now, we duck into a café. It's crowded enough that no one pays us any attention. We find a set of bathrooms in the back and one of them is unoccupied. We step inside and lock the door behind us.

As far as bathrooms go, it's fairly clean. Toilet and sink and urinal. White and blue and oddly futuristic. Not the worst place for some emergency triage.

Because there's blood on my hand and it's not my blood.

A steady drip of red is falling from Sam's sleeve, striking the floor in little pats. Her arm is hanging from her side like a piece of meat.

She turns the sink on hot and tries to pull off her jacket but has a tough time, so I step behind and help. I hang it on a hook on the wall and she turns to reveals a tear in the shoulder of her gray sweater. There's red underneath. She pulls the sweater over her head so she's down to her beige bra. It's uniform, lacking of any kind of adornment. It's the bra I would have expected her to wear.

There's an oval cut into her shoulder. Probably the bullet that was meant for one of our heads, diverted by the flash bang so that it grazed a deep path through the surface of her skin. She kneels down and roots around in her bag, comes out with a little bottle of brown fluid and what looks like a toy handgun. She hands me the gun and turns to look at the wound, pulls a wad of paper towels from the dispenser, douses it in the brown liquid, and places it on her arm, wincing a little as she does it.

"Looks like five staples to get it closed," she says. "Maybe six."

"This is a stapler?" I ask, turning the gun over in my hand.

"I don't have any anesthetic," she says. "Do it quick. This is not going to be fun."

She reaches her hand over and presses the sides of the wound closed, so instead of an open red eye it looks like a pair of dark red lips pressed together. She breathes out hard when she does this and closes her eyes. I'm standing slightly behind her and I can see the full of her back, save the part obscured by the bra strap.

She has a lot of scars.

Some fresh, pink and mottled, raised from the skin. Others faded, thin and white. A few that are round. Others long and narrow. Her back is a roadmap of pain and it says more to me than anything else she's said.

She opens one eye and peeks at me. "C'mon, Ashley. Do it."

I press the gun to the middle of the wound and wince, phantom pain leaping from her to me as the gun makes a hard click. The staple bites into her skin and she exhales hard, grits her teeth, but doesn't move.

"Quick now," she says, desperate. "Quick."

I shoot staples into the rest of the wound, working my way in one direction, and then the other. Fresh rivulets of blood trail down her arm. Five staples. It looks properly closed. When I'm finished, she looks at it and nods and presses the wad of paper towels to it again.

"In my pack," she says. "Bandages and gauze."

They're easy enough to find. I pull out a large bandage and press it over the wound and wrap it in tape.

"Tight, tight," she says.

I wrap it hard but not too hard, spinning the tape on so it'll keep pressure on the wound. When I'm done, she walks to the toilet and drops her pants and sits, peeing loudly. I turn to the wall to give her some privacy. When she's done, she gets up, flushes, and picks her sweater off the hook.

"At least it's clean in here," she says.

"You need to stop lying to me, you know," I tell her.

She pulls her sweater back on, maneuvering carefully around the bandage. "What does that mean?"

"You said you don't have any cool spy shit," I

tell her. "What do you call a flash bang disguised as a pen?"

"It's not that cool," she says.

"It's kinda cool."

"Shut up. We have a train to catch. If we can, I'd like to pick up a new jacket. Maybe a new shirt. Mine has a hole in it."

"Sure."

She nods, closes her eyes.

For a moment she looks like a balloon about to deflate, and then she falls against me. Her small body pressed close to mine, and I don't know what to do. This feels like the universal sign of wanting a hug, and I am never really opposed to obliging that kind of thing, but the thought of putting my arms around her makes me think of hugging a bear trap.

Eventually I settle on putting my hand on her back, under her neck and where her shoulders meet. Think again about the scars underneath her clothes. Feel the weight of them against her.

That's the thing about scars. People like to say time heals all wounds. Wounds do heal, but the scars they leave behind are tight and they tug when you move. You never forget about them. Not entirely.

She breathes, long and deep, and exhales. The warmth of it spreads across my chest. I can feel the loneliness radiating off of her. I hold her tighter because I think that's what she wants.

As I press her against me, she surrenders, nearly going limp.

As much as I want to provide her the comfort she seems to need, my own level of comfort is dwindling.

Is this the future I'm running toward?

A life where you do the work and then you die alone?

And in this moment, I know: that is not the life I want.

"You okay?" I ask.

She pulls back. Looks up at me like she thinks I'm a moron.

"I'm always okay," she says, smiling like she didn't just get shot.

We wait across the street from the train station, under a bus shelter. Three buses pull up and leave while we stand there. The wind is picking up and my ears are cold enough to sting. Neither of us has spoken and Sam doesn't need to explain what we're doing.

Waiting for Chernya Dyra.

I look over at her every now and again, and sometimes catch a small wince or grimace on her face, but otherwise, the wall is back up. She's in a coat that looks remarkably similar to mine. The best option we could find inside the mall.

The emergency surgery makes me think of last year, Bombay sewing my forearm at his kitchen table after some asshole cut it open. He used purple thread because he thought it would be funny. Looking back now it was a stupid thing to do—I didn't even use something proper to sterilize it, like Sam did. I used vodka. The scar is a little ugly but you don't even really notice it unless you're looking close.

My scars having nothing on her scars.

When we're fifteen minutes out from departure, Sam walks away from the bus shelter and I follow, pulling my new baseball cap down over my eyes. We move quickly through the station. There are a lot of people, and every time someone makes even brief eye contact with me, I wonder if they're a plant, for Roman or Chernya Dyra or Ansar al-Islam.

Moscow rule. *Everyone is potentially under opposition control.*

Or, every person is this place is potentially someone who wants to kill us.

That's probably not the truth, but it's definitely what it feels like.

We board the train and it's the same kind of layout—long hallway, wood paneling, cheap dingy curtains. It might even be the same train. The conductor is a hard-faced man, probably my age. He nods curtly to us as we load into our room. Sam disappears to handle the passport situation, and reappears a few moments later.

"Do you think we're safe?" I ask.

"If we're not dead within an hour of the train pulling out of the station, then probably," she says. "She's got to be working alone. She probably has great access to information but there's no way she'd crack the number of layers between me and how I ordered the tickets."

"Good, then," I tell her. "So what's the plan?"

"The plan is I need some rest," she says, pulling the sweater over her head. "My body needs to heal. I need to sleep. I'm taking a little dose of what I knocked you out with. Not as much. Enough to get me under. You stay up in case someone tries to murder us."

"You trust me to do that?"

"Sure. Why not?"

"And if the Dyra shows up?"

"Then we're dead either way," she says. "And I'd rather be asleep for that."

Sam turns to the mirror and removes the bandage, which is heavy with diffusing shades of brown and red. After a few moments of inspecting it, she takes out a bottle of water and the brown liquid and proceeds to clean it and place a new bandage.

"You know, the Dyra doesn't seem so tough," I tell her. "We got away twice, didn't we?"

"Yeah, the odds of that happening even once are pretty remarkable," she says. "The thing is both of those situations—the bridge and the apartment—were locations she couldn't control.

Don't be surprised if in the next day or two you're walking into a room and you have a bad feeling and you don't even know why you're there. That's the moment the lights go out."

"Unless you kill her first?"

She gets the clean bandage in place and pulls a black t-shirt out of her pack. "We'll see how that goes."

The train whines and moves slowly out of the station, picking up speed.

"You said we should know within the hour?" I ask.

Sam pops a pill into her mouth and washes it down. "The countdown begins. Night night, sweat pea. Don't wake me unless it's an emergency."

"Can I have the knife at least?"

She takes it out of her pocket and hands it to me, then climbs onto the top bunk, pulls the blanket over herself, and turns away from me. The knife is heavy in my hand. I flick it out, look down at the blade. I snap it closed and slip it into the coin pocket of my jeans, but it doesn't make me feel any better. Locking the door to the compartment doesn't make me feel much better, either. It feels like a formality.

Tonight I learned something about myself. I really like Agatha Christie. *Murder on the Orient Express* is a great book.

Though it's bumming me out a little because

this train is far less luxurious than the Orient Express. And I'm not being called on to consult on a murder investigation where everyone sits around and the biggest threat is whether the tea is too hot. That'd be a nice change.

I don't have a phone and there's no clock in here but I'm sure it's been a few hours since we left, which is encouraging, because we are not dead. Still, I'm afraid to step into the hallway to pee. I'll have to risk it soon. At this point I feel okay about the Dyra and less okay about the conductor. I've got my New York driver's license but no passport, and no Sam to run interference if something happens.

I'm thirsty though. I get up and take a sip from the bottle of water sitting on the counter. Look up at Sam, who's still facing away from me. Wonder if at this point I can risk sleeping a little bit, but don't really want to.

If I can't sleep, I can at least be comfortable. It's boiling in here, and even with the window cracked it's not helping much. I take off my socks and pull off my shirt, get ready to climb in the bunk and get under the thin blanket and find out who among the aristocrats on the Orient Express murdered Samuel Ratchett.

I'm in a nice groove when the train slows and stops.

After a few moments, there's a commotion outside the door.

I get off the bunk and look at Sam, who hasn't moved. I slide open the door a little and hear a man talking hurriedly in Czech or Polish at the other end of the hall. I can't make out what it is. But the person repeats himself it in English.

"Border control. Passport please."

Of course.

I move over to Sam and nudge her shoulder. She doesn't move. I nudge her a little harder. Nothing. I put my fingers to her neck to make sure she still has a pulse, and she does, which is great, but doesn't exactly help me. I tap her cheek lightly, leaning back as I do, expecting her hand to shoot out and hit me in the throat, but it doesn't. She's dead to the world.

The inspector is starting on the other end of the car and working his way down. I don't know how many doors are between us. I have a few minutes at best.

If they find me without a passport, I could be detained. Stuck in a cell or a holding room somewhere. Roman is waiting for me. What if I don't show up? Will he assume I skipped town? Decide to move against my mom in retaliation?

Only a few minutes to solve this.

Think.

We can't hide. The conductor knows there's someone in this room. Can't get us out of the train because the window is too small and where the hell would we even go? I could find Sam's ID but that doesn't really help.

I move to the crack in the door and peek out. They're glancing at papers. Not examining them too closely.

Look back at Sam, and she's prone in the bunk.

It's a random security check. I need them to look in and not want to come in here. To not think about checking us too closely. I need to distract them with something.

How do I do that?

Think think think.

Oh shit.

I've got an idea.

It's not a nice idea, but it's an idea.

Quick as I can, I strip down to my boxers, tossing my jeans into the corner, making sure to leave the door closed but unlatched. I put the ladder against the bunk, climb up until I'm next to Sam, turning her so she's lying on her back. I drop her arm off to the side so she's more visible from the doorway, climb on top of her, and pull the sheet over us.

She makes a little face but doesn't wake up. I hold myself mostly in a push-up position, my back pressed up against the ceiling. It hurts like hell to hold in the narrow space. I look down at Sam and really hope she doesn't wake up at this moment. I'm thankful the knife is down in my jeans.

The door slides open and I thrust forward like

we're having sex. In the doorway is a short, stocky man in a uniform and a funny hat. I put on my best attempt at a Czech accent, and yell, "*Jdi do prdele, kokot!*"

Which roughly translates to: "Fuck off, dick-head!"

There are only six words you need to learn to cut it in another country.

But curse words help, too.

The man in the uniform pauses. His mouth drops open.

And then he smiles and nods, his face a swirl of embarrassment and approval. He says something and I don't know what it means but he winks at me and throws a thumbs-up before he slides the door closed.

The latch clicks and I exhale.

Then I look down and Sam is staring up at me, her face twisted in fury.

She brings her fist into the side of my head, making contact with my ear. The blow rattles through my skull and I tumble off the bed, hitting the far wall before landing hard on the floor, my arms up, trying to protect my head.

Sam jumps off the bunk, blocking the door. Her eyes are heavy with sleep and rage. She searches her pants for her knife and remembers that I have it. I make it as far as my knees when she grabs me by the throat and slams me into the wall. Immediately my oxygen supply is cut off.

"As soon as this train is moving I am going to start carving you up and dropping parts out the window until we get to Prague and there's nothing left," she says. "I bet you know which part I'm going to start with."

I try to speak but can't so I shake my head and wave my hands, try to get her attention.

"What?" she asks. "You got something to say before I get started?"

I nod against the force of her hand. She drops me and I fall to the floor, take greedy breaths of oxygen.

"There was . . . a passport check," I tell her. "I thought if it looked like . . . we were having sex . . . they would be embarrassed and move to the . . . next cabin."

She doesn't move, doesn't acknowledge what I've said, just watches as I climb to my knees again. My jeans are behind me. I reach back, feeling around for the knife. It's not close enough. I would have to turn all the way around.

"I swear," I tell her. "It was the best idea I could come up with. And it worked. They moved on. I'm sorry. But I tried to wake you up. You were out."

She takes a deep breath in and out. I wonder if she's going to start choking me again. She looks very angry.

After a few beats she says, "That was actually kind of clever."

"Kind of clever? I'd say it was very clever."

"Yeah, it worked because you rubbed your gross body all over mine," she says.

"And what would you have done?"

"Handled it better than that."

"Oh, why the fuck didn't I think of that?"

"Will you get dressed? It's weird talking to you like this when you're on your knees and half naked. This feels like the start of a weird fetish video."

I get up and put my jeans back on. Sam reaches around me to take the bottle of water off the counter. She takes a deep drink and climbs onto the bunk.

"We must have passed back into the Czech Republic," she says. "Only a few hours now. I'm going to try to sleep a little more. You good?"

"Now that you're not going to kill me, yes, I'm good. I'm almost done with my book. I'm about to find out who killed Mr. Ratchett."

"It was everyone," Sam says. "All the people who hated him teamed up and took turns stabbing him so the crime couldn't be blamed on any one person. They all get away with it in the end because Mr. Ratchett is an asshole."

"C'mon," I tell her. "Did you have to spoil it for me?"

"The book was published eighty years ago," she says. "It's not a spoiler anymore."

"Jerk."

"Shut up."

I go back to reading anyway. Not like I've got anything else to do. After a few moments, I notice that my heart is still racing so I close the book and put it in a mesh basket next to me and stare at the top of the bunk for a little while.

Sam pushes me to wake me up.

"We're almost there," she says.

I climb out of the bunk and get myself put together. By the time I've got my boots on the train is slowing to a stop. We move quickly off the train and make our way through the station.

"So what's the plan?" I ask.

"Let's go back to Kaz's," she says, checking a phone. A new phone, apparently, since she smashed the other one. "Shower, clean up. I'll make contact with Jeremiah and find out where the password is stashed. We have to get that first. Then we go see Roman. Once we have your passport back, we get you out of the country quick as we can. It's a short train ride to Budapest. You can get a flight home from there."

"And the Dyra?"

"We'll see. With any luck she'll just be after me at this point."

"Yeah, about that. Why not kill her when you had the chance?"

"I could barely see. Plus she had a gun. Smart move was to get out. Moscow rule. *Pick the time and place for action.*"

"Okay. And once I'm gone, you'll handle the release of the information about the bank?"

She hesitates. So briefly I wonder if it's even a hesitation. Maybe it's my mind playing tricks. But the way she says "yes" gives me a moment of pause. I file that one away, to the "that's interesting but maybe nothing" file in my head.

"So what exactly is the plan with Roman?" I ask. "Are you going to kill him? Do I have to do it?"

"Well . . ." Sam starts as we exit the train station into the bracing winter air, and standing there in the bright morning sun is Roman, flanked by Pug and Vilém.

"Huh," I say. "Speak of the devil, and he appears."

Roman is smiling that Day-Glo smile of his that I hate so much.

"You know nothing about anything," Sam whispers to me.

"My little golem," Roman says. "I thought you could do with a welcome party. Better this than have to worry about coordinating things later." He turns to Sam. "And this must be your little friend."

"Roman, Sam," I tell them. "Sam, Roman. Something tells me you two are going to get along great."

SIXTEEN

There are two rows of seats in the white SUV. The windows are tinted so there's no way to see what's happening if you're looking in from the outside. Not comforting. Roman makes us sit in the middle, and then climbs into the row behind us. Pug and Vilém are up front. Pug is driving.

No one is talking, which makes for a pretty somber mood.

The buildings yawn and spread out. The architecture becomes blander. Communist-style. Big, blocky concrete. The crowds thin until there's only the occasional person, walking a dog or riding a bike or carrying groceries. The silence is awkward and I hate awkward silence.

"So I guess the only person I don't know here is the driver," I say. "What's your name?"

"Don't talk," says Roman.

"C'mon. I already know Vilém's name."

"Vilém . . ." Roman says, his voice heavy with reproach.

Vilém turns. "I did not see the harm."

"František," says the driver in a heavy Czech accent.

"I'm going to call you Fran," I tell him.

"Most people do," he says.

"You know my pain," I tell him.

He doesn't get the joke. No one does. Tough crowd.

"Now we're all friends," I say. "Doesn't that feel so much better?"

"Be quiet," Roman says.

"Fine."

I look over at Sam. She's staring forward. I want to catch her eye, try to get some kind of reassurance that she has a plan. But she doesn't budge.

Roman's hand appears from the back, holding a bundle of black cloth.

"Please put these on," he says.

Sam takes the bundle and splits it into two hoods. She hands one to me. I pull it over my head and I'm left with a tiny bit of light trickling between the strands of the fabric, and the musty smell of someone else's breath.

"I hope you clean these things between uses," I say.

"I am very close to shooting you," Roman says.

"I doubt that. I mean, then you'd have to clean up the car. This is a pretty nice car. Granted, you'll get your stooges to do it for you. You don't seem like the type who enjoys getting blood on his hands. But still . . ."

He smacks me on the head with the flat of his hand. My head snaps forward. It's more of a warning, but still, I really need to stop getting hit in the head.

"I said be quiet," he says.

The last few times I was forced into a car and taken somewhere against my will, it was in a trunk. This is a nice change of pace. After a little while, though, I have to wonder if we're even still in Prague. The city is made up of districts, and I've only ever been in the first and second. That's the city center, and where most of the Crash Hop apartments are. I don't know how long it would take to drive out of the city.

I'm about to ask another question—something, anything—when the car stops and the engine turns off. Roman says, "You can take the hoods off now."

We're in front of a long row of warehouse type buildings, or an office park. I can't really tell. Everything is gray and utilitarian, with harsh corners and no real sense of style. Fran and Vilém open the doors for us. We get out and follow the two of them inside, Roman behind us.

The building is falling apart. I don't know what it once was. There are long, dark hallways shooting off from the main lobby. There's garbage on the floor and an occasional colorful burst of graffiti. The whole scene looks vaguely apocalyptic.

"Upstairs," Roman says.

We climb the stairs, going up five flights until we're at a hallway washed in harsh yellow by construction lights hanging from pipes along the ceiling. We march past gutted offices with glass doors. There's a pulsing sound from the end of the hall. Bass-heavy music.

We walk into a cramped room with a skylight. It's full of tables holding computers and cups of coffee and containers of takeout and a variety of disassembled electronics. There are six men in the room, talking among themselves or typing at computers. They barely register us. They're listening to rap with the volume turned way up. Nas, I think. The source of the music is a big wireless Bluetooth speaker.

"Turn that off," Roman says, yelling to be heard over the music.

One of the men picks up his phone and taps it. The music stops.

Roman leads me into a bathroom with all the fixtures ripped out. Green tile and holes in the wall and floor. He nods toward a pipe running from the floor to the ceiling. I put my hands around it and he ties my wrists together with a heavy-duty zip tie. He cinches it tight and pulls Sam out of the room.

"Hey, where are you taking her?" I ask.

In response, he closes the door. It's dark, save the sliver of light coming from underneath. After a few moments, my eyes adjust and I can make out the boundaries of the room. That's about it.

I pull against the pipe a little to test it. It's solid. I twist and turn but the zip tie stays taut and cuts into my wrists. I lean back with all my weight, put my foot on the wall to brace myself, and yank back hard. Nothing. After a few minutes I give up and sit on the floor.

And I wait.

I guess we're pretty much fucked now. The only silver lining to this is that Roman will probably leave my mom alone. There'll be no sense in killing me and then going after her.

I hope eventually someone finds me and they can at least identify my body. Give her that peace of mind. Maybe even ship me home.

Give her something to bury.

I don't believe in an afterlife. Maybe reincarnation if I'm feeling romantic. Energy can't be created or destroyed, just moved around. The energy that makes up me has to go somewhere. But even not believing in the afterlife, it makes me wonder which way the scales have tipped. If there actually were a heaven or a hell, which one I'd be going to. My guess would be on the latter, but I've always been a bit of a pessimist.

I don't know what else there is to do, except to apologize.

Sorry, Dad.

Sorry, Chell.

The two people I loved most in this world, and the two people I feel like I've let down.

The two of you are here with me now,

somewhere on the edge of the room where I can't see you. But I know you're here. The two of you have hung very heavy over my life, and the things I did, I did them because I thought I was living up to the standards you set for me.

In a lot of ways I failed to meet them, and for that I am sorry.

But I love you both, and I'm glad you're with me.

I turn myself the best I can until I'm comfortable, pressed up against the wall, and place my head against the cool tile. Try to rest.

The door opens and the room fills with light. I blink as my eyes adjust. Look up and Roman is standing there. It looks like he's wearing gloves. When the gloves start dripping on the floor, I realize they're not gloves.

I guess he is the type to get his hands dirty.

In one hand, he's holding a small towel. Once he's sure I've seen his hands, he proceeds to wipe them off with the towel, which he tosses against the wall close to me. It makes a wet smacking sound, leaving a big red splotch and a streak as it slides to the floor.

"She's a tough one," he says.

"Is she alive?"

"Do you care?"

"Yes."

"She broke quickly," he says. "And when she

did, she admitted that she was going to sell you out the first moment she got. She called you a couple of choice phrases, none of which I feel inclined to repeat. But take it from me, there's no love lost."

He steps out of the room and comes back with a metal folding chair, brings it to within a few feet of me, and unfolds it. He sits and puts his hands in his lap. He is calm and poised.

That scares the shit out of me.

"Is she alive?" I ask again.

"For now. She tells me that you played a pretty big role in all of this."

I think about Sam's last words to me. That I know nothing. And the idea of her breaking, I don't believe it. He's trying to bait me. For now I'm going to stick to what I assume was Sam's plan in the first place: play dumb.

"She wouldn't tell me shit," I say.

"What happened in Kraków?" he asks.

"She had to meet someone. I don't know who. She wouldn't let me come. She got back to the apartment and said we had to come here. Then Chernya Dyra attacked. We barely got away. I imagine you saw that Sam took a bullet."

"I did, yes," he says. "She's lucky that's all that happened."

"You lied to me before," I tell him. "You know exactly who the Dyra is."

Roman exhales, sits back in the chair, looks

263

around the room. "I didn't want to scare you away. If I told you the truth about her, then maybe you would have run."

"What's the truth?"

"She is exactly who Sam says she is. A ghost you have every reason to be afraid of. I heard that back during Gorbachev's reign, there was a Russian dissident making trouble. The Dyra was instructed to eliminate him. I guess she took what he was doing personally. He had two small children and a wife. She killed them while he watched. Then locked him in a room with enough water so that he'd only starve to death, which takes far longer than dying of thirst. I am no stranger to cruelty, but that seemed a bit much."

"Says the guy who threatened my mother."

He raises an eyebrow. "You have to use what works."

"You know what? You all play like you're tough but you're a bunch of fucking cowards. The only way to get to me was through my mother. The only way to hurt this guy was kill his children. All of you. Can't stand and fight your own battles."

"Again, you have to use what works," Roman says, not at all bothered. He reaches into his pocket and comes out with the jump drive that Jeremiah gave Sam. "She must have told you something about this."

"Nope."

"Do you know what's on it?"

"No idea. It'd be nice to know what I'm about to get killed over."

Roman nods, sits back in the chair, thinking.

"Look, I know this didn't work out as planned and you're probably not too thrilled with me right now, but after you kill me, can you report it to the cops?" I ask, my throat getting thick. "Anonymously. Leave my body somewhere. My mom . . . I'd like her to have my body back."

Roman smiles. "I'm not going to kill you."

I'm flooded with a feeling of relief, but try not to get too excited. "Really? You don't seem like the 'loose end' type."

"Here's the thing," Roman says, resting his arms on his knees. "Killing you, not killing you, they both carry complications. I prefer to not kill people, when I can manage it, because ultimately, it raises too many questions. I get the sense you're a good little soldier. That if I promise to destroy everyone you have ever loved, you will believe me. Do you believe that?"

"I believe that," I tell him. Now that there's not a noose around my neck anymore I can't help but adding: "Because you're a coward."

"This whole thing went off the rails," he says, ignoring the jab. "But I'm feeling generous. And anyway, you could tell this whole crazy story and you'll be lucky if anyone believes you. You'll never find me or her or anyone else involved in this thing. You'll sound like a lunatic. It's all pretty far-fetched, if you think about it."

"Does this mean I'm done? Can I go?"

He smiles again. "Not yet, little golem. There's still the matter of the password. There's a message on the phone. I assume it's from her contact. I'm sending you and Vilém out."

"So I get the password, what happens?"

"You go home."

"Just like that?"

"Just like that."

"And what about Sam?"

"I'm keeping her alive for a little while longer," he says. "To see what she knows. To make sure the password is legit. Then I'll kill her."

"Why?"

"Keep asking questions and I'll kill you, too."

"Why not send your goons?"

"Because this is the decision I've made. I don't need to explain myself to you."

"It seems dumb. Honestly."

He sighs. "Because you've been traveling with her for the last couple of days. You might have overheard something useful. Or there might be someone watching and seeing you might give whoever is on the other end a little comfort. Does that make sense?"

"Okay, fine. What's the plan?"

Roman takes out a knife. Sam's knife. He leans down and cuts the zip tie. "Vilém will come and get you. You'll have Samantha's phone. You'll figure it out. You don't have much of a choice."

He gets up and leaves the room without saying anything. I rub the deep red grooves the zip ties left in my wrist. Wonder where Sam is.

If he's even telling the truth. If she's still alive.

The sun is down. The air quiet. Vilém opens the passenger door for me. After I get into the car, he walks around to the other side, climbs in, and starts the car. He hands me a black hood.

"Really?" I ask.

"You must understand that I have a gun," he says. "I am under strict orders to shoot you if you do not listen to what I say."

"Fine." I pull the hood over my head. Once it's all the way down, the car starts moving. After a few moments of silence, Vilém asks, "How are you liking Prague?"

The way he asks it is like a cab driver making conversation.

"All this bullshit aside, it's a wonderful city," I tell him.

"It is a very nice place. I was born here, you know."

"I can tell from the accent."

He laughs a little.

"What?"

"Most Americans can't tell the difference

between accents. I have been to America, once. Everyone thought I was Russian."

"Russian has a heavy L and puts an I sound in front of vowels," I tell him. "Czech is more precise and it substitutes V for W, whereas Russian is the other way around."

"This is very astute," he says. "You know your accents."

"I grew up in New York City. I hear a lot of accents."

Vilém's voice brightens. "New York is a wonderful city. That is where I visited. I have a cousin who lives there. He owns a cab company in Queens. Very crowded. A little like Prague."

"A little," I tell him.

"Do you miss it?"

"Yeah."

"You will go home soon?"

I laugh. I can't help but laugh. This is a very pleasant conversation.

"That'd be nice. But, level with me. Are you going to kill me at the end of this trip? Just give me that much."

"Roman is not going to kill you, and neither am I," he says. "I assume he gave you the standard threat, yes? Friends and family and loved ones will suffer greatly?"

"Along those lines, yes."

"You have to understand he meant every word of it."

"I'm erring on the side of caution."

"That is good of you. Roman is a dangerous man. An even more dangerous enemy. This is all very unpleasant. But in time, you will forget it."

"Is Fran as nice as you?"

"No, Fran is not nice. You should feel lucky that Roman sent us out together."

"I do. Can I take the hood off?"

"I will tell you when you can."

"Fine."

We drive in silence for a little while. I was hoping he would put on the radio. The car comes to a stop, probably at a red light, and I ask, "So how do you even get into a business like this?"

"It is a long story," he says. "There is not enough time to tell it."

"Give me the quick version."

"Bad job market," he says.

I expect more but he doesn't say anything else.

"That really is the quick version," I tell him. "You seem like a nice guy. If Roman is such a bad guy, why do you work for him?"

"First, I am not nice," Vilém says. "It would be a mistake for you to consider this an act of friendship. I am simply doing a job and feel no need to be rude. Second, sometimes you find yourself in a position where you have to make difficult decisions."

"I know that," I tell him. "Sometimes you just don't have a choice."

"Is that true for you?" he asks. "I have overheard things. You have a mother at home who loves you. If you did not love her, Roman would have no sway over you. You have that, and you choose to run from it? Hide all the way here? You did have a choice. You made your decision."

I want to say something back to that, refute him in some way, and find I can't. It's a harsh but fair assessment. I am hiding. I am afraid. This liminal space, this Kafka-esque assortment of bland European apartments I find myself stuck inside, it's a hiding spot. Nothing more than that. Coming out of hiding means committing to something.

Taking a step forward in my life.

"Are you doing this because of someone you love?" I ask.

"I have a family. Wife and boy. I must do the things I do because I can do them, and because it keeps a roof over their heads, food in their bellies. I have tried many times to find decent work. It is very difficult. It is very typical of you Americans, you know, to think you have been backed into a corner when you can do anything you want in the world. I hope you never learn what real desperation feels like."

The light is picking up on the other side of the hood, which makes me think we're getting closer to the city center. Vilém says, "You can look now."

I take it off and find we're back in the heavy part of Prague. We're stopped at a light in a long row of cars somewhere alongside the Vltava.

"Why don't you check the phone?" Vilém asks.

I pick it up, click the button on the side. There's no password, which is a little surprising, given who Sam is and her profession. But then I realize why: a little trace of blood comes off the fingerprint sensor. Roman must have made her unlock it and turn off the security features. I look at the splotch of blood on my finger for a moment, and try to put it out of my head.

There's a text message waiting. It's a set of coordinates, and they're even highlighted blue. Easy enough. I click that and a map opens, showing a bar on the other side of town. I tell the name of it to Vilém and he says, "I know that place."

It doesn't take too long to get there. It looks like a British-style pub. When we pull up in front, Vilém asks, "Now what?"

"I have no idea. We should go inside, I guess?"

We have to park around the corner and then maneuver through crowds of drunken revelers. Inside, it's all wood and brass and stone. Mostly quiet, which is surprising given the amount of people out tonight, but this looks more like a place for locals than a party spot. We sit at the bar.

"Do you want a beer?" Vilém asks. "My treat."

"Sure."

He flags the bartender over and orders two Pilsners. The bartender puts the beers in front of us. We clink our glasses together and I take a long swig of mine. He takes a tiny sip and puts the glass down, scanning the room.

Moscow rule. *Go with the flow.*

"I don't know if this is impolite to ask," I say to Vilém. "But have you ever killed anyone?"

He takes a sip of his beer, puts it back down on the coaster, doesn't act like he even heard the question. I figure that's answer enough, but then he says, "Two men."

"Was it justified? In your mind?"

"You can justify anything."

"I don't like the sound of that."

"I am not going to kill you."

"We'll see."

"What about you, then?" he asks. "Have you ever killed anyone? Roman indicates that you have."

"Once. Yes."

"Was it justified?"

I take a sip of beer. Place is on the coaster. Inspect the glass. Think about it a bit. "You can justify anything," I tell him.

"Sometimes that is the best we can do," he says.

Sam's phone buzzes. I look down and find a text: *No job is finished until the paperwork is done.*

That sounds familiar. I take another sip.

"What is it?" Vilém asks.

It's what Jeremiah said to us before he went to the bathroom at that pub in Kraków.

"I've got to take a piss," I tell Vilém.

"I will come with you," he says.

"You want to hold it for me? I can't get a little privacy?"

"No, you cannot," he says as he places bar coasters over our beers to signal to the bartender that we're coming back.

I push into the men's room and find it empty. Vilém comes in behind me and locks the door. I stand there for a minute and look around the space. One stall, two urinals that are uncomfortably close, and a sink with a mirror above it. I crouch down, look around the floor for vents, then do the same along the ceiling. Test the mirror to see if it budges, but it doesn't.

"What is it?" Vilém asks.

"I think this is where we're supposed to be."

What did Jeremiah say? That the password wouldn't last long where it was.

"Hold on, I changed my mind," I tell Vilém. "Switching to number two."

I step into the stall, close the door, and lock it. Vilém bangs his palm on the door. His voice takes on a heavy, urgent tone. "Open this up, right now."

There's an old-fashioned toilet with a tank on

the back of it. I take off the lid of the tank and flip it over. Scrawled on the back of it in blue pen is: *Eogih23t9h4gLwfjh39kDjg8f.*

I dip my finger into the water inside the tank and rub at the last letter, F, in the string. Vilém is banging harder on the door, yelling for me to open it. I've got a few seconds before he rips it off the hinges. Lucky for me the letter erases pretty easily.

I commit it to memory: F.

F as in 'fuck Roman'.

Vilém reaches up, grips the door, and leans back. It twists down and toward him, the metal groaning. I unlock the door and it swings open, throwing him back into the wall. I hold up the tank with the code facing out.

"Found it," I tell him.

He yanks it out of my hands.

We pull up in front of Kaz's building. Vilém extends his hands to me. I look at it for a second, wondering if I should take it. If he'll grab my hand and pull me forward and stick a knife in my throat, then send me tumbling out of the car.

But it feels impolite to not accept, so I take his hand. It envelops mine and he squeezes. It hurts, the bones in my hand grating against each other.

He lets go. Reaches inside his jacket for what I figure is a gun, but comes out with my passport. Seeing it makes me want to cry with relief. I flip through it to make sure it's intact, and stick it in my pocket.

"The girl's phone," he says.

I take it out of my pocket and hand it over, feel like I'm letting down Sam in the process.

"So we're done?" I ask.

"Not quite," he says. "You are to stay here. You are booked on a flight leaving Prague tomorrow. You will be escorted to the airport and someone will make sure you get on the plane and go. Until then, we will be keeping an eye on you."

"I could really go for a trdelník," I tell him.

"Have someone bring it to you," he says. "You are smart young man. This is almost over. You must continue to be smart. Roman will be posting someone by your mother, too, to make sure you comply. My understanding is they have found her, and this man is already on a plane. He will be there in a few hours. He is not a nice man. Do you understand?"

I climb out of the car. Vilém lingers, like he wants to say something.

"What?" I ask him.

"You understand we are not friends, correct?"

"I don't expect a Christmas card."

"No one here is your friend." He glances up and looks back at me. "No one."

"I get it. Everything sucks. Thanks." I salute him and he drives away. I watch as the car turns the corner and check my passport again. A light snow begins to fall and I know Sam will be dead soon. I stare up into the night sky for a minute and then scream "FUCK" at the top of my lungs, so hard it makes my throat hurt, the word echoing off the buildings around me.

It doesn't make me feel any better.

Because I want to believe that I have no choice but to run.

As I enter Kaz's building, I notice a rotary phone hanging from the wall. I go over and pick it up and it's got a dial tone. I should call my mom. Make sure she's okay before I hunker down.

Should I warn her?

Should I tell her everything?

Maybe. Let her know that her son is an idiot and a coward and got himself into so much trouble halfway around the world that the weight nearly came down on her. Maybe I should tell her to get a motel room somewhere, pay in cash, wait until I'm home.

I dial her cell. Should be early afternoon.

She picks up on the third ring. "Ashley?" she asks, her voice a little tired.

"How'd you know?"

"The caller ID. It's a foreign number. Is everything okay?"

"No, Ma. Not really. Look, I need to tell you something. And it's going to sound a little crazy. But I need you to listen and trust me, okay?"

She sighs. "Can't be any weirder than the day I'm having."

"What happened?"

"I got a fraud alert from my credit card company. So I checked my account. Someone got the number and ordered plane tickets and a hotel room, all in my name. Which makes no sense. Why would they do it in my name?"

"That is weird. Where did the fake you go?"

"Florida."

Florida.

Is Florida nice this time of year?

Oh, fuck.

Sam asked for my mother's name. She asked about Florida. There's a man on a plane to her location, but you wouldn't take a plane to Aunt Ruth's because there aren't any airports around there. You drive or take the train.

Sam did this. Created a paper trail that would send Roman's men in the wrong direction. Bought her some time.

Tried to protect her.

My brain starts spinning so fast I can barely keep up with it.

I'm formulating the plan as I'm speaking.

"Ma, I need you do me a favor," I tell her. "I need you to trust me. Do you trust me?"

" . . . Yes?"

"Do not dispute those charges. Not until tomorrow. Do you understand me?"

"Ashley, why in the world . . ."

"Please trust me on this. I'll talk to you soon. And listen . . . I love you. I love you so much."

"Ashley, you're scaring me."

"Don't worry, Ma. I just . . . I drank too much. I'm feeling a little sentimental. I'll call you in the morning. Everything is going to be fine."

That last bit feels like a lie.

". . . Okay," she says.

I click off.

Sam saved my mom's life.

Or at least she tried.

Which means I'm sure as fuck not going to sit around and wait to go home. I have been running away from fights for a year. No more. There's a job that needs getting done and I'm the only one who can do it.

Roman thinks I'm smart enough to keep my head down and follow orders.

Too bad for him I'm not that smart.

Moscow rule. *Don't harass the opposition.*

You know what?

Fuck the Moscow rules.

SEVENTEEN

Kaz takes a big chug from his bottle of vodka, places it on the coffee table, and gestures toward it. I shake my head. A mouthful of vodka would be nice right now but I need to be sober for this.

He leans close to me. He has to. Gogol Bordello is playing loud over the surround sound stereo system in the living room. It was the first thing I did when I came in; turn on the music nice and loud in case Roman is listening in addition to watching. I don't know how deep his abilities go, and no sense in playing around.

"So I am to understand all of this," Kaz says, his voice barely audible over the music. "You mean to go up against these men, rescue Sam, retrieve the information they have stolen, and evade an assassin in the process."

"Yup."

"Why do you need to do this? You can go home. You are free."

There are a lot of things I can say right now. About guilt. About atoning for past mistakes. About the foreword momentum of a goal. More than anything, it's that Sam tried to protect my mom, and for that, I owe her.

But really, there's only one thing to say.

"Because it's the right thing to do," I tell him.

Kaz nods, like he gets it.

"So we have a couple of problems we need to solve," I tell him. "I need to get out of here without them following me. I need to find out where they're holding Sam. And I need to take down at least eight people quickly."

"The weapons, I have you covered on," he says.

"How so?"

"I told you," he says, smiling. "I know people. We need to get out of here first. Do you think we could escape across the roof?"

"Roman's not stupid. I don't think it'll be that easy."

"Then let me think on it," he says. "How do we find Sam?"

"She left her laptop here. She found me using a tracking device. Maybe she still has it on her. I can check her laptop and see."

"Well, then do that," he says. "I will work on getting you out of here."

I head into the bedroom Sam was using. There's the bed and the dresser and no closet. The bed is neatly made, to military precision. There's a charged laptop and a few articles of folded clothing on the dresser.

When I open the laptop, I see a fingerprint scanner, like the one on Fuller's computer. Well fuck. That's not going to work. I think about it for a few minutes. Look around the room.

How do I get Sam's fingerprint?

The doorknob.

There's a smudge that looks like a thumb on the inside knob, which she touched when she last came out of the room. I head into the living room, where Kaz is typing on his laptop.

"Need some tape," I tell him.

"Drawer under coffee machine," he says.

There's a roll of masking tape in the drawer. I take it back into the room, lay it over the thumbprint, and pull up a faded outline that looks to be more than three-quarters of her thumb. I lay that over the fingerprint scanner and then use the back of my pointer finger to press down, feeling a rush of pride and accomplishment.

Nothing happens.

Well, I guess I'm not as clever as I thought.

I toss the laptop aside, lie back on the bed, hanging my boots off the end so not to dirty the sheets. Think about that long hallway. Roman leading us down toward the end. There was the room with the computers. The bathroom. Nothing in either of them that could have revealed a location.

Everything so bland and vague and old. No details.

I close my eyes, try to re-imagine that hallway. But I was pretty sure I was about to be killed so fear clouds my memory. I can remember my panic and heavy breathing more than I can remember the details.

The sound of our footsteps on the tile. The smell of dust. There had to be something.

But nothing comes up.

It's a hallway, in a building, somewhere in an entire city that I don't know a thing about.

When I come back into the living room, Kaz sees it on my face but he says it anyway: "It did not work."

"No, it didn't."

He sighs, sits back in his chair. "I think it is time to leave this be. You are alive. Your mother is alive. These are all good things. This was a game you never had any business being in. Maybe it is best to move on?"

He's right. I fall into the couch, reach over, and pick up the bottle of vodka. The thing I said I wasn't going to do anymore. No more hard liquor. Another promise broken. Because that's all I can ever seem to do: break promises.

As I'm pressing the bottle to my lips, the sharp smell of it stinging my sinuses, Kaz says, "That will help, my friend."

And I stop.

Think about what Vilém said, about not having friends.

The words pulse in my ear.

Kaz is usually so amped up with nervous energy, but right now his muscles are taut. His eyes are darting around the room. He's trying too hard to be casual about getting me to drop this.

And if that wasn't enough, Vilém really fucked up.

Because he took me here without me asking him to.

I put the bottle down. "Kaz . . . there's something that strikes me as a little strange."

"Yes?"

"You let us stay here. Which was risky, considering my current situation. Especially considering Roman and his men were pretty good at tracking me down. But they never showed up here."

Kaz nods slowly, trying very hard to keep his face even. The music still blasting, up-tempo gypsy punk filling the air around us.

"I'll allow that you and I have a pretty tenuous connection, but at some point, Roman should have showed up here," I tell him.

He's holding his breath. "I trusted Sam. She said it was safe for you two to be here."

"You trusted Sam," I tell him.

"Yes."

"I thought we were friends."

"We are friends."

"You sold me to Roman."

He looks around the room. When he speaks, his voice is slightly chilly. "I do not know what you mean."

"You know exactly what I mean. Do you scope out targets for him? Expats who might have some skeletons in their closet that can be exploited? Is that why we became friends?"

"I don't think . . ."

"Kaz, we fucking sang Johnny Cash together."

He picks up the vodka bottle and drinks too much of it. Places the bottle back down and looks up at me, his eyes suddenly sad. "I did not mean for any of this to happen."

I want to leap over the table. Grab him around the throat. Scream in his face. Hit him, hard. "You set this whole thing in motion. What did you get?"

"Money."

"Was it worth it?"

"No, it was not. I did not even think anyone got hurt. It has never been like this."

"Do you know where Roman took us? The place he took Sam and me to? Where he's keeping her?"

"I had to drop something off to him once. A list of names. I met him right outside the city. Old building, being torn down."

"Good. Now we know where she is."

"I do not think this is . . ."

"You better start thinking about how you're going to get me out of here and over to there. You fucked me and now you're going to make it right."

"Roman is not a man to be crossed."

"At the end of tonight, either he's going to be dead, or I will be. Either way, you'll be fine."

"My friend . . ."

I stand up. Tower over him. He leans back a bit in the seat. "Don't call me your friend. We're not friends."

He looks at me like a child being scolded.

More importantly, he looks regretful enough to do what I say.

A cup of coffee and twenty minutes of pacing and I've got no idea how to get out of this building. The basement was a dead-end. I checked. No egress. There's only one entrance, at the front of the building. I could play the roof trick but that's too obvious.

Kaz has been pacing and thinking too, but carefully avoiding my path, like if he gets too close to me, I might strike him.

Which I've considered.

Throughout this whole mess, I've had Kaz to fall back on, and that was a real source of comfort. And now I don't even have that. Now I'm completely alone, save Stanislav. But by now I'm sure he knows something went down at the apartment in Kraków. I'm probably on his shit list, too.

Whatever. I'm not here to make friends.

"Ash."

I turn and Kaz is standing at the entrance of the kitchen, holding something around his back.

"For what it is worth, I truly am sorry," he

says, his eyes rimmed in red. "I will help you. Whatever you need. I will make this up to you. I think I have an idea."

He brings his hands around to his front, holding a deflated blow-up doll with blonde hair and a round O-shaped mouth rimmed by pink lips.

"Are you kidding me?"

"Trust me," he says. After a moment, he adds, "Please."

It's not too long before the bell rings and there's a gorgeous brunette strolling into the apartment wearing a white fur coat. She looks at Kaz and says, "This will cost a lot extra."

He nods at her and turns to me. "Ash, this is Lenka."

"We have met before," she says to me, smiling.

It takes me a minute, but I realize she's the porn star who warmed me up after I took a swim in the Vltava.

"Right," I tell her. "Thank you for that, by the way."

"You are looking a little better, at least."

She places a small, sleek piece of machinery on the counter, about the size of a car battery. A portable inflator for an air mattress. It has a built-in battery supply so it doesn't have to be plugged in.

The plan itself is pretty simple. Lenka will take the doll and the compressor and get her car. When she pulls up out front, I get in the passenger seat. Once we're sure we're being followed by whoever is watching the building, we wait for the first hard turn. I bail at the same time as we hit the inflator. The doll pops up and from the vantage point of the car behind us, it's like there are still two people in the car. Lenka will continue to drive in the opposite direction of the warehouse where they're keeping Sam.

Kaz will then get me and we hit the road. This way, even if Roman is pissed at me for not staying put, he won't know I'm headed for him. Kaz insists this is a real spy trick he found on the internet, but I find that claim pretty dubious.

We dress the doll in a spare jacket and hat and hit the compressor. It takes a little less than minute for the doll to inflate.

Lenka leaves, taking the doll and inflator, and promising to be out front in five minutes. I feel a little light-headed, bouncing on my toes, clenching and unclenching my fists.

I've done some boneheaded things in my life. This ranks pretty much near the top.

"I will go meet my driver," Kaz says. "We will be behind you."

He hugs me and claps me on the back, then kisses me on the cheek. Again I think about hitting him but I think he's trying to make up for things, so I'll roll with this until I'm proven otherwise.

I wait two minutes after he's left and head down the stairs after him. Outside the front door there's a small red car waiting with Lenka in the seat. I dive into the passenger side. The interior is heavy with the smell of cigarettes.

Lenka pulls away from the curb and another pair of headlights turn on behind us. A black car swings out from the curb in. In the dark, I can barely make out the driver, but I don't think it's Vilém or Fran. Definitely not Roman. And it's only one guy.

I pick up the doll and inflator off the floor under my feet, trying to keep everything out of view. The machine hums as the doll slowly inflates with air, filling the small space under the dash.

"Can I have a cigarette?" I ask. Feeling guilty for asking because it's been months since I've had one, and I considered myself quit, but if I'm going to die tonight, it may as well be with a little bit of nicotine in my blood.

She proffers a pack and I pull one out. A slim, some brand I've never heard of. She puts the pack away and hands me a lighter.

"Thanks," I tell her.

As I light up, Lenka uses the controls on her side to lower the window. I take a drag, and immediately want to puke.

God, this is unpleasant.

I changed my mind. I don't want to smoke any more of this, but I also don't want to be rude, so

I hold the cigarette up toward the window, where the wisps of blue smoke are ripped out into the night air.

"So who beat you up the other night?" Lenka asks.

"If I tried to explain, it wouldn't make any sense," I tell her.

"And yet here you are, running toward the danger instead of hiding from it. That is very noble. Maybe not the smartest thing, but nobility is not always the smartest thing."

I can't help but smile at that. It makes me think about my dad.

Our paths in life are very different. He was a firefighter. Took the more traditional hero route. Mine has been a little less typical, a little more twisty, and at times it's branched in some pretty bad directions. But the thought that I might be getting closer to the example he set makes me feel pretty good.

"Thank you for saying that," I tell her.

"Welcome," she says, a little confused about why it matters. "How does the turn up here look?"

I toss the cigarette out the window, check on the doll, and it's only half full. Check the inflator and it's slowing down a little. "Need a few more minutes."

By the time Lenka takes the turn, the inflator has switched off. I flick the button on the side and nothing happens. Those practice runs must have drained the battery more than we thought. The doll hasn't taken on nearly enough air to stand on it's own.

"Ah, fuck," I say.

"What?"

"The battery is dead."

I pull the nozzle off and lean down to blow it up manually. The angle is all wrong and I'm heaving lungfulls of air into the doll until I'm dizzy, but it doesn't inflate.

"You know," Lenka says. "Upon thinking this through, we should have had a third person in the back seat hiding out and they could have jumped in front while you jumped out."

"Great," I tell her. "You should have been in charge of this plan."

We drive a little more until we have to stop at a red light on an empty street. The trailing car pulls up right behind us.

"After the light changes, I can gun the engine," she says, excitement creeping into her voice. "We can lose him. I know these streets."

While the idea of a car chase piloted by a porn star through Prague sounds like a fun way to spend an evening, it also sounds like a good way to end up dead.

"I've got a better idea," I tell her. "Pop the trunk."

I open the door, climb out. The car that was

following us is practically touching Lenka's bumper. A little further down the block is an SUV that pulls to the curb. Hopefully Kaz. Lenka's trunk clicks.

The driver of the car behind us gets out. He's a tall, thin guy with his long black hair tied back in a ponytail. I open the trunk all the way and he comes at me. "You were not supposed to leave," he says. "Now I must report to Roman."

As he pulls his cell phone from his pocket, I lean down and grab a chunk of ice and snow and wing it at him. It hits him square in the face. He staggers and I hop over the hood of his car and kick him in the balls. As he doubles over, I drag him toward Lenka's car and push him into the trunk. Pat him down. No weapons. I take his cell phone off him and slam the lid closed. He immediately starts banging against it.

"Are you fucking kidding me?" Lenka asks, now standing beside me.

"It's a solution," I tell her. "Drive around for a little while. Then pop the trunk and gun it after he gets out. It'll save me some time."

"You are crazy."

"Sorry for the trouble. And thanks for the help."

She mutters something in Czech and returns to the driver seat. I check the guy's phone and find a half-composed text to Roman, informing him that I left and he's following me, which he didn't send. Good.

I throw the phone and pull the driver's car to the curb, turn the engine off, toss the keys into the car, lock the doors. Once that's done, the SUV pulls up. Kaz sticks his head out the back window.

"Good job, sticking to the plan," he says.

"Inflator died," I tell him as I climb into the back. There's a mountain of a man in the front seat who doesn't acknowledge me.

"Onward," Kaz says, patting the seat in front of him.

The driver drops us off on the main drag in Wenceslas Square, at the bottom of a slight hill. I don't recognize the area. Moments after we get out of the car, we're swarmed by a large group of African men speaking in different languages, grabbing our jackets, pulling at us, promising to take us to cheap girls.

The red light district.

I've been meaning to check this area out. Purely for curiosity's sake.

"Fuck off," Kaz says with a great deal of force, and most of them move off, albeit pretty slowly. Some of them still seem to be insistent, but Kaz walks with the confidence of a local, which is enough to break free of the scrum.

"What's with the welcoming party?" I ask.

"They work for the clubs," he says. "Convince scared tourists to follow them. They get a cut for every person they bring in."

As we get further up the hill, the clubs pop up. Lots of neon signs and women in heavy coats but not much on underneath, lingering in doorways. They call to us in a mix of languages. A woman leans out of a window and yells, "One hour for only forty euro."

"No, thank you," Kaz yells back. "Not tonight."

"That's not terribly expensive," I tell him.

"You get what you pay for. Forty euro gets you the clap."

"Is prostitution legal here?"

"Yes and no. Technically, organized prostitution, like brothels, are illegal. But enforcement is lax. It drives tourism. The trade is worth something like six billion crown a year. The government knows this. They intervene when they choose. Look the other way most of the time. Are you interested in a pit stop?"

"I've never paid for sex."

"It is two consenting adults agreeing to a contract. I believe it to be far more truthful than the dance most people submit themselves to."

"Well, still. Tonight is not the night for me to explore my moral boundaries on this."

"Maybe next time, my friend."

We stop in front of a black metal door. Compared to all the other clubs with the screaming, buzzing signs, this doesn't look like much at all. Kaz enters and holds the door for me. Inside is a turnstile, like you'd see outside a subway platform. Kaz pays some money to the scary man standing behind it. We step into a bar area, which is long and winding and reaches a few hundred feet toward the rear of the place. Kaz turns to me and says, "I will be back. Do not buy a drink for anyone."

"Why not?"

"Do not. I will explain later."

I slide up to the bar and am immediately beset by a series of half-naked women in tiny, glittering outfits. They seem to be jockeying for position, until a tall black woman with almost impossible measurements plants herself in front of me with a smile wide enough to fall into. She puts her hand in the crook of my elbow and leads me to a stool at the bar, and sits on the stool next to mine.

"What is your name?" she asks, her voice sweet and drippy like syrup.

"Ash."

"Ash?"

"Short for Ashley. I'm not making that up. What's yours?"

"Serenity."

I think she's probably making that up. "And where are you from, Serenity?"

She gives me a little smile. Like this is not the kind of thing people tend to ask her in this place. "Swaziland."

"I have never been to Swaziland. Do you miss it?"

"No, I do not."

She doesn't seem interested in expanding on her answer. The bartender comes over and she asks if I'll buy her a drink and I tell her no. The bartender pushes a laminated menu across the bar like I didn't tell him no, and Serenity points to what she wants.

"I'm not buying you a drink," I tell her.

"But I'm thirsty," she says, batting her long eyelashes at me.

"Sorry," I tell her, and shrug.

"So if you're not interested in a drink, can I tell you what else is on the menu?" she asks, trying to temper her annoyance.

"Sure."

"A handjob or blowjob is fifteen hundred Czech. Sex is twenty five hundred Czech. We can bring in another girl. That's an extra two thousand Czech . . ."

"Wait, wait . . . a handy and a blowie cost the same?"

She squints. "Yes."

"Do you set the prices, or does the club? Like, does each girl get a custom menu? How does that all work?"

She's a little taken aback by this line of questioning, but lucky for her—or me, probably—Kaz appears and says, "He's ready for you."

I nod to Serenity and follow Kaz to the rear of the club.

"So why wasn't I supposed to buy her a drink?" I ask.

"It is a game they play on tourists," he says. "Especially Americans. She will order a very expensive glass of champagne and the bouncer will force you to take the money from the ATM if you can't cover it."

"Got it. Thanks for the save."

We reach a staircase, guarded by a giant Asian man who reminds me a little of OddJob from *Goldfinger*. Same hat and everything, to the point where I wonder if it's an affectation. We climb two flights and find ourselves at a door. Kaz knocks and it opens.

We step into an office straight out of a '70s movie. Lots of shag and bright primary colors, with a decidedly retro feel. Sitting behind a mammoth mahogany desk is a thin black man in a plaid suit. Right off, I can tell he's a player and it's best to tread lightly. It's that earned confidence. Most people look at me—broad shoulders, bad attitude—and they see me as a threat. The way he looks at me is like he's bored.

There are other men here, too. Bodyguards, I presume. They're perched on chairs and couches, watching Kaz and me warily.

"This is him," Kaz says to the man behind the desk.

The man stares at me for a few moments. I want to compliment him on the suit. It's a nice suit. He looks like a zany college professor who would slit your throat over a late assignment. Just when I think I ought to say something, he speaks.

"My name is Fenomenal, with an F," he says in a British accent.

"Well, Fenomenal with an F, what have you got for me?"

His face turns down. "No need to be sarky, is there?"

I look at Kaz. His eyes are wide and fearful, in a way that makes me think I'm fucking up.

"Sorry," I tell him. "Didn't mean any disrespect."

He nods toward us. "Arms up, bruv."

I put my hands in the air. One of the bodyguards pats me down. They don't do the same to Kaz. I guess he's been searched already.

"Shit, I don't have any cash," I tell them.

"We take credit," Fenomenal says. "It'll show up on your statement as Creative Enterprises. Very discreet." He turns to one of the guards. "Go get the card reader."

Nice to see weapons dealers are adapting to new technology.

Fenomenal gets up and beckons us to follow. There's a door at the back of the office. He opens it to reveal a small, dark room. He flicks on a light and we're surrounded by guns hanging from racks on the wall, from little handguns to the kind of stuff I would expect to see a space marine carrying in a video game.

"You weren't kidding when you said you knew people," I tell Kaz.

"You meet some interesting people in my line of work," he says.

Fenomenal gravitates toward the handguns. He takes a small boxy model off the wall and holds it my way. "A personal favorite. Small, so it's easy to conceal. Polymer so it's light. Low-recoil, and it has a rail for a laser sight, which I can hook you up on, too. Doesn't get more tried and true than this."

He hands it to me. I turn it over, feel the weight of it. "To Keep and Bear Arms" is stamped on the barrel, which strikes me as a little obnoxious.

It doesn't feel good in my hand.

People feel a lot of different ways about guns. I understand that for a lot of folks it's cultural. It's about family and history and hunting and protection and survival. But the way I know guns is how they rip families apart. How if someone takes one out, they want to kill you or scare you into doing something.

I've had to think a lot lately about the kind of man I'm going to be. And the path is still pretty long, but there's one thing I know: I don't do guns.

It's important to have principles.

Even if those principles might get you killed.

I hand it back to Fenomenal. "I'd rather not."

"My friend," Kaz says. "I thought you were American."

"I am."

"And you don't like guns?"

"Funny." I turn to Fenomenal. "What do you have in the realm of blunt force trauma?"

He steps toward a series of drawers, opening one of them. There's a long row of knives nestled in felt. I pick one up and put it on the counter. I'm not looking to stab anybody, but I imagine it'll be useful to have.

Next to that sits a pair of what looks like brass knuckles, but they're not made of brass. They're hard plastic, and thicker across the knuckles, with a shiny strip of exposed metal. I run my finger along one of them. "What's this?"

"New item," Fenomenal says, smiling. "A cross between brass knuckles and a stun gun. It holds enough charge for a couple of strikes. Activated by pressing the button on the side."

"Holy shit."

I take it out and put it on the counter, along with the knife.

"Zip ties?" I ask.

Fenomenal turns to a shelf and comes back with a pile.

"I know I'm being greedy, but how about night vision?" I ask. "Be nice to try to cut the power. If I can even figure out how to do that."

Fenomenal goes into a different drawer and comes out with a pair of chunky ski goggles. "State of the art. Lighter and slimmer than any pair on the market. These are not cheap, bruv. I hope you can cover this."

"We'll get to that. Mind if I root around a little bit?"

He holds up his hand, allowing me to proceed. I pull open the odd drawer here and there. The deeper I dig, the weirder it gets.

I come across a drawer with swords set in felt. Two samurai swords and a scimitar. They look fun but I'd probably hurt myself more than anyone else. One drawer has an assortment of spiked rings and machetes, which is way too grisly for me. Below that, I find pens. Lots of pens. Pick one up and it feels stamped out of the hull of a warship. In a close fight you could ball your fist up around this and do some real damage. But it feels a little slight for the job I've got to do.

In another drawer, there's just a crossbow. Not a modern one either. This looks like it was lifted from a medieval battlefield. Not even sure I would know how to work it.

Another drawer has nightsticks and asps, which seem a little more my speed. They're piled in there so I root through, take out an asp. Click the button on the side and it shoots out to full length, but I don't like the weight of it. Feels light. I want something with heft. Fold it up, put it back, keep looking.

Nun-chucks. No way. Again, I'll do more damage to myself.

A leather sap. Nope. This isn't a Prohibition-era raid.

The guy with the card reader comes back in and I fish out my credit card, hand it over, go back to looking. Fenomenal quotes me a price that seems like a lot. Kaz interjects. "Can you do a little better than that? He's a friend."

Fenomenal gives him a long, hard look, but finally nods and quotes a price slightly lower. I nod at him and feel something familiar at the back of the drawer, pull it out.

And I am filled with wonder and light and happiness.

"What is that?" Kaz asks.

"Providence," I tell him, smiling like a goofball. I turn to Fenomenal. "How much for this?"

"It's a novelty. Consider it a fairing." He looks up at me and sees the confusion on my face. "A gift. Take it along with the rest."

I pick it up. Give it a swing.

And I smile.

Now it feels like I have a chance.

EIGHTEEN

The building is a monolith against the night sky. There's a fallow construction site behind it, the machinery covered in snow. Kaz and I duck behind a bulldozer. There's no discernable light coming from any window on the row. No sound but the wind.

Even given Kaz's betrayal, I'm suddenly worried for him.

"You're sure about this?" I ask him.

"My friend, I told you," he says, clutching the chrome six-shooter he pulled out of his car's glove box. "I will make this right."

"You could end up getting killed," I tell him. "You might be surprised to hear this, but I'd really rather that not happen."

"What do you want me to do, leave you here all by yourself? Anyway, it might put me in good with Sam. She is very pretty. The worst thing she can do is say no."

I laugh at that. "I don't think that's the worst thing she can do, but sure, why not."

"After I cut the power, I will come up and help," he says.

"You will not," I tell him. "You'll stay down there and out of sight."

"How come you get to have all the fun?"

302

"This isn't fun. There is a very real chance I might get shot. You don't want any part of that."

"My friend . . ."

"It's going to be hard enough to get past everyone in there. I don't need to have to worry about protecting you, too. Kill the power, stay out of sight, don't move until I get you. Okay?"

"Fine."

"And do me a favor. If something happens, my mom is on Facebook. Find her and get a message to her. Tell her I'm sorry and I love her. Make sure she knows I was trying to do a good thing. I doubt it'll be much comfort."

"You will come through this," Kaz says.

It actually sounds like he believes that. I want to ask him how he knows but figure it's better if I don't. Because he can't. I could very well die in this building. And maybe I should be afraid, but I'm not.

What I feel is clarity.

"One last thing," I ask. "Do you have your phone? And does it have Bluetooth?"

He nods, takes it out of his pocket, hands it to me. I turn off the ringer and stick it in my pocket. I've got the makings of a poorly formulated idea. Something to serve as a distraction.

Kaz hugs me again. "I am sorry, my friend."

I pat him on the back. We hold like that for a few moments and then pull away.

"You still smell like a French hooker," I tell him.

He smiles. "You are jealous."

"Ready?" I ask.

He nods, and we take off at a run through the open space between the construction site and the building, dodging the occasional trench or piece of equipment or pile of cinder blocks on the ground.

There's a small padlock on the door, so I pull out the lock picking kit that Sam got for me. Slide in the tension wrench, go to work, visualizing the clear lock, the way the guts looked, the way the pins lined up, how if I nudged them right and put enough tension on the wrench . . .

The lock pops. I pull it off and push the door open. We both slip inside. There's a staircase leading up and down. Kaz heads down, I head up.

My plan was to have Kaz cut the power and I would crash down through the skylight I noticed in their main room, taking everyone by surprise. Luckily for me, Kaz did insist on coming, and then dissuaded me of this very stupid idea.

We spent a lot of the ride over talking video games.

Specifically, two main styles of action shooters.

There's *Halo*, in which you run into a room full of alien monsters and you fire gigantic weapons, expending thousands of rounds of ammo, and throw a bunch of grenades, and if you die, you die. Then you re-spawn a few minutes later back at the checkpoint. You're free to try as many times as it takes to clear the room.

Then there's *Splinter Cell*, which is about stealth. You sneak around and hide in the shadows and there are some levels you straight out lose if someone detects your presence. You carry a silenced pistol with a finite number of rounds and a couple of gadgets. You get shot once or twice and you're dead.

Splinter Cell strategy is probably the way to go since I don't get any re-spawns.

At the top of the stairs, I check my watch. Ten minutes until Kaz is supposed to cut the power. Hopefully enough time to get into position. I move carefully but my boots crunch on the floor. I am not a great fan of this, but there's not much I can do. Still, I wish I was wearing sneakers. The things you realize only when it's too late.

The night vision goggles come in handy. The hallway is pitch black. It takes me a second to get them comfortably over my head and figure out how to turn them on, but when I do, everything is cast in a sickly green light. The view is crisper than I would have thought.

As I move down the hall, my heart rate increases gradually, until it tops off somewhere around the speed of a jet engine.

Off in the distance I can see the hallway leading into the computer room. I duck into an empty room alongside me. It smells like mildew and dust, light barely trickling in through the windows. I consider dropping my coat but figure

305

it's easier to leave it on. It's a little heavy but the way it spreads out around me when I move might provide me with some cover. Plus, I'd rather keep the stun knuckles in my pocket until I need them.

And then there's the matter of my new special little toy.

That's strapped to the inside of my coat.

I creep down the hallway, stop on the edge of a pool of shadow, a few feet from the door of the stairwell we entered through when Roman brought in Sam and me. At the mouth of the long hallway, I can hear voices and see shapes in the distance. The construction lights hanging from the fixtures are all individually plugged in. I don't think there's a common switch that will kill them all.

Glad I brought Kaz's phone. Time to see if my backup distraction plan will work.

The Bluetooth speaker I noticed earlier shows up in the settings menu. I scroll through Kaz's playlist, figure on playing something loud to disorient them. It's not much, but even if it covers my footsteps, or makes someone turn their head for a moment, it'll be worth it.

I've never been in a fight where I've gotten to pick a playlist.

It raises the question of what I should pick.

I could go old-school. AC/DC or Metallica. Plenty of that. Kaz has a nice punk collection, too. He's got Cock Sparrer on here. "Take 'Em

All" is the kind of song that makes you want to pound a beer and clear a bar full of hooligans. That's my top pick but I give the list one more swipe to be sure I'm not missing anything.

Then I find it.

The perfect song.

So perfect it makes me smile like an idiot.

I pull the song up, pause it, and crank the volume so it'll come on at full blast.

Okay, now, need to map out the route.

There's the hallway, about sixty feet long, with three empty offices on each side. All the doors are ajar. That's helpful. I can duck in and out and it gives me plenty of cover.

There were six men in the room Roman marched us through. Could be less but I doubt there's more because there weren't a lot of seats and it's not a big room. So six, plus Vilém, Fran, and Roman. That makes nine. I would like to not have to go after Vilém because he was nice to me and bought me a beer. But this is a take-no-prisoners type of scenario. I've got to incapacitate as many of these goons as I can with enough time to get Sam.

As for Roman, I should probably kill him.

I wanted to be the kind of person who didn't kill people.

Too bad for Roman, I will kill for my mom.

The lights click off.

Guess Kaz figured it out.

Showtime.

I flip down the goggles. There are some herky-jerky beams of light at the end of the hallway. Flashlights. Frantic voices, too. Someone comes marching down the hall. A guy I don't recognize. I step into the office opposite the staircase and peek out. He's got something in his hand. At first I think it's a gun and the sight of it freezes me. He's walking slowly, using his other hand to guide the way. Must be going downstairs to check the power.

He stops and slaps the thing in his hand against his palm. A little beam of light erupts out of it before it goes dark.

He gets close to me. I slow my breathing, try to keep from giving away my position. Slip my hand into my jacket and grip the stun knuckles.

Once he's within a foot of me I hit the button on the side with my thumb. There's no arc of light, no crackle of energy, just a gentle hum I probably wouldn't notice if I wasn't paying attention. That's almost disappointing.

I make a clicking sound with my mouth. He turns to look in the office. I pop up and hit him in the shoulder. There's no sound and nothing happens to indicate it's turned on, but he goes stiff and tries to scream but his muscles have seized, so it comes out as a groan. I grab him with my other hand and pull him into the office, drop him to the floor. I pull a zip tie out and lash his hands together, and then his feet. Pull off his boot and then a sock, which I cram into his mouth.

The whole thing happens quickly, and doesn't make enough noise to alert anyone. I drag the guy into the corner. He's whimpering but the shock took the fight out of him.

That leaves eight.

Eight against one.

Still sucks, but better.

Someone calls down the hallway in Czech. Calling to the guy I just took out, I think. I peek out again and see another guy coming down the hallway, this one with a working flashlight. I duck into the office before the beam of light hits me.

I press up against the flat of the wall until the guy is close, then pick up a shard of sheetrock from the floor, toss it against the far window and it makes a *clink* noise. He comes in to investigate. A punch to the abdomen and some more zip ties and a sock in the mouth and we're down to seven.

I notice a fire alarm on the wall above me. It was a good idea when Sam did it at the Crash Hop building. I'm not sure I want to alert the authorities, though, in case it's hooked into some kind of broadcast system. I'll save that for later.

I check the hallway again and hear Roman's voice. "Where is everyone?"

"Anton and Konstantin went to check the generator," a voice replies. "Ivan and Jakub are still assigned to McKenna."

"Have either of them reported in?" Roman asks.

"Ivan, yes," the voice replies. "He has seen nothing. Jakub has not reported yet. I will call him again."

"You do that," Roman says. "And you, go see if you can help them with the generator."

Not seven, five. Maybe fewer than five.

It's about to be four.

Footsteps come down the hallway. I pick up another piece of sheetrock, crouch down, toss it against the far wall. The guy turns into the room but swings his flashlight up so that the beam hits me in the face. There's an explosion of white, like turning on a bright bathroom light in the middle of the night.

Fuck, I got cocky. I pull the goggles off my head and blink away the blue lights hovering on the edges of my vision as the man yells and drives his knee into the side of my head.

At the same time, the overhead lights snap on.

Either there's a backup generator, Kaz fucked up, or he's been compromised.

I go down hard and land on my back, but sweep my legs to the side and manage to catch the man with enough force to send him tumbling. He nearly falls on me, and I roll off and over until I'm on top of him, drive my fist into his face a couple of times. No stun knuckles this time. He's not a bruiser and the fight goes out of him quick.

I lash his wrists and hear more footsteps coming down the hall and I guess I've lost the element of surprise. I put on the stun knuckles, than take out Kaz's phone, click on the song.

The hallway fills with Nena's "99 Luftballoons." Time to work.

I turn the corner and Fran is coming at me, a gun held with both hands, pointed at the floor. But he's looking over his shoulder, trying to find the source of the music. I jab him hard in the chest with the stun knuckles and he screams and arches back.

His hands stay gripped to the gun so I stand to the side, out of the firing range, pry it out of his fingers, then fling it into a corner. I slip off the knuckles and zip-tie him.

I charge into the room with the computers and find Vilém standing over a small man with a rat-tail haircut and a bad mustache, typing furiously on a laptop. He sees me, shakes his head like a father disappointed in a son.

"I told you to go," he says.

I slip the stun knuckles into my pocket. It's a little ridiculous, but I feel like I owe Vilém a fair fight.

"Before we do this, did you kill Evzen?" I ask.

He nods. "Yes."

"Okay."

He reaches behind his back for his gun. Well, if that's how he wants to play it. Before he can get the gun all the way up, I pick up a heavy glass ashtray and fling it at his face. He turns to the side so it glances off his back but I'm already coming at him too fast, driving into him and pushing him into the wall.

The gun goes flying. He tries to swing at me but I'm too close to his midsection so he has no leverage. I hop back and throw my fists into his stomach. Once, twice, three times. On the fourth blow he leans forward and I spring up with an uppercut that snaps his head back.

Vilém looks more angry than hurt so I pick up a folding chair and hit him over the head with it. His face goes red and he throws a fist at my face. I duck just in time for it to slam a hole into the sheetrock wall behind me. I back up from him, stumbling and landing on my ass. Sliding backward, trying to put some distance between us.

"I am sorry," he says. "But this is the job."

I'm thinking of something clever to say back when a red dot appears on his chest.

He looks down, sees the dot, and his face turns into an expression of confusion.

The window on the far end of the room shatters as a bullet tears through his chest.

I slide across the floor, behind a desk, out of view of the window. Vilém tumbles to the floor and hits it hard. His body is limp, eyes vacant.

Even though he killed Evzen, even though he

would have killed me on Roman's orders, I feel bad. He had a family.

Before I can dwell on it, the computer guy stands up and his head explodes in a spray of red, sending a hot splash of viscera across my face.

Seems like Chernya Dyra found us.

Which is good.

That means all of this ends one way or another.

I crawl over to the computer where he was working, pull it off the desk and down onto the floor with me. The thumb drive is sticking out of the side. I find the password prompt screen and type in the final letter—F. A folder opens. I expected something dramatic, like a cascade of flashing documents. I click some buttons and pull the drive out, and crawl to the other side of the room, looking back to make sure I'm not visible to the window.

Once I'm clear of that room, I stand up. Find the bathroom I was held in. No one inside. There's another hallway branching off the main room. I slip the stun knuckles on my right hand and head down the hallway until I get to the room at the end.

It's another gutted bathroom, the tile pink, harshly lit by construction lights. Sam is sitting in a wooden chair, her hands tied behind her back and ankles zip-tied to the legs. She's stripped down to her bra and jeans. The wound on her shoulder is open again, the skin jagged. It looks like the staples were pried out.

There are small puddles of blood underneath her. Some fresh, some not. Next to her is a rolling cart, laden with wadded-up paper towels in varying shades of red and brown. She doesn't appear to be conscious, but she also doesn't appear to be dead.

Roman is standing behind her, one handing holding her hair to tilt her head back and expose her throat, the other holding a scalpel against her neck.

I stop. Put my hands up. Calculate the distance between us. He'll open her throat before I get halfway across the room.

"There's more going on here than you could possibly understand. Do you know how many people would lose their jobs? Do you know how much suffering this would cause? You put these people out of business, the ripples are going to be catastrophic."

"That's your argument," I tell him. "We should let someone do an evil thing because of the collateral damage? You want to talk about collateral damage? How about all the innocent people Ansar al-Islam is going to kill?"

"They're a bunch of dumb kids trying to make a buck."

"Doesn't make it right."

He tenses like he's about to draw the scalpel across her throat. I wave my hand to bring attention to the flash drive.

"What about this?"

"Useless. I was about to destroy it. That was the job anyway."

"But you wanted the password."

Roman pauses.

"Yeah, funny thing," I tell him. "I have the password."

"The one you found didn't work," he says.

"Actually, it does work," I tell him. "I just didn't give you the full key. So here's the deal. Back off and leave her alone. I'll tell you what the full password is and you can open the drive and do whatever the fuck you want with it."

Roman's face goes red.

"You . . . asshole," he says, his voice rising and shaking. "You fucking asshole. I can't . . . why . . . for her? What the hell is wrong with you?"

"Roman, please," I tell him. "That kind of language is uncouth."

His eyes go so wide they nearly fall out of his head. His hand tenses. I get ready to charge forward when I hear movement behind me. Roman looks at something over my shoulder. I throw myself to the side as something explodes. A bullet strikes Roman in the chest and his arms fly up, flinging the scalpel.

Three more bullets strike in succession.

The adrenaline tearing through me makes time slow down. The way Roman falls, backward, face pointed to the ceiling, palms spread, is almost graceful.

I press myself against the wall and prime the stun knuckles.

As soon as I see the gun clear the door, I grab the barrel and drive my fist into Chernya Dyra's forearm.

As I'm doing this, I'm thinking, hey, this worked out pretty good.

Then I realize I'm holding her gun.

Mostly I realize this when every muscle in my body tenses so hard it feels like I'm being torn apart. I fall back, my hand still holding onto the gun, pressing the stun knuckles into her forearm, the current traveling through the gun and into me.

Feels like being back in the Vltava.

But hot.

We both hit the floor. I can move, but barely. Feel like I'm drunk, except without the fuzziness. Hopefully it hit her harder than me.

Really should have thought that through.

I manage to crawl over to Sam, pull my knife out, and cut the zip ties holding her legs to the chair, then the ones binding her wrists behind her. She falls to the floor and groans, doesn't open her eyes. She's alive, but not by a wide margin.

Roman, on the other hand, is definitely dead. His head is facing me, his eyes staring through the wall behind me. The final expression on his face was one of confused fury. I don't care enough to try to close his eyes.

Good riddance, fuckhead.

When I turn, Chernya Dyra is climbing to her feet, pulling the shovel from her back. Seems she wants to do this the old-fashioned way.

I pat Sam on the shoulder. "Could really use your help on this."

She doesn't move.

I get to my feet, too.

"99 Luftballoons" ends and starts up again.

I pull the weaponized umbrella off my belt.

The one Fenomenal so graciously gave me for free. I click the button on the side and the shaft extends to its full length, just under three feet.

It's not the umbrella I used to carry. This one is heavier, and it's completely black, whereas on mine, the canopy was blue. It reminds me of a time in my life when I may not have made the best decisions, but damn could I hit.

No hesitating this time. Before Chernya Dyra has her bearings, I charge and swing. She gets the shovel up to block and is a little surprised at the force with which the blow lands. I pull up to swing again and she jabs the handle of the shovel into my stomach and I stumble back, swing the umbrella up and catch one of her hands. I hear a crack and I'm sure I broke a finger or two.

She rears back and grimaces but doesn't yell out. She grips the shovel in her good hand and swings the flat of the blade. I drop to the floor but it's a feint and she kicks me hard in the stomach. I flip over and try to crawl away as she advances.

I swing the umbrella out at her feet and she kicks it away. I crawl a little and knock over the rolling cart next to Sam. Metal tools clatter to the floor. I pick up a wrench and a hammer and throw them at her. She deflects them. Then I pick up a scalpel and heave it. She's not quick enough for this one, which embeds itself in her stomach, the handle sticking out.

Not that it stops her.

She plucks the scalpel from her stomach and tosses it aside.

I pick up the tray and throw it at her face. She puts up her arm to block and I push myself up and run at her fast and hard. She may be strong and she may be a better fighter, but I outweigh her by at least fifty pounds. I need to use that to my advantage.

We collide and I drive her back. She trips over something on the floor and I fall forward, first landing on her, and then scrambling to straddle her so I can hit her in the face enough that maybe she stops trying to kill me.

Before I'm even all the way up, she jabs me in the stomach. I reach down to protect myself and she uses her fist like a hammer, bringing it down hard on my thigh. Pain blooms through the muscle and I roll off her and back against the wall.

I stand up and she grabs me, pushing me into a sheetrock wall that splits under my weight.

My head cracks into a beam and it's enough to

make me see stars. I hit the floor and get lost in a wave of dizziness. Try to climb to my feet. She picks up the shovel and comes at me. Pointing the sharp end of the blade at me, preparing to drive it into something soft.

Bad move. The umbrella is within reach. I grab it and swing it at the same knee I kicked on the bridge. She's favoring it. When I connect, something crunches. She screams and falls onto her good knee, her bad leg now stretched out in front of her. I get up and throw my fist across her jaw, make contact so good a pulse travels up my arm.

Then another.

And one more.

Her nose breaks, red welts that'll grow into bruises framing her eye sockets.

The shovel is lying on the ground. I go to pick it up.

Again, with the killing. I can't risk this falling back on my mom. That someone else will use her as leverage to get to me. It doesn't make me feel good, but it's got to get done.

But I've made a major mistake.

One stupid mistake in the heat of the moment.

I looked away.

When I turn, Chernya Dyra slams into me, hurling us into a darkened room where the floor feels loose and uneven. It crackles and buckles under us and gives way.

My stomach twists from the sudden change in gravity. I put my arms up to protect my head and we tumble through space.

We land in another room, this one empty, and darker, since there are no lights on this floor. Just what's floating in through the windows. I mostly land on the Dyra, which saves me from splitting my head open. But my ribs absorb enough of the blow that it suddenly hurts to breathe.

The two of us roll away from each other to regroup, tripping and falling over the debris of the collapsed ceiling. I try to climb to my feet but find I'm unable. My body has decided to pack it in. I can barely breathe, choking on the dust we kicked up.

Chernya Dyra coughs and spits blood on the floor.

But then I hear it. Scrambling above us.

My salvation. The thing I was waiting for.

She stands up at full height, keeping the weight off her bad knee, takes a deep breath, and looks at me like we haven't been beating each other to death. Like she's caught her second wind.

"You cannot win," she says, her voice heavy and flat, but labored.

"I didn't need to win," I tell her. "I needed to keep you occupied."

She pauses, confused.

She figures out what I mean when Sam leaps from the floor above us onto her back, reaches around and plunges a knife into her chest.

Everything pauses in that moment.

Sam holding onto Chernya Dyra, whose face is twisted in surprise and pain and fear. Sam digs the knife in, yanks it hard to the side. Chernya Drya bucks like a wild horse, throwing Sam to the floor, and pulls the knife out of her chest, holding it in her hands, her eyes on fire, staring at me.

Even though blood is pumping out of her chest in time with her heart, it looks like she's prepared to stab me with it.

Then she drops the knife, gasps, and falls facedown on the floor.

After that, it gets real quiet.

My body is an echo chamber of pain. It bounces around, getting louder as it rings off various surfaces. I drag myself over to Sam, who's vacantly staring at the ceiling. For a moment, I think she's dead. As I'm reaching for her neck to search for a pulse, she turns to me.

"You came back," she says.

"You saved my mom. Least I could do."

She laughs and then winces, pulling her legs up and curling into a fetal position.

"You okay?" I ask.

"I'll live," she says, attempting to climb to her feet, not doing a great job of it. She falls back to the floor and lies there. "Where's the drive?"

I take it out of my pocket and hold it.

"Give it here," she says.

I remember the way she hesitated before.

"I'm going to hold on to it," I tell her.

"Why?"

"Until I can be sure it'll get into the right hands."

"Ash, give it to me."

"No."

"I can take it from you."

"I don't think you're in any shape to do that."

"You're not in any shape to defend yourself," she says.

"Who do you work for?"

"What does it matter?" she asks.

"What happens to the information on the drive?"

"Ash," she says, her voice soft, almost pleading. "Please. Give it to me. This is the job. The one I was hired to do. Fuller died. He was my mentor. I loved that man like a father. I would not compromise the integrity of the mission."

I think about it. And then I shake my head.

"No," I tell her. "Just to be safe."

"Fine," she says.

She rolls toward me and holds her knife to my throat.

That flat lizard look back on her face.

Everything that's happened in the past few days is erased. She'll kill me. I know it. I drop the drive on the floor.

She picks it up, looks at it, and puts it back

down. Picks up a chunk of rock that broke off when I crashed through the ceiling and brings it down hard on the drive, shattering it.

"Are you serious?" I ask. "After all that?"

"Sorry Ash," she says, her voice cold and distant. "That was the mission."

"People deserve to know the truth."

"People aren't smart enough to process the intricacies. Deal with it."

I crawl a little closer, so that I can look her full in the face. "Who do you work for?"

"A government agency," she says. "You wouldn't recognize the name if I told you."

"You told me agencies like those don't exist."

"I told you a lot of things."

"Who did Roman work for?"

"Hemera Global."

"And the Dyra?"

"Probably the Russian government. They would have had a field day with this. Oh, and Roman told me about the baby terrorists who came after us. They wanted to stop us because they wanted to protect their payday. Which makes sense."

"If Roman was working with the bank, why did he have the Ansar Al-Islam jackoffs killed?"

"He's an outside contractor. And they were sloppy."

"What about the guy who came after you at the Crash Hop office?"

"Oh my god, shut up," she says, rolling onto her back. "It doesn't even matter. It's over. We have more important things to worry about. Like not bleeding to death."

I lie back, look up at the exposed guts of the ceiling. Hope the spinning stops soon, and that I don't have another concussion.

"You're no better than Roman," I tell her. "You're a coward, just like him."

"I'll live with your disappointment," she says.

But there's a crack in her voice. It makes me not believe her.

She tries to get up again, but still can't.

"You stay here," I tell her, climbing to my feet. It feels like my body is held together by old rubber bands. Most of the pain is in my left side. Every time I breath it feels like I'm getting punched. "Kaz is downstairs. I'll have him get help."

"No hospitals."

"He has a guy. A doctor. Patched me up. He can do the same for you."

"Why?"

"What?"

"Why would you help me?"

Her voice is suddenly sad. Vulnerable. It sounds the way it did in the bathroom, after I stapled her arm shut. I turn back and she's propped herself up on her elbow, looking at me with wide, expectant eyes.

"Because it's the right thing to do," I tell her.

I want that to sting, and from the look on her face, I think it does.

She rolls onto her back and closes her eyes.

I backtrack through the space, going slow. Feel like I'm on the verge of shattering. I head upstairs to check on the guys I tied up.

All dead. Mottled red holes in their foreheads.

Chernya Dyra executed helpless, unarmed men.

Another reason I'm glad she's dead.

I stop at Vilém's body. He's lying on his back, staring at the ceiling. I press my fingers to his eyelids, close his eyes. His skin is still warm. I make sure he has his wallet on him, so the police can identify his body.

Out in the hallway, I hear footsteps. Kaz comes up the stairs.

"I'm sorry, my friend," he says. "I killed the main line but they must have a backup generator somewhere in the building. I thought I heard gunshots. I stayed out of the way . . ." He stops, gets a good look at me. "Are you okay?"

"Surprisingly, yes," I tell him. "C'mon. Sam is hurt pretty bad. We need to get her help."

We head back to the room where I left her, but when we get there, we find only the body of Chernya Dyra and a small pool of blood on the floor where Sam was lying.

NINETEEN

The waitress, a gray-haired woman with bright blue eyes, wearing what I can best describe as a frock, takes my order. Roast boar and gingerbread dumplings and a Pilsner. Her English isn't great so my order involves a lot of pointing at things on the menu. Still, I am very happy about how all this is working out.

The place is nearly empty, just a few locals huddling around drinks. I pick a spot where there's sunlight streaming in through the window, barely illuminating the space, which looks stuck in time somewhere around the Middle Ages. A mysticism that's broken by the Wi-Fi password written on a dry-erase board above the bar.

I pop open the laptop and look up Pete Fernandez. A reporter I met in Jersey years back, when I was on a job. Nice guy. Figure he might want to break the story. After a little searching, though, I find that he's left the reporting business and he's become a private investigator.

Well. I should call him once I'm settled. See if he can give me some tips.

Next, I look for Molly Rivers, who, lucky for me, is still a working reporter.

Her Twitter account has her job listed at a

newspaper in Los Angeles, so I ring them up and get a receptionist who directs me to her desk. The phone rings until her voicemail picks up, which offers Molly's cell phone number, so I call that.

She answers the phone with a curt: "What?"

"Molly Rivers."

"Who is this?"

"Ash. Remember me? We met in Portland. I gave you the Mike Fletcher story."

The tone of her voice shifts substantially. She almost sounds like she's happy to be talking to me. "I do remember you. Thanks for the tip. Got me away from that paper in Kansas and onto a sinking ship with slightly fewer holes. I owe you a drink. Or at the very least a sad handjob."

"I've never thought a handjob could sound unsexy. I think I'd prefer the drink. But listen, I have something else for you. What's the top prize in journalism?"

Pause. "A Pulitzer."

"Do you want one?"

"Don't be cute."

"What if I told you a U.S. bank conspired with terrorists to push into oil fields in the Middle East to destabilize the market and push up the price of the barrel so they could recoup on drilling investments?"

There's a pause on the other end.

So long I wonder if maybe we got cut off. But then she comes back: "What you said is literally better than the best sex I ever had . . . if it's true."

"My name goes nowhere near this. You got it from an anonymous source and you can't reveal that source under any circumstances."

"Oh my god, for this? I will Judith Miller this shit."

"Good, then. I'm not going to e-mail this to you. I saved the link in a draft folder in a dummy account. I'm going to read you the login information now. Got a pen?"

"Shoot."

I rattle off the details. When I'm done, she asks, "Why me?"

"You're the only reporter I know. And you did right by me on the thing with Fletcher. A lot of people died to keep this story from getting out. Which means it needs to get out."

"Well . . . thanks."

"Good luck. Don't fuck this up. I almost got killed over this."

"Are you serious?"

Click.

I put the phone down next to the laptop. I look up the town on Google Maps and find that there's a river nearby. The Vrchlice. Another river in need of a vowel. It's right by the train station. I'll drop the laptop and phone in the drink before I catch my train back to Prague.

When I dragged the folder off Jeremiah's flash drive onto the desktop to create a copy, I didn't know why I was doing it. It felt like a moderately clever thing to do.

Turns out it was more than moderate.

After Kaz and I got to safety, I tried to read through the information and couldn't really make sense of it, but I suspect someone with actual resources and time and a decent education will be able to figure it out.

A small part of me wonders if this thing hits, whether Sam will be forced to come after me. Not that it'll change anything, but I did completely derail her mission.

Maybe. If so, it won't be pretty. For as weird as it sounds, it would be nice to see her again. Even though I'm mad at her for following orders rather than doing what was right. Even though she treated me like a stupid child and there were a couple of moments where I thought she might kill me.

Until it happens, I'll keep an eye on people's shoes.

Specifically, for gray Nikes.

The food arrives, and it is so good I want to cry. I'm going to miss the food in the Czech Republic. I'm going to miss a lot of things about it, but mostly I'm going to miss the food.

Once I'm done, I leave a generous pile of money on the table—I'm not going to need much, since my flight leaves tonight. Stand up, and the plastic wrap around my midsection shifts.

I go to the bathroom to re-wrap it. Turns out I did crack a rib crashing through the ceiling, and Étienne offered this as a way to keep things in place while I healed up.

After that's all set, I walk in the direction I think I need to be going, through quiet streets covered in a heavy blanket of snow. Around buildings that went up before my native country was even a concept.

I cut through a square and find a holiday market. I browse a bit and find a booth selling hand-carved Christmas ornaments. I find a skull about the size of my fist, carved from a piece of oak, to replace the dragon that got all smashed when I wasn't smart enough to take it out of my coat pocket before storming a heavily guarded warehouse.

My mom will get a kick out of this.

I stop at another booth and even though I'm not terribly hungry, I get a trdelník.

One for the road.

As I'm leaving the market, I pass a booth selling hats. They've got newsboy caps. I've always wanted one of those, but was never able to find one that fit right. I pull a few off the rack and try them on. I'm about to give up when I find a brown one that fits perfectly, and doesn't look too bad either. I've got some money to burn, so I pull off the tag, hand some crown over to the old woman working the booth, and head out.

Off in the distance, up on a hill, three spires of a massive cathedral poke at the sky, and I wonder if I have enough time to stop inside.

Kutná Hora is a beautiful town. I wish I had come here sooner.

As I make my way through the quiet streets to the Sedlec Ossuary, I run through the checklist in my head. Try to figure out if there's anything I still need to do. I had my dinner with Stanislav, and lucky for me, I heard nothing about the Kraków apartment. Chernya Dyra must have covered her tracks. He made his offer to hire me any time I want, but I told him this isn't the work I want to do. Not that there was anything wrong with it, but I'm ready to make a change. He understood. Even seemed happy for me.

I had a long night with Kaz in Pats. I drank a little more beer than I should have and woke up with a bit of a headache, but I'm glad I did. We worked through some of our shit. Yes, he sold me out, but then he stepped up, so that's what I'll judge him on. I can look back on this and say I came out of this with a friend.

It used to be I wasn't so good at making new friends.

Other than that, I think I covered everything. Except this. When I got my passport, the woman at the expediting office told me to visit the Sedlec Ossuary and I told her I would. I don't know that I'll ever be coming back to this part of the world.

I'd like to, but there's a lot of world left to see, and a lot of living to do, and I may as well do the smart thing. Do it now, rather than regret it later.

Outside the ossuary, I stand close to a tour group. An elderly woman in a puffy black coat speaks German-accented English and explains the history of the church. That in 1278, the church's abbot was sent to the Holy Land and returned with a small amount of earth from Golgotha, the site where Jesus was crucified. He sprinkled it on the ground and it became a popular burial site for people throughout Europe. The land was expanded after the Black Death and Hussite Wars. Around 1400, the Gothic church was built, with a vaulted upper level and the ossuary underneath. And after 1511, a half-blind monk was charged with exhuming skeletons and stacking their bones in the chapel.

Satisfied that I've gleaned the bullet points, I head inside, pay the admission fee, and walk the stone staircase down into the ossuary, the place full of ornately stacked remains. Many of the piles are behind cages, but others out in full view, and it all culminates in an obscenely beautiful, impossibly intricate chandelier of human bones hanging from the ceiling.

I walk the space slowly, taking it all in. The woman in Georgia was right. I forget her name now and I'm sad about that. But she was right. It's incredible to see. I stop in front of what looks like a crest, and a raven built of human bone—a hand and a hip and split femur—pecking at the eye of a skull. A dark-skinned woman next to me is looking at the same thing.

After a moment, she clears her throat. "It is so sad," she says in a Spanish accent.

"What's sad?"

"All these people. There was so much life here once. And this is all that is left."

I look into the skull's eyes. Wonder if it was a man or a woman.

If the person was good or bad.

If his or her life was regretted or celebrated.

Where they are now.

"I don't know that it's sad," I tell her.

"But these people were loved. And now they are here for tourists to take pictures. For our entertainment."

"Is it for our entertainment? The care and thought that went into this, it's like the people who made it wanted us to know that even death can be beautiful. That even after a person is gone, the thing they left behind can be special."

She smiles. "You are an optimist, then?"

"I'm coming around to it."

She turns to me and smiles. She's beautiful, like a museum statue taken on life. She's also incredibly polite, because she doesn't mention anything about my face.

"Then what about you?" she asks. "Would you

like to be displayed like this after you are gone?"

There's something about being here, alive after the last few days, and the comfort of anonymity—we don't even know each other's names—that compels me to dig a little.

"Maybe," I tell her. "I don't know. There was a time not too long ago I was indifferent to the concept of dying. I felt like I would blow away in a stiff breeze."

She arches an eyebrow. "And now?"

"I don't feel that way anymore."

"You are very strange, Mr. Optimist. You are an American?"

"I am."

"Are you on holiday?"

"Not exactly," I say.

"Where will you go next?"

"Home," I tell her. "It's time to go home. I've been away too long."

ABOUT THE AUTHOR

ROB HART is the author of three previous Ash McKenna novels: *New Yorked*, which was nominated for the Anthony Award for Best First Novel, *City of Rose*, and *South Village*, which was named one of the best mysteries by the *Boston Globe*. He is the publisher at MysteriousPress.com and the class director at LitReactor. Previously, he has worked as a political reporter, the communications director for a politician, and a commissioner for the city of New York. He is also the author of *The Last Safe Place: A Zombie Novella*. His short stories have appeared in publications like *Thuglit*, *Needle*, *Shotgun Honey*, *All Due Respect*, *Joyland*, and *Helix Literary Magazine*. His non-fiction has appeared at *LitReactor*, *Salon*, *The Daily Beat*, Mulholland Books, *Criminal Element*, *The Literary Hub*, *Electric Literature*, the Powell's bookstore blog, and *Nailed*. He has received both a Derringer Award nomination and honorable mention in *Best American Mystery Stories 2015*, edited by James Patterson. He lives in New York City.

Find more on the web at www.robwhart.com and on Twitter at @robwhart.

Center Point Large Print
600 Brooks Road / PO Box 1
Thorndike, ME 04986-0001 USA

(207) 568-3717

US & Canada:
1 800 929-9108
www.centerpointlargeprint.com